© Amanda Beesley

About the Author

NICHOLAS WEINSTOCK is the author of the nonfiction book *The Secret Love of Sons* and the novel *As Long as She Needs Me*. His writing has been featured on National Public Radio and in the *New York Times Magazine*, *The Nation*, *Vogue*, *Glamour*, *Nerve*, *Ladies' Home Journal*, *Poets & Writers*, and many other publications. A former volunteer firefighter, he serves on the council of the Authors Guild and works as vice president of comedy development for 20th Century Fox Television. He lives in Los Angeles with his wife, the writer Amanda Beesley, and their three children.

The
GOLDEN
HOUR

ALSO BY NICHOLAS WEINSTOCK

As Long as She Needs Me

The Secret Love of Sons

THE GOLDEN HOUR

NICHOLAS WEINSTOCK

HARPER

NEW YORK • LONDON • TORONTO • SYDNEY

HARPER

A hardcover edition of this book was published in 2006 by William Morrow, an imprint of HarperCollins Publishers.

HarperCollins books may be purchased for educational, business, or sales promotional use. For information please write: Special Markets Department, HarperCollins Publishers, 10 East 53rd Street, New York, NY 10022.

FIRST HARPER PAPERBACK PUBLISHED 2007.

Designed by Jeffrey Pennington

The Library of Congress has catalogued the hardcover edition as follows:

Weinstock, Nicholas.
   The golden hour : a novel / by Nicholas Weinstock.—1st ed.
   p.cm.
  ISBN-13: 978-0-06-076086-1
  ISBN-10: 0-06-076086-9
    1. Hudson River Valley (N.Y. and N.J.)—Fiction. 2. Volunteer fire fighters—Fiction. 3. Married people—Fiction. I. Title.

PS3573.E3969G65 2006
813'.54—dc22   2005050383

ISBN: 978-0-06-076087-8 (pbk.)
ISBN-10: 0-06-076087-7 (pbk.)

07 08 09 10 11 ❖/RRD 10 9 8 7 6 5 4 3 2 1

For Amanda

Every man is two people, and one hardly knows whether it is in the morning or in the evening that he reverts to his real self.

—ROBERT MUSIL

ACKNOWLEDGMENTS

For their very generous help and support, I would like to thank: Jane Friedman, Meaghan Dowling, Maureen O'Brien, and Stephanie Fraser at HarperCollins and William Morrow; Tina Bennett, sterling agent and true-blue friend; Svetlana Katz at Janklow & Nesbit; John Spada, Garrison Company's Rookie of the Year 1998, for his firefighting expertise; Anthony Gellert and the entire staff of Livingston Capital for their finance-world wizardry; Jennifer Belle, for her beloved intelligence; Rich Appel, for his keen friendship; the New York State Frederick L. Warder Academy of Fire Science; and the men and women of the Garrison Volunteer Fire Company of Garrison, New York, for their hard work, good deeds, and great lessons.

I also want to thank Savannah, Derek, and Lincoln Weinstock for their patience, and Amanda Beesley for her guiding wisdom and her graceful ability to make better everything she touches.

AS ONE LEAVES MANHATTAN

and drives up the Hudson River into the rural and unimaginable territory to the north, the tensions of the city fade gently away. In their place loom the terrors of the country. I clung to the steering wheel, sticking close to the blue-brown river. I voluntarily crossed the George Washington Bridge for the first time in my life. Here the arguments of portable radios, the car-alarm anthems and the other clashing noises of my home were distilled to the hum of traffic. Then, somewhere along the Parkway, even that went away. I steered up the Thruway with only the occasional growl and blinker of an automotive rival and with a sense of dread and freedom like nothing I'd ever felt. Hills bulked on all sides, barnacled with yellows and reds, like surfacing leviathans of the deep. Roadside telephone wires cut up and abruptly down and up again: dwindling connections to civilization that could be severed with the fall of a tree.

Two and a half hours out, the land grew howlingly empty. The occasional electric appeal of fast-food signs was replaced by the lower-wattage colors of dying leaves on trees. In Ulster County the river disappeared. In Delaware County it coldly returned. Passing the Catskill Mountains, according to my fucking unfoldable map, the car filled with the scent of pine and with the sharp, green knowledge that this was only the beginning: that I had lived my whole life on a slim island off the southern tip of something bigger, this clean slate, this triangle of woodland stretching from Coney Island to Canada. Here the sleekest of New Yorkers find themselves fish out of water, wide-eyed and gasping in the state of New York.

I was in sorry shape to begin with, given recent events, and wasn't likely to be soothed by a rare and clumsy turn behind the wheel of an automobile. Pippa had always been the one to drive us to the country house. Now, for all intents and purposes, there was no Pippa. Which left me with the challenge of shifting and pedaling and handling the unruly power of a new BMW with its steering wheel jammed in my gut, with the sales sticker still on the window, with my rearview mirror useless thanks to the wall of boxes in the backseat. In the passenger seat, miles away, rolled my survival ration of top-shelf gin. Having lived for forty-six years with the clattering efficiency of the New York City subway system—and for the last decade with the slower nosing and unloading of its limousines—I was at a loss in any vehicle requiring my guidance. I did own a driver's license, albeit one that had expired in 1986. The dealer hadn't seemed too persnickety on that point, hardly glancing at my boyish photo as he leaned over it to count my cash.

The signs beside the highway were barely legible through the leafy spill of Mother Nature. Towns seemed to be arranged in descending order of appeal, from the lordly Arden and Oxford and New Windsor past increasingly ominous village names ending in *hook* and *kill*. Pippa got the apartment, I thought as I accidentally flipped on the wipers and pawed at buttons in an attempt to turn them off. Which left me the rest of the world.

Or at least a house perched on the edge of it. Who'd have thought I would ever elect to live in this gilded shack in the boondocks? The country, as I'd explained to Pippa more than once, was not my forté. I did not do mosquitoes. I had no primal longing to hike through poison sumac. When it came to greenery, I preferred mine creamed and served beside an $80 steak at Peter Luger. The clever residents of New York City floss their teeth, they wax their fruit, they pay good money for razor-scraped tablecloths and the pressing of dress shirts on command. Such commands, in a place like Harristown, fell upon the deaf ears of the cornfields. Men like me drew the snickers of trees.

But what choice did I have? She had ordered me out. She had staked her claim to our apartment, and having disappointed her for nineteen years of marriage, I was not prepared to fight her as well. Which left me few options; fewer and fewer as the days went by. I could have stayed in a downtown hotel. I could have stayed at my job. A more reasonable man might have absorbed the grim twist of fate and moved on, kept at it, kept the trains running on time. I, however, had run away to the country house. This was my great escape, my mad dash to the last place anyone would look for me. The only place I could go. I had tried to get in touch with friends, but I seemed to have lost custody of them, judging by their uniform failure to return my phone calls. *Not a man,* she must have called to inform them soon after she'd shrieked the words at me. *You're no man.*

I left the highway for a road, the road for a winding lane. The buildings scattered and soon shrank to the size of houses, finally turned into barns. There were no people, it seemed: no pedestrians, no neighborhoods. The inhabitants of this outback sheltered alone. I tried two right turns and recognized nothing before I found the steep and appleless dirt path marked Apple Hill Road. I drove up the incline, spitting rocks, past the weathered shacks of the locals. The long-fingered woods closed in. The smell, now, was of soil, of mold, of rabid farm animals, and I found myself suddenly nervous at the prospect of having to get out of the car. Then the glossy white-and-blue sign for Ridgepoint Circle appeared on my right. My wheels hit the tarmac and sighed with relief. The branches fell away from our landscaped clearing of sky. After three hours in a motor vehicle, I was almost happy to see the trim lawns of emerald green rise, like a butler, in welcome.

Our house—my house—was second in the neat row of them, distinguished by a front-yard cluster of yellow trees and boasting the same royal blue mailbox as all the others. I rolled past the redbricked Georgian monstrosity owned, it was said, by an Albany television-station owner and his stepfamily. I turned into the driveway before my other neighbor's tall Swiss chalet of blond wood and glass. Across the street was the gigantic stucco fortress of an insurance tycoon from Hartford, its pale bulge that of a papier-mâché school project gone awry. From a distance these luxury homes would appear to have been air-dropped into this dirt-poor county, plunked down in a hasty row like Red Cross care packages for the desperately wealthy. Mine was arguably the least garish, with its small yard and generous use of locally harvested cobblestones. Still, the twin turrets and stained-glass windows were enough to have led me, that first day with the real estate agent, to question aloud the lack of a moat and drawbridge, to holler upstairs for Sir Galahad—at which point Pippa lanced me with one of her stares. She strode to the foot of the staircase and declared the place sold. It had everything, she informed us. Peace and quiet. Sauna and Jacuzzi. She would take it, she announced to the awestruck Realtor and me.

Who, of the three of us, could have predicted that ten months later I'd take it back?

I turned off the ignition. I spent a minute imagining what my former associates would be doing in the office right now. Changing the world. Redistributing global wealth. Milling at the windows with their shoes off, tapping putts across their carpets, yelling at the speakerphone and fuming at the drop in the Nasdaq and biding their time and their reputations until they could go home and fail to relax. I wouldn't miss the life. I didn't miss it already. Nobody left the life. Only I had left, only me. I suppose it took something like this. There would be times, and this was one of them, that the whole barbaric incident with Pippa would seem a twisted excuse to leave my job. This, after all, was a circumstance beyond my control—all right, maybe within my control, maybe if I were stronger, but awful enough to knock anyone for a loop and change his life.

I took a last deep breath. I shouldered open the car door. I exited the vehicle to the thin smell of wood smoke and the spooky silence of a country afternoon. The boom of the door behind me. The stretching of legs. The trees of Ridgepoint Circle nodded in uneasy greeting. The orange-speckled hills above them rolled over and went back to sleep. The grass was crowded with pine cones and the gaudy leaf heaps of fall. Nothing a good raking (hell, I could learn to rake) wouldn't fix. My cell phone rang amid the boxes on the backseat, where I'd thrown it the fourth or fifth time it had rung before. None of my neighbors appeared to have come to the country for the weekend. It occurred to me then that it wasn't the weekend. The phone gave up and I closed my eyes, nudged by the breeze. Hair riffled on my head and unshaved face. There was quiet here: not the cumulous, tangible quiet that hangs between events, but a vapid soundlessness, a permanent emptiness, that made me feel as if the top of my head had been removed.

I unloaded my boxes in staggering laps up and down the stone front steps. The house was dumpier than I remembered it. There was a rakish tilt to the Viking stove, clouds on the satinwood dining room table, incriminating grit on my index finger when I knelt, with heavy effort, to inspect the dulled parquet floors. There were enough brown rings in the drained hot tub on the third floor to count its age. The stained-glass windows were peppered with bird shit, and there was a smell emanating from the olive green divan in the piano room that suggested something with fur had burrowed in and died. Worse, and gratuitous, were the two used mugs in the den, left out for all to see on the glass table between the easy chairs. The shriveled tea bags had been plucked out and carelessly left to dry in a silver ashtray beside the mugs. Two mugs. His and hers. I had never drunk tea in my life.

By the time I had kicked over the table and deposited my property on all three floors, wide as a life, darkness was falling across the Thomas Cole paintings and down the sculpted front banister to render the gold velvet of the living room sofas a mortuary gray. I dropped the last box in the master bedroom. I stumbled to the picture window on the third-floor landing. With the thinning and blushing of the treetops, our view of the Hudson—my view—had improved in the months since our last visit. The river was a strip of metal, tinged red at its edges as if recently forged. The sun was in mid-drop behind the hills. I stood there for several minutes, scratching my gut, king of the castle, overseeing the end of the day.

I retrieved my bottle of gin from the passenger seat. I found the tonic in a kitchen cabinet, a dusty glass above the sink, and poured myself a triple with which to seal my vow. I would retreat to the woods. Nature and nurture myself back to life. I would hole up in the country house I had bought to save my marriage in the bleak hope of salvaging myself instead.

With the arrival of night came a mean chill. A swallow of gin helped. I found the chandelier dimmer and twisted on the lights. I was visible now in the nearest kitchen window, fatter than I had been in years, all belly and woe as I hung over my drink. I toasted myself and my downfall, the gesture reflected in place of the dark outdoors. To the ex-urban ex-husband. To a fresh start.

MORNING CAME WITH AN
assault of unfamiliar morning
sounds. The *chock-chock* of a lumberjack in the distance. The
scrabble of something like a squirrel, or perhaps Sasquatch himself, on the roof. A repetitive squeak just outside the bedroom
window—a kind of *woo-YEEP, woo-YEEP*—that would have been
promptly repaired by the superintendent of any decent building
in New York City. My lower back was tied in its usual knot.
Only when it loosened could I sit up in bed and swing my feet to
the cold floor.

I rose to the first day of the rest of my life with two sore
shoulders and a crimped neck. Those of us born and raised in
the city are not accustomed to moving objects heavier than taxi-
cab doors or making anything more substantial than a deadline.
The usual clench of my lumbar region was matched by knots in
both biceps that prevented any straightening of arms. As I eased

myself out of the bedroom and down the hallway, my legs joined the mutiny. A dozen lifted and lowered boxes and I was broken at all my hinges. *You're no man,* whispered the walls, in her voice, as I slid my hands along them for support.

To travel anywhere in this house, a circuitous path had to be charted between stately cupboards of black walnut and whimsical Aalto armchairs, around standing screens of mahogany from the '20s and over carpets of hand-spun nomadic wool from the Southwest. There was no rhyme or reason to be detected in the array, rhyme and reason being hopelessly advanced concepts for a novice interior designer in a frenzy to acquire. The cedar-lined hot tub stood beneath the conical ceiling of the eastward turret, a round master bed in the westward turret behind me. Cluttering the hall between them were enough antique iron day beds and Hepplewhite settees to suggest a Victorian slumber party. Her Dutch bell-metal candelabra was hung in perfect position, there in the third-floor hallway, to receive my forehead and my shouts of *shit* and *son of a fuck* before I swung it wildly aside and pushed on. Faintly stained by the stained-glass windows, I teetered at the top of the staircase. Then I limped down.

Our country house was Pippa's storage facility, her practice ground and her display case, all of which left little room for a man of my size. Still, the place was perfect for her. She was interested in the country, inasmuch as the city could no longer contain all her furnishings, but she was not about to bunk in a barn. Pippa was no more likely to settle in a modest clapboard house on some hunk of untamed acreage than I was. She had come to New York from a nation in disarray and had worked ever since to adopt an American semblance of panache. This flimsy structure and its overpriced contents, this grandiose front foyer with its tinny ringing after every footstep, these faux-cathedral ceilings and fabric-coated walls were a shrine to the divine power of image, a slapdash mock-up of richness, as was she. Here she could smell the roses through the open dining room window while setting the brushed-copper banquet table with her leopard-skin place mats and Limoges. Perhaps she was reminded of her African origins by the calm that shivered the grass here, by the quiet that pushed the clouds across the long empty minutes between her flustered adjustments of the Federal bull's-eye mirror on the maid's-room wall. This idiotic house might have been snapped together like a toy, painted by numbers; but it gave her the feeling (and for this I was once grateful) of success.

All that the house lacked, I thought as I hobbled down the last few front stairs, were the three bags of Italian coffee I'd left in the door of the Sub-Zero freezer in the apartment. How the Christ could I have forgotten coffee? A country house ought to be supplied with the stuff on a regular basis, topped off by the kind of wheezy tanker trucks that pump the place full of gas and oil. I stalked across the living room and into the kitchen. I pillaged my boxes and managed to dig out the electric grinder, hoping—what? That it would have rebrimmed magically overnight, like a well? That my life could return to normal, that a mistake so large might be erased and that I could simply pluck up my wits and return?

The new car started with a thrumming self-importance. BMWs are designed to be effortless, or so I'd been assured at the dealership the day before, yet this one seemed more of a surly opponent. The vehicle was obviously aware, deep in its digital brain, of the incompetence of its handler. Convinced of it, then, as I zigzagged along the driveway and down the avalanche of a dirt road to the street and barely managed the hard-right turn toward town.

Town was a shabbier outpost than the word might imply. The sloping doze of crayon-colored hills and gray river and off-season farms gradually gave way to a main street of actual buildings. The storefronts appeared to be plywood and to tilt precariously against one another for support. The tattered awnings and rotted wooden benches were hopelessly outdated without being quaint. The feeling that cracked the pavement, that dusted the empty sidewalks and creaked the useless store signs, was that of a place abandoned in a hurry, the site of a recent plague or receded flood. There was no trace of youth or spontaneous human activity: no razz of a skateboard, no snarl of a motorcycle, no teenage laughter or yuppie couple strolling anywhere along the brief length of what must have passed for The Strip. No inkling of renewal. Nothing I could have done. The tobacco shop that I might have arranged to be purchased and converted to a Cinnabon would continue to sag and stink where it was. The clothing store whose window displayed a single sun-blanched tracksuit would never be born again as a Foot Locker or a Gap. There was no possible investment for an investment banker: no future, no equity, no growth potential whatsoever. This was it, this row of has-been businesses servicing the same collection of old-timers who ordered the usual and shambled out the door. I found what had to be a bar, Henry's Place, and shambled in.

The door smacked closed with the shimmy of a sleigh bell.
"Coffee?" I called out.

"Hm," replied the mustachioed man, denim shirt, who stood
behind the bar. This, absolutely, was Henry. There was an unmistakable air of ownership in his slouch and in the hamlike
hands he planted on the long counter of imitation oak. Drifting
somewhere above the half dozen stools, two tables, and open
metal trash can was the promising scent of old grounds.

I repeated: "You got coffee?"

"Hm."

"Is that a yes? Great." I glanced around. "I take it you don't do
espresso."

"Machine's busted," he said, with a gruffness that suggested
he might have been the one who had sauntered over with a two-
by-four and busted it. His craggy country face was etched with
self-satisfaction, its wrinkles and scars the honorary decorations
of a veteran of the outdoors. Even his eyes appeared to have
been faded by the weather to a durable blue. Only his prepos-
terous silver mustache, lovingly combed and waxed to points
like the horns of a water buffalo, betrayed the soul of a dandy.

"You don't by any chance have the *Times*," I said. *"New York
Times."*

"Hm."

"Didn't think so. I'll just take that coffee."

"Be a minute." The mustache rose and fell absurdly as he
spoke. "Make a new pot."

This was not, I presumed, a command. His denim eyes traveled down to take in my rumpled Bergdorf shirt, to scowl at its
monogrammed cuff—I hadn't changed, or bathed, since my last

day of work three days before—before returning to my face to inform me, without bothering to inform me, that the previous pot of coffee had long since been consumed by the earlier risers with earthier jobs who belonged here.

He moved away into the dark door hole that must have led to the kitchen. I leaned an elbow on the counter. It was an inside-out sensation to be slumped in a dim bar at nine-fifteen in the morning as daylight bathed the street out the dirty window to my left. A flier taped to the door begged the enrollment of volunteer firefighters. The sawdust on the planks beneath my feet would have been a folksy embellishment in the city. Here it was pure neglect.

A body filled the kitchen doorway, but instead of Henry there materialized a woman with a lopsided mass of curly brown hair and wearing a black Violent Femmes T-shirt and undies.

"Whoopsie," she said, noticing and turning toward me. She pushed a fist through her hair, a gesture that raised her shirt enough to show a blue corner of her panties. "Morning." Smeared makeup, big boobs, she turned and was gone. There was a blunt conversation in the kitchen (it was impossible to picture old Henry uttering more than two syllables at a time) and the fading scratch of feet as she padded back to the bedroom upstairs. Then more silence. Dead silence. The specialty of the house.

I called out unnecessarily: "How's business?"

"How's yours?" Henry shot back.

Fair enough, I figured. "Not so good." I thought I heard a *Hm*. "Left my job."

It was, I realized, my first conversation concerning the event. What is it about bars that prompts the belching confessions of men? What was it about me that needed so badly to talk—me, who'd talked candidly and emotionally to no one in thirty years? I hitched both elbows behind me as if moseying about a saloon. *Lost my wife,* I was about to say when he emerged with my coffee. The coffee cost approximately one-sixth as much as my daily espresso at the Wall Street café by the office; but those were served in easily one-sixth the time, and by slender Italian women who pretended to admire me as I smoothed my Charvet tie, tapped my Rolex. This man pretended no such thing.

"Where from," he asked. He had taken out a rag and was slowly polishing his bar.

"Me? New York."

"You're in New York."

"Right." Sipping my coffee, I turned to watch a cat walking down the middle of Main Street, slinking past the shut stores and abandoned trucks. Across the vacant main street, beneath those gigantic tawny hills, an antiques furniture mart was closed, a feed store open next to that. Two clock-repair shops competed lamely side by side. It might have been the Hollywood set for a B-grade gunslinger movie. It could all have been pushed to the ground with a groaning fall and cough of dust. "I mean Manhattan."

"Hm," he said. This appeared to confirm something. "Car break down?"

"Better not have. I just bought it." I indicated out the window with my Styrofoam cup.

He examined my parking job. "Seven series."

"Excuse me?"

"That'd be the 745i."

I reassumed my cowpoke slouch. "Think that's right."

"Eight cylinder?" he asked. "Or straight six."

I drank my coffee again quickly, as if the cup might contain knowledge of cars. "At least," I said. The coffee tasted like liquid rust.

"McPherson struts?"

"Sure does."

I might have thrown in a *reckon*. *Reckon he does*, I should have said. *Reckon they do. To reckon*, I conjugated: *I reckon, you reckon, he reckons*. Henry's fists were balled on the bar. He looked at the door. He was waiting for me to leave. There was a mean gleam in his eye, effective as a stun gun. I finished the coffee with three long, difficult swallows.

"One more thing," I told him, crumpling the cup in one hand and throwing it at his open trash can and missing by a good two feet. "I reckon I'm going to need a couple bottles of gin."

THE OFFICE WAS CALLING

again as I parked before the house. I reached into the backseat and swept the cheeping phone onto the floor. Then I shoved out of the car and mounted the steps with my paper-bagged goods: the bottles of gin, the six-pack of tonic, and the dented cans of Maxwell House and salted peanuts I'd purchased at a gas-station grocery store. I entered the kitchen and threw my keys onto the counter, tripped over one of a knee-high clutter of brown boxes. I wrenched the plastic top off the coffee. Couldn't find a can opener. I opted instead for a tall gin and tonic, numbing myself with four good slugs and a fistful of nuts before moving to the boxes, squatting with a grunt and starting in.

First out of the cardboard were my hundred-plus bottles of wine, stripped of their newspaper wrapping and stood in a darkly glinting army. My 1900 Mouton-Rothschild led the troops through the dining room, a '64 Cheval-Blanc bringing up the rear. In the next box was all my industry memorabilia, the spoils of wars past. The Colonel Sanders cap I was awarded for my role in Pepsi's purchase of Kentucky Fried Chicken. The Cracker Barrel apron I was given after securing the company's hold on key sections of highways across the Midwest. A vintage menu from the Pig Stand, the first drive-in restaurant opened in Hollywood in 1932. It took a disappointingly short time to unload my treasured baggage. I stood before the window to stretch my back. It was then, with a shock, that I glimpsed a movement at the far edge of my lawn.

An intruder—flash of blue—ducked out of sight. A second later he had vanished between a couple of trees. There was a man on my lawn. Someone was casing the property. The guy could have been leisurely scheming to plunder the empty house for months, not imagining that the owner might return all of a sudden and with nothing to lose. I glared at the crease in the woods that had swallowed him. The bastard didn't reappear. I could picture the break-in. The clumsy violence of burglary. The feel, once again, of a marble floor against my hands and face.

Then I saw her. It was a girl, walking plain as day past a bunch of crimson trees. Back-strapped to a purple book bag, reaching out to slap trunks, she was heading down the footpath that must have wound through my woods. She vanished again into a thicket. A buzzer sounded nearby. There was the watery noise of children's voices. There must have been a school down the hill, buzzing and squealing several times a day; but I'd only been to the house on weekends, three or four of them in all. There was a church somewhere, too, to judge by the dreary chimes that decorated the top of the hour. I suppose there would have to be. Post office, probably. Rotary Club. Hair parlor. An entire hokey human civilization where I had pictured only me and my square of grass, my mustering of strength, a house in which to hide.

With the brusque departure of the sun the big house went cold. Gin and tonics, I had discovered, can serve as a meal. For dinner I had a half dozen of them at the dining room table, watching the gloom thicken and the colors fade out all the windows. Somewhere was a credit-card-size remote control for the digital thermostat, but I had neither the energy to hunt it down nor any idea how to adjust the temperature by hand. Instead I remembered the wood-burning stove. Legs still sore, off-kilter from the booze, I retired to the east wing.

The stove was in the den, beyond the dining room and maid's room, just past the upended table and broken mugs. Here were the suede easy chairs on which Pippa used to curl up with her home-decorating magazines and shout for more wine. Her magazines, there on their shelf of greened copper, appeared to be ordered not by date or publication but according to some more superficial criterion (era? budget?) that eluded me as I inspected their rows. She had issues, my wife, hundreds of issues. She would spend hours scanning and dog-earing and tearing out their pages, fondly dwelling on the images stored there as others do with lapfuls of family photo albums. These were her loved ones: this Nepalese throw rug, that Edwardian bedstead; not fixtures of her past but candidates for inclusion in her future. I used to watch her fiddle with her magazines as I made my angry, urgent, idle weekend calls to associates' mobile phones and beach houses. She was—I was convinced—purposely wasting the evening, pretending to be reading in the hope that I would give up and go to bed alone and be snoring by the time she joined me (without having to *join* me) in bed. But then I would catch sight of her face as I lumbered over to top off her glass of Viognier or Cabernet. Her fine features would have gone heavy with effort, lips twisted, white-blond hair fallen flat, neck muscles tensed with the pressure of conjuring an offhanded elegance she desperately lacked. She would gulp the wine as if I'd handed it off at the fourteen-mile marker of a marathon, practically splashing it over her head and picking up her pace. She wasn't dawdling with those magazines. She was actually striving, suffering for her art. I felt for her in moments like that: far from home, distant from her goals, trapped in the lower regions of the upper crust with a fat banker like me.

I creaked open the side door of the stove. Across the Mexican tile floor was a meticulously distressed pine cabinet full of Duraflame starter logs. No ragged lengths of actual wood, no splinter-bearing bark requiring the fireside tongs of gleaming brass that had been purchased at auction and unblemished since. I crouched before the dark window to slide a fake log into the stove. I clonked a second one on top of it. One more for good measure. I had never made a fire, having not been sent by my parents to any of those khaki-clad camps named with the American Indian words for homesickness and masturbation. Summers, according to my parents, were for ordering in Chinese and lazing before a Yankees game with the apartment windows thrown open, the breeze nearly fresh, the waterfall tinkle somewhere of dropped coins on concrete. The idea of sending their only child off somewhere greener—hell, of buying a houseplant—was the unacceptable equivalent of admitting defeat. This was the conviction of die-hard New Yorkers. The rest of the earth's population could prune hedges and seed yards to their hearts' and small minds' content while we in Manhattan pounded the pavement for real.

Paper, I figured, was part of the equation. I unwedged two or three magazines from the top shelf and stuffed them in above the fake lumber. I found matches in an ivory saucer and lit the casing of the bottom log. The flame trickled across the Duraflame wrapping, catching and eddying, spreading to the next. The things worked. I rose and crashed into a chair to relax.

I allowed my eyes to close, my mind to swim, my thoughts to paddle out to the underwater wreck of what had happened. I shook my head, working to think of something else. What I needed, I thought, was a goddamned TV. Pippa's refusal to put a television in the country house had seemed her prerogative, as I wasn't planning to spend much time here, and had served as a nostalgic reminder of her un-American childhood. Thanks to the sanctioned isolation of her country during the apartheid years and to the severity of her father, a crabby former farmer in Cape Town, she had been raised without an addiction to television and movies: a quirk that rendered her charmingly and almost unfathomably foreign to me. Television didn't arrive in South Africa until 1975, by which time I'd spent more than a decade glued to *The Honeymooners, Newhart,* and *M*A*S*H.* On our very first date, over rice and beans in the Spanish diner favored by Columbia grad students, she quoted Steven Biko, expounded on pivotal laws and events in her nation's history, and taught me the lyrics to "Nkosi Sikelel' iAfrica," the underground anthem of South Africa composed by a black schoolteacher and sung in defiance of the Afrikaans song mandated by the government. In return I taught her the entire songbook of *Guys and Dolls*.

I was raised, after all, a child of the city: feeble of limb, soft in the gut, yet with a brawny knowledge of mayoral politics and Midtown traffic patterns, a headlock on the history of the Yankees. I was taught to see trees as sidewalk decorations. The sky existed between building tops, blue inches at a time. It wasn't that the rest of the world held no interest: I caught informative glimpses of it between commercials on television, skimmed whole paragraphs about it in the international section of the *Times*. The people and cuisine and film festivals of the world came to New York City in unending droves; why scurry abroad to try and collect them? As a boy I traveled once to Long Island to visit my grandparents. I journeyed as far as Washington, D.C., on an eighth-grade school trip. And that was it. I was born into the privilege of Manhattan: into the knowledge, narrow and cozy and as securely locked as an apartment, that there was nowhere else like it. Therefore I went nowhere else.

Where I went was to PS 75 and IS 77 for high school, downtown to New York University, and then a full hundred blocks north to Columbia Business School. My father was a stockbroker from suburban Long Island who had moved to the city at age nineteen and, whether out of resolve or fatigue, never looked back. My mother was a cheery and lousy housewife who prodded me to take after her husband while communicating, with secret smiles over her plates of burnt waffles, that I could do better. And I did. I excelled at math in elementary school, read the stock pages in middle school, and developed a passion for outwitting my fellow baseball-card traders that grew more serious from there, as did I. In eleventh grade I started selling doughnuts in the hallway between classes. As a senior I merged my business with the school's dining-hall services for the sake of cross-promotional opportunities and expanded distribution. Freshman year of college I discovered a way to rig the student-housing lottery that won me hand-slapping congratulations and a gaggle of false friendships and a sense of forbidden achievement that I had never known. Upon graduating, having already gotten my feet wet, I simply waded forward into the worldwide sea of numbers and dollars that beckons and embraces those of us keen enough to hear its call.

It was at business school that I met Pippa, who had swum from further away. I can still see her there in the cafeteria where I'd first seen her, milling with the herd of foreigners who foraged together in doe-eyed self-defense. She was wearing a typically shapeless green sweater, aiming a delicate finger at the tin of peanut butter on the salad bar and asking an Eastern European acquaintance what it was. She was white skinned, blond haired, but anointed invisibly with the exoticism of her continent, a darkly thrilling background that made her round face glow like a moon. With her corn-silk bangs, her giant eyes and her impulse to agree gratefully with strangers in midsentence, she might have been Nebraskan. The truth was betrayed by her accent, clipped and flighty, the ends of her sentences looping in the audible signature of Cape Town. She had grown up speaking Afrikaans, the bastardized Dutch of the inventors of apartheid; but she was a liberal and, as she was forced to testify repeatedly to inquisitors in New York, on the side of the *bleks*. In fact, it was her belief in the rightful rule of her country's native majority that had led her to brave the sanctions—*hi?*—and break through the red tape—*sjoe!*—to get herself and her girlish South African expressions to America. Here she would be armed with long-winded lectures on urban economic reform and sent home to make a difference. These were the late-seventies, a time when hair was blow-dried into elaborate wings and idealism was just as puffed and stylish. It would have been impossible for Pippa to believe that Nelson Mandela, a convicted criminal known in the white newspapers as the Black Pimpernel, would one day be freed from three decades in prison and elected her country's first democratic president. It was difficult for me, frankly, to picture where exactly South Africa was.

But I learned. That's how I've done things. I've sat down with the facts and crammed them. The unspoken secret of growing up is that everything you need to know can, and must, be improvised. Life comes naturally to no one; yet its sacred rules and mannerisms can be memorized, convincingly imitated, hastily swallowed and regurgitated on cue. None of us owns our knowledge. We must borrow and rent it, steal it when we can. We are frauds, every one of us. We can be anything we want. I had proved this throughout my decades of preening and posing as a top investment banker at the top investment bank in New York. Pippa had seized on this notion with the time-honored zeal of the American immigrant. I watched the process, marveled at her passion and her dispassion, witnessed her cold ascension with the mixture of awe and sadness that might be called love. I never had a chance of keeping her. She had necessarily passed through me, like homely Ellis Island, because better things lay beyond. I was lucky to have and hold her, to cling to her, for as long as I did. I was unlucky, too. And I was, in the end, to blame.

I was almost asleep with this when a log shifted in the stove. Opening my eyes to gloat over my fire, I sat bolt upright in the face of it. One of the magazines had cartwheeled out the open door and come to rest, breathing red, at the bottom edge of the nearest curtain. Flames rushed upward, licking the wall. I was on my feet. My first impulse, strangely, was shame. Spreading fast before me was a mistake that had to be rectified before anyone saw. But no hand pats or blown breaths could halt the spread of what I'd done wrong. Nor was there anyone here to see this. There was only me and my fire.

The flames rapidly climbed the curtains and lapped at the ceiling. The heat knocked me back. That surprised me; there was no gradual warming of the room, only instant hell. The ravaged curtains fell off their rod and were swallowed in slow motion, disappearing into the roar. My mind was burned blank. What the Christ did people do with a fire? They sprayed water. They hurled blankets. I had nothing like that. Nothing but the urge to run.

I ran for the safety of the dining room, the cool length of the hall. There was quiet in the kitchen. The distant crackle of the den. I grabbed the gin off the counter and ran back to duck and gape in the hot doorway before summoning my nerve, cracking off the bottle at the neck against the door frame and lunging forward to slosh the liquid—cold liquid, there we go— onto the fire. I was nearly incinerated by the explosion of orange blue.

The flames claimed the room. The fire owned the place. It

had spread to the ceiling, where it pulsed like the roiling surface of the ocean seen from beneath. I turned in a panic and grabbed the mohair throw off the back of one of the chairs and cast it like a net at the wall. I winced as it zapped and vanished. Above me the fire emitted a proprietary crack, a pop, another crack, an unstoppable grumbling power. Scalp burning now, face smarting, I covered my head and bolted.

"Help!" is what I yelled as I crashed out the front door. It sounded halfhearted in the vast darkness. I stopped running. I cupped my hands around my mouth and shouted: "Fire!" The neighboring mansion didn't budge. *"Fiiiire!"* I bawled, giving it my all. I turned to direct the alarm down the whole huge row of houses. *"Fiiiire!"* Someone had to be home. Somebody somewhere had to hear that. *"Fiiiire!"* I yelled again, aiming it up to cold heaven. But there was nothing but the cruel winks and distance of the stars.

I MUST HAVE BEEN SITTING

on my lawn when the rosy whirl of sirens announced the tramping of a half dozen strangers into my home. An hour might have passed, or else a couple of minutes, time having crumpled in the heat like everything else. I was helped to my feet. I followed the firemen into the house. To my surprise, I recognized a face: the one with the drooping silver mustache that approached me as I sank onto the bottom step of my front staircase to watch.

"Flue was shut," Henry said. He wore a wobbling fireman's helmet—a full fireman's outfit, in fact. The effect was as comical and incongruous as a dream. I half-expected him to hand me a well-made gin and tonic in a golden goblet and welcome me to the great beyond. "Nothing getting up your chimney there. That's why it spat on you." He scowled down at a burnt scrap of something, maybe rug, and kicked it aside. "Lucky a lady on

Apple Hill saw the blaze. Called it in. Gotta open your flue when you use the stove."

"I know about the flu," I said.

He nodded, unconvinced, gave a "Hm" and was gone. The room around me no longer contained fire but rather meandering firemen, chewing the fat and pushing around my debris with their brooms. Slumped with my head against the banister, I watched the mop-up of my den. Evidently the blaze had petered out once it had rushed through the shelves of magazines and bubbled and burnt the paint on all the walls. The lounge chairs were unharmed. The tile floor was singed but intact. There was disappointment at this, it became clear as my vertigo settled, my head cleared, my hearing returned and I listened to what was said.

"Close call," grumbled a man as he towed a brown pile of something across the room with a rake. "Thought we had one there."

"Could've been a burner," said a smaller fellow with a long, scraggly beard. The beard was tied off at the end, as if for the sake of neatness, with a rubber band. He fiddled with a lever on my stovepipe that I'd never noticed, peered up at the ceiling, thumped his glove on the pipe and listened hard: the forensic scientist of the bunch. "Jumps into the dining room there? Gets onto those fabric walls? You're off to the races," he said. "New house like this? Cheap wood, flimsy beams? Goes up like nothing."

"Not this time," came the response from a colleague. "Crapped out." And then, at last, a desultory: "Lucky break."

Looming over me, then, was a shockingly tall man, his fireproof coat parted to reveal a T-shirt that read "Harristown Fire."

He had the thick red chin stubble of a lumberjack. His neck was draped with some kind of heavy plastic camera: a fireproof camera, apparently, despite the absence of flames. His white helmet suggested a more regal office than the other yellow hats, its stiff leather badge decorated with royal red numerals and—now that I noticed it—the word "Chief."

"How you doing there," he rumbled down at me. He straddled the space before the stairs as if to block my escape.

I managed a nod, fighting nausea.

"Want some water? Glass of water?"

The firemen had arrived, I thought, bearing water. I shook my head.

He had opened a small notepad. He took a minute to read over what he'd previously jotted down and readied a pen to jot more. He was older than I'd first thought, his fiery beard flecked with ashes. "How about spelling the name for me."

"Schoenberg," I said. I spelled it as slowly as I could without vomiting. J-E-W, I thought. That's right, Chief: with a J.

"Why don't you tell me what happened here, Mr. Sheinberg."

"My house caught fire."

He tapped the pen against the notepad. "And how do you think that happened."

"I got the flu. Or didn't get the flu. Whichever's worse. You can ask Henry over there."

"Neglected," he said slowly, "to open the flue." He added it to the page. "And how old are the premises."

"The house? 1998, I think."

"Nineteen." It took him some time to get this down. "Ninety. Eight. Test your fire alarms?"

"Be my guest."

"Nossir. Do *you* test your fire alarms."

"Every chance I get."

"And how often is that."

"Not often enough," I gave him.

"Not often," he repeated, "enough." He wrote down the reprimand. "So you understand what happened here."

I slouched farther down. The stairs were hard against my back and then soft, turning slippery, dissolving behind me.

"You understand that you have endangered the—buddy. Yo there. Sheinberg."

I might have responded. No way to be sure.

"You listening? You with me? Henry. Pete. We got a diver. Help me out here."

I DID MY FIRST EVER LOAD of laundry in the washer and dryer in the basement, careful to follow the cartooned directions on the back of the carton of Tide. I returned upstairs to clean myself in a similar manner (Jacuzzi cycle, quick sauna, shower rinse) and dripped across the bathroom. I stood before the mirror. Apart from the glistening size of me, I appeared to be all right. I was sleeping better in the country; more, anyway, without a job. There was an undeniable pinkness to my complexion——right there, on the part of my cheeks not hidden by the brown-and-white growth of a beard. The beard was the color of snowfall on soil. It was the look of my father, post-retirement, pre-death. Little about him looked Jewish, or *was* Jewish, in practice. My childhood was a careless assortment of improvised Hanukkahs and an eventual reversion to store-bought Santafests: stockings, even, a new dreidel tucked every year in the toe. But in the last years before my father's final stroke there was something of the rabbi in his grizzled visage, in his drooped lower lip and collapsed posture, something like the look that sagged back at me now.

There came the heart-stopping noise of the phone. By the time I'd encircled my girth with a towel and pounded down the stairs, I was too winded to speak.

"Yes," I managed.

"Bull," came the voice. "Hey, Bull, is that you?"

"Me."

"Fuck, you sound terrible."

Gradually I caught my breath. "Who is this?" I said. Although I knew.

"It's Mark, man. Who'd you think?"

"How did you get this number?"

"I got this number by getting this number. What are you, on the lam? Someone said you're in Pennsylvania Dutch country or something."

I propped my elbows on the kitchen counter. Rubbed at my beard. I could hear Mark's other line ringing and being forwarded, with a jab of his stubby finger, out into the hall to his assistant, the pimpled Shelly, where she would be sitting in her fishnet hosiery and big-heeled pumps, her stale blouse, her customary cloud of vanilla perfume and armpits. I could sense, like a blind man, every dismal corner of that fourteenth-floor hallway in that sixty-story black building. I could still hear the bleating of the phones, the wail of the fax, the reckless misery of the people who lived at that job.

"I'm in New York," I said.

"I knew it. Wouldn't last two fucking minutes among the Pennsylvania Dutch. Take away your Blackberry and you'd go postal. Am I right? Make you churn your own butter and you'd go nucking futs. So what's this, new cell number? Couldn't get an answer on your old one."

"I'm upstate."

"What are you talking about."

"In the country."

As if on cue, a bird whooped by the window.

"Which country?" he asked. "Not that house in Jersey or wherever."

"New York State."

"I didn't know you actually went to that place. Shit, Bull, I didn't even know you quit"—he lowered his voice—"*quit* until this morning. Marty won't say word one about it. Even Slick isn't talking. Daria said you groped her in the hallway and that's why you got canned."

"What?" I said. "Daria said *what?*"

"Kidding, man. I'm kidding. Daria didn't say anything."

"I didn't get canned." I let my forehead lower until it rested against the chilled kitchen counter. "I just stopped coming to work."

"That's what I heard."

"I thought you hadn't heard anything."

"Heard a few things," he said. "Heard about Pippa."

I pulled up my head. "What did you hear."

He moved something around on his desk, probably the pedestaled model of his boat that he proudly displayed beside his in-box. I used to stop by Mark's office. We were friends, you'd have to say: colleagues, and generally collegial, despite the elaborate descriptions of sexual affairs and female anatomy and television-industry revenue streams that I had to thereby endure. Mark did for the media industry what I did in the retail and restaurant sector. We would share knowledge, exchange war stories, analyst-to-analyst, man-to-man. I would watch him fiddle with his miniature boat like a baby with a bath toy during his phone calls to Vivendi, while waiting for faxes from Warner and Sony, fumbling with the tiny rudder, flicking a finger into the back of the sails, thumb-polishing the nameplate. *Blow Me,* the sailboat was called. Beside it, the picture of his rigid wife and sons.

"Sorry about what happened," he said then. "That's the worst."

"Yes, it is."

"That's the worst you can ask for."

"Okay, Mark."

"I mean, the thing at the apartment. Son of a bitch."

I looked again out the window at the bushy red trees. I longed for more distance. If I were on the second floor, I'd be able to see clear to the glimmer of the river.

"Tell you this, though, buddy. From what I heard"—and here Mark took a moment for emphasis, or else to manipulate the miniature spinnaker, maybe trim the plastic jib—"wasn't anything you could do."

There was no point in answering that. Investment bankers hate to be corrected.

Someone was speaking to him in his office now. "Just can't believe it," he told me, pretending not to be distracted. "Fucking

Bull." He was mouthing to his visitor: I could hear the working of his jaw. The quiet closing of a door. "So you've basically checked out."

"Something like that."

"For how long."

"Don't know."

"Couple weeks?"

"Couple months, maybe."

"Well, good for you," he said. "Good for fucking you."

"I don't know."

"Hell, I do. This place is a shithole. You know that, man. Market's crap. Turns people into animals."

I was watching an actual animal out the window. A fox, maybe a weasel, snooping around the garbage shed and trotting away. I realized that we always griped about our work to anyone who'd listen, to everyone outside the game, and that this was the routine I was getting now from Mark. These were boasts disguised as complaints, testimonials to the weekly difficulty of what we did, to our victories against invisible enemies, to the might and monetary value of the forces we wrestled with and nearly, occasionally, tamed. We alone had the nerve to ride the Nasdaq, to hold on through the dips and leaps that follow quarterly earnings calls, the bucking of market trends, the shake-ups of the Federal Reserve. We were the precious few—the workaday thousands—who knew the grim pleasure of lucky guesses, of the tallying of millions, of moving and stacking and jumping and removing billion-dollar corporations like so many pieces on a checkerboard, of fighting poison pills and contradicting institutional investors because we say so, because the share price is sure to follow our predictions and the next deal to follow after and our wealth to follow as well. We complain (they, I should say now, complain) even about the money, bemoaning the hefty income and the lack of time to spend it. Such are the woeful songs and dances, the ulcers and divorces, the crumpled suit pants after red-eye flights that serve to bolster resolve.

"So what the fuck," Mark was asking, "are you going to do in the country?" He was tapping out something more important on his keyboard as he continued to speak to me. "Lay eggs?"

"Could be."

"Lay a farmer's daughter?"

"Listen, Mark—"

"I mean, because, seriously. You're going to die out there."

"Maybe I'll get a job." I was thinking out loud: always a mistake with Mark.

"You're not going to get a job. Come on, Bull. Cut the shit. It's me, man."

"Read books. I don't know. Get some exercise. I'm going to take—"

"Oh, for fuck's sake. You're going to die."

"What happened to 'Good for you'?"

"Good for you for leaving. But, I mean, at some point you've got to come back."

"Hey, Mark," I said. Something had occurred to me.

"What's up." Tap ta-tap on his keyboard.

"How'd you get this number?"

"I told you, Bull. I just got it." Tap, tap. "That's how I do things: I just get them done. If I didn't, they wouldn't kiss my hairy ass with the kind of year-end bonus that makes yours look li—"

"You saw her."

"Who."

"You saw Pippa. She gave you the number."

There was silence, then, from Mark and his keyboard. "Ran into her," he said. "Lincoln Center. Totally unplanned."

"Shit."

"And I'll answer your next question. She was with him."

"Jesus, Mark. I don't—"

"And I'll answer the question after that. She looked great."

"I really don't want to kno—"

"Just fucking great. Healthy, happy, whole nine yards." With a creak he leaned back in his chair. "Never seen the guy before. Not exactly what I expected. Didn't catch the name. What's the name?"

"I don't know."

"What's he do. This guy."

"I don't know, Mark. I don't know who he is."

"Kind of a schlub. You seen him?"

"No. I haven't seen him. I've never—"

"But shit, did she look good. You know how she can look. Just booming. Total fucking wow. To be honest with you."

The phone slid up my head as I slumped against the cold counter.

"Know you appreciate the honesty," said the phone into my hair. "I figure I owe you that."

I HAD NEVER BEFORE HAD

time like this—*felt* time like this, wallowed in it, sensed its congealment around me until I shrugged it off to finish my drink. I had basically been drunk, been sleepwalking, for two weeks, fueled only by the canned peanuts and frozen burritos from the gas mart and the half-hearted will to live. It was ten forty-five in the morning. I was on my third gin and tonic of the day. I flipped through the local paper, browsing for anything remotely financial. Where were the stock prices, the news articles, the slightest evidence of any occurrence beyond this meaningless stretch of lawn? Where was the goddamned *New York Times,* here in the heartland of New York? I had barged into every coffee shop (two) in a twenty-mile radius, called every bookstore (one) and stationer (none) I could find. There was nothing but these six pages of farm gossip and guesses at the weather, a half-page ad requesting volunteer firefighters—and, on the front page, me. A blurb detailed my mishap, now more than a week old, beneath the grainy photo of the black wall and window that had been dutifully snapped by the chief. I examined the photo, my square moment of small-town fame. I walked across the house and into the charred smell of the actual den. The walls were oiled black in great flame-shaped streaks. The ceiling was a lighter brown mess of cooked plaster. Where the curtains had been, the fire had eaten dark divots into the wall. I supposed I should repair that. I had no interest in learning to repair that. Mark was right: I would die here. I needed something, absolutely anything, to do.

The sound of a machine growled in the distance. It came closer, louder, growing ugly, shuddering the house. The roar from the road escalated to thunderous proportions, scraping and twanging branches as it neared. I walked to the front door and opened it in time to watch my driveway fill with the gray sight of a garbage truck. The vehicle moaned and was jammed into park. With a sigh of pistons, the dirty truck ejected from its cab a limber man in overalls. He appeared to be no more than four feet tall—although he had to be taller, his grizzly beard at least that long. It took me a moment to notice that the beard was cinched at the end by a rubber band, and to remember the little fellow as having been at the fire in my house.

"Hullo!" He threw a wave. His jaunty arms were sheathed in bright orange gloves to the elbows. He hustled over to my trash shed and hoisted the lid to find the first full barrel in months. He snatched and tossed the bag with surprising ease into the metal mouth of the truck. As if pleased, the truck idled louder. Then he crossed the driveway to meet me. "Hullo," he said again.

Reluctantly I descended the steps. "How are you."

He yanked off his gloves, hell-bent on shaking hands. "Pete Karl."

His finger strength was murderous, a garbageman's grip.

"Thought you folks only came up on the odd summer weekend." Pete Karl stepped back to size me up: to determine, as I watched him, that I was overweight. Undernourished. Drunk as a skunk. This was a man who knew his trash. Pete Karl was not only short but thin as a wire. I could have eaten him whole. He appeared, twitching before me, to be thinking the same thing. With his jumpy manner and pipe-cleaner beard, he seemed a kind of leprechaun of the garbage, the sort of filthy sprite who springs out of trash sheds in the nightmares of children.

"Nice time to spend a few days," he was saying. "Changing leaves and all."

I leaned against my car. "Actually, Pete Karl, I'm here for a while."

"That so?"

"I live here," I said. I twiddled my fingers, longing for my glass.

He nodded and pushed the back of his hand across his bristled mouth. The orange gloves went back on. He spanked them together. Spanked them again. The sound came back to us, echoing off the huge row of houses. "So where's the wife, Will."

"It's Bill," I said. "There's no wife."

"Don't say." He didn't appear to believe me. "Talked to a lady here one time. Tall lady. Blond. Good-looking." Spank. Spank. "Don't mind me saying so. English lady. Right here on your stoop."

"That," I told Pete Karl, "was an ex-wife."

"Well." Spank. "That happens too."

"I'm afraid it does."

I looked away at the hills, up at the ice blue sky, around at the pottery colors of the leaves on the trees. There was a damp smell in the air that suggested things were moldering beneath us. There was the sound of shifting branches, brittle and repeated, like the shuffling of cards. Pete Karl had met Pippa on a weekend when she was here and I was not.

She came out early, and repeatedly, once our purchase had closed and the house was hers to be flamboyantly overdesigned, stuffed full of her crap. But in truth she had come out for another reason. And Pete Karl had caught her. I, too, had caught her—but only gradually, cumulatively. I had seen a leaf in the city. That had been my first clue. The Harristown number on our phone bills. The mugs on the table. News of a run-in at Lincoln Center. And now a glimpse by the garbageman: this undercover sanitation worker, my bearded spy. The leaf was obvious enough. It was stunningly out of place in the foliage-free apartment, a place of onyx counters and high-gloss floors, that I was cleaning for no reason at something like two A.M. That's what I did, late at night, when she must have assumed I was still hunched in the office, or else conked out in our big bed, and that it was therefore safe for her to slink home anytime. I cleaned that goddamned apartment until it gleamed. I put things back the way they should be. I reordered our marriage in those lonely late nights, restored it one grudgingly folded camisole at a time. I was determined, I suppose, to keep things together like that, to keep her extramarital romance (and, maybe worse, her marital indifference) from wrecking the life I'd so neatly arranged.

The leaf was hooked into her limp sweater when I lifted it to within an inch of my blazing eyes. I stared at it, seeing things clearly for the first time. There were no leaves in the city. It was a man in the country. Some guy at the fucking country house. Without a word, as usual, she had told me herself.

I wondered what else Pete Karl might have seen through the spade-shaped windows that punctuated the stone front of the house, who else had received his nod and neighborly *hullo.*

"See anyone else?" The question slid, more or less casually, from the side of my mouth.

"Not these days," said Pete Karl. "Not at Ridgepoint. Week-enders, mainly. Don't come up much from October on."

"I mean at my place. When you saw Pip—the lady you saw."

He stared up at me, his head at my chest. His beard, I noticed, bent slightly with the breeze.

"Was she *alone,*" I said loudly.

This he got. I could tell by the nervous two-step of his boots, his stalling sniff.

I figured I'd make it easy for him. "Was her *brother* here."

"Oh, sure. That's right. Thought I saw someone in there. Didn't meet the guy." He looked relieved. "*Thought* I saw someone else. That'd be him."

"But you didn't meet him."

Another spank of the gloves. "Nope." Spank. "Good guy?"

I considered this. "Nope," I said.

And still—with the garbage taken care of, the truck messily idling, the day passing before our eyes—Pete Karl didn't leave. He scratched at the edge of his beard with the distant, pleasured expression of a dog digging at fleas.

"So." I gave in. "Get you a drink?"

"No-no. I thank you, Will. Never touch the stuff."

"It's Bill. And I touch it all the time."

"Volunteer firefighter," he went on. "Have to stay sharp."

"That's right. You were here."

"Stove fire," he confirmed. He added modestly, "Part of the job." He patted a square device attached to his belt. "Pager goes off all the time."

We both watched the pager, then, waiting for it to go off.

"Two or three calls a week, nowabouts. Plenty going up in smoke. Dead leaves. Dry ground. Drier and drier these days. That's everywhere. That's your global warming."

"Huh."

"That's why we need volunteers out this way," he said then. "Big guys like you."

"Oh, not me."

"We're hurting pretty bad. Working nonstop. Fire season's twice as long as it used to be."

"How about that."

"Got your brush fires. Lawn fires. Your occasional forest fire. Few weeks and it'll be winter, with your chimney fires and what have you. Lot more electrical fires in winter, with your shorter days and longer nights. Car wrecks on the ice."

I nodded. I looked over my shoulder toward my faraway front door.

"Spring you're talking barbecue fires." He was progressing seasonally. "Propane fires. People grilling out in their backyards. And then you're into summer."

I agreed: "Right after spring."

"Plenty busy come summer. Lot more civilians, for one thing. Heck of a lot more. Got your chain-smokers. Motorcycle riders. Folks who don't know thing one about public safety."

"Tourists," I said. "City folk."

"There you have it."

"Bastards."

What I could use, I thought, was a good long soak. I would have to call someone to come clean and fill the hot tub. Maybe Pete Karl could take care of it for a crunchy handshake with a hundred-dollar bill. Straighten the stove while he was at it. Pull the cork off my '63 Quinta do Noval and stay for the house-warming celebration. A festival in honor of my one big mistake: a commemoration of violence and the untimely lack thereof.

"Sure you can't help us out," he was saying.

"What, as a fireman? No. Yes. Positive."

"Just don't have the manpower these days."

"Yeah, well, neither do I."

"Don't see that many new faces around," he said. "Thought I'd ask."

"I understand."

I stood on my stone steps as the little fellow backed his big rig down my drive. The *wheet-wheet* of a garbage truck in reverse was a welcome urban strain amid the strange peeps and quiet of the place. And as I watched him—as I planned to return inside to get drunker; as I stalled there, adrift in invisible wood smoke and the comments of birds and considered how far I'd run from my problems, how little I'd done in the face of them—it dawned on me that this might be my chance to change. A man can learn lessons. Here in the middle of nowhere, there was room to turn around. I could, it seemed at that moment, be saved by the crew of the Harristown Volunteer Fire Company: not exactly dragged from the orange jaws of flame-roasted death but rather taught a few ways, and the previously unknown impulse, to set things right. Of course, those helmeted yokels wouldn't know what the hell to do with an actual fire. Nonetheless they showed up, bulging bellies and shrinking hairlines and all, to give it a shot. They were over the hill and took action, took a stand in silly boots. They heard tell of an emergency and stood tall (and, yes, short; and, sure, fat; but stood) to try and stop what shouldn't be happening. It was high time for me, now that it was too late, to learn how.

The truck had braked with a scream and lurched forward toward the neighbors' when I halted Pete Karl's progress, a raised hand over my head, and waded forward through all the fallen leaves to have a word.

I WOULD HAVE HOPED

for something more handsome. I had envisioned the sort of boxy wooden firehouse, hand-painted red, that weathers the seasons behind a yapping dalmatian in the rural backwaters of urban minds. This beige building, boringly constructed of cement and aluminum, could have been the forgotten branch office of an insurance agency. The black letters spelling "Harristown Volunteer Fire Company" were plastic and stuck crookedly over the tall steel doors where the trucks must have been kept. The place was furnished, I saw once I walked through the open side door, with third-hand folding chairs and New England Patriots banners. Not a brass pole in sight. No whiff of stove-top chili, no dog. There was a hallway, a doorway, a small office and the overwhelming smell of gasoline, as if the floors were scrubbed down with it daily. There was the hum of fluorescent lighting, the caw of a bird outside. The faux-wood walls were crowded with plaques and framed photographs of ancient men in badges and hats. Polaroids of someone's baby were tacked to a bulletin board by the bathroom. A sign-up sheet for a class in auto extrication was scribbled with names like Finelli and Murph.

"Hello?" I called.

There was the sound of whisking. I followed it through a doorway and across a room full of hissing radios and out onto the cement floor of the truck bay. Two fire engines glistened, enormous, like gorgeous new ships, titanic vessels of tomato red. My face appeared as a smudge on their nickel rails and shiny panels as I made my way around them. Racks of fireman outfits lined the wall, soiled yellow jackets hung under a long shelf of yellow helmets. The quilted yellow pants all had boots stuck within them. Propped in the corners of the room were mops and rakes, lengths of rope, coils of hose. The reek of petrol made my head spin.

Another whisk on the floor. And now the *jink, jink* of metal being struck. Beyond the second fire truck a squat-bodied man turned toward me, steering a broom. He wore a plaid flannel shirt and tall rubber boots. His mutton-chop sideburns were substantially thicker than his hair. The close set of his beady eyes gave him the look of a mole.

"How you doing."

"All right," I said.

"From the other week. With the stove fire."

"That's right."

"Okay now?"

"Sure."

"Full recovery." He startled me with a smile. His teeth were the teeth of vermin, tiny and variously colored. "There you go."

"Y'ought to be dead," came a high, sneering voice from somewhere else, ricocheting off the metal walls.

I turned quickly, too quickly, and had to fight through a whoosh of dizziness that may have been the result of breathing gas. I focused through the vanishing dust motes of what was almost a dead faint to see a man in a baseball cap, sleeveless T-shirt, his arms emblazoned with tattoos, leaning against the wall and sharpening (was I imagining it?) a blood-stained ax. The blood, now that I got a good look, might have been the remains of antique paint. The old ax, to be fair, may well have needed sharpening. But the twisted scowl of the man didn't resolve into anything less menacing as he continued to jab a stone against the blade edge, the length of the handle braced under his ink-littered arm. His baseball cap said "Harristown Fire" and was yanked low over a beak of a nose, its brim bent to a point that looked recently sharpened as well.

I turned back to the mole man and to the larger task at hand. I reconsidered my decision. Reinforced it with a deep breath. "So," I said, "I'd like to joi—"

"Sure, yeah. Pete said something about that," he snapped. "Sounds good. Be glad to have you. What's the name?"

"Schoenberg."

"Tom!" Megaphoned by both hands, his voice was startlingly loud. His broom handle fell to the floor with a smack. "Tom-*may!* Yo, Chief! Got a guy out here!"

A door groaned open beyond the back fender of the far truck. Unfolding himself from the doorway was the red-bearded Goliath who had interrogated me in my home. He stood unsteadily, as if he'd just woken up. "What's up, Sully."

"Got one," Sully called over. "Volunteer right here." His tiny eyes flashed with pride. "Mr. um—say again."

I pushed my hands into the shallow back pockets of my suit pants. "Schoenberg."

"That's our chief. Tom Moore."

Chief Tom Moore swayed toward us across the concrete, growing taller and taller as he neared. He walked with excruciating slowness, savoring each long step, a lavish side-to-side approach that suggested the manly absorption of a past injury—pins in a knee after a motorcycle crash in the Painted Desert, crushed pelvis beneath falling horse—and left no doubt who was chief.

At last he stood before and above me. "Soooo," he said. "Want to join the company." Kindness and condescension mixed richly in his baritone. The ax sharpening of the guy in the baseball cap had finally stopped. "Got any training?"

"None whatsoever."

"Any kind of physical problems we should know about?"

All kinds, I thought as I shook my head.

"Heart trouble?"

In a sense. "No."

The chief examined me from several feet above. "Serve any time?"

I gradually deciphered the question. "You mean prison?"

He nodded.

"That would be no."

"Military service?"

"Not me." I rubbed at the stubble on my cheek. "Served

some corporate time," I said. "Went AWOL a few weeks back."

None of the men offered a smile. The psychopath behind me started in again on the ax, honing his weapon with whack after whack.

"Not going to bullshit you," announced the chief. "Could use the manpower. All the help we can get these days. More and more property sites out this way means more and more lumber, more and more wiring. For us"—and here he leaned forward, teetering above me like a redwood—"that means more and more fires." He spoke the way he walked, indulging himself in his words and their deliberate pace, basking in the hierarchy, not to mention the height, that kept his audience trapped. "Record number of residents in this town. More people you got, more mistakes they're going to make. Lot of them living in fire zones. Means less room for natural fires to burn themselves out and take the fuel with them. So what we got is a lot of fuel." He shifted the angle of his lean hips. "Dry season, too," he mused, "with the leaves down. Can't afford to be picky, from a personnel point of view." With these disclaimers issued, he took a long breath that seemed to pull all the air and gas and tension from the room. "So basically," he said, with a slow rubbing of his ginger-haired forearm, "you're hired."

Sully pumped my hand at the news. "Tom's the chief," he explained again. "Big cheese. Me, I mainly drive the truck. I'm exterior. See, there's interior and exterior. And I'm exterior. Someone's got to stay on the radio, operate the pump. That's me." He kicked at the fallen broom. "No stretching the hose, no putting on the air pack. Screw that. That's what I say. Screw it. I'm not twenty years old." He gave me a pleading look. "What about you."

I bent over and pried up the broom by its handle. I squinted down the shaft, as if sighting a rifle, before handing it back to Sully. "I'll do interior."

His rodent eyes didn't leave me as he accepted the broom. "Don't have to."

"Zip it, Sully," said the chief. "Could use someone interior. Good timing, too. Course starts in a couple days."

"There's a course?" I asked.

"Training course. You do need training," he intoned from on high, "to be a firefighter. State requires thirty-nine hours of EF."

"Essentials of firefighting," Sully translated.

"Thursdays and Saturdays up at the training center in Freemont. Half hour north. Get you a pager when I can. Just ordered some. Gary order those?"

"Shit if I know," Sully answered.

"You're a probie until you graduate from the course." The chief was looking down at me. "Come out with us on calls, but can't go interior. Not yet."

"Get your light, too, when you graduate." Sully waggled his thick eyebrows. "Got mine. Not supposed to yet. But you gotta have a blue light. You know: car light."

He flashed me another feral smile. The ax hitting grew louder, and I could feel the glare from beneath the brim of the baseball cap without having to turn around to see it. The chief said something about getting me fitted for turnout gear. He had lowered his head to better gauge my physique, confronting for the first time my full fatness, my oldness, his shoulders sagging in dismay—but I was busy looking over the fire engines, gazing up toward the metal roof, intoxicated by the smell and the shiny clanging notion, for once in my life, of saving the day.

I WAS LATE FOR MY FIRST CLASS.

It took me an hour and fifteen minutes of start-stop driving to locate the town, the street, and the upstairs training room of a larger and better-looking fire station than our lame little outpost in Harristown. I strode belly first into the room, fending off the stares and glances of the men who were seated in bunches at round wooden tables like overgrown kindergartners. It occurred to me, then, that I might be something of a small-town celebrity. These were firemen, after all, and I was a guy (as they knew if they read their papers) who had seen my share of fire. Then again, I had run away. They might have been snickering; their expressions, though aimed at me, were hard to read behind a spectacular variety of facial hair. A scan of the room revealed every possible option—pencil-thin mustache, full beard, soul patch, Fu Manchu—with the exception of freshly shaved. Their eyes and growled comments followed my progress as I wove between the tables.

From across the room, Sully called out once and waved.

"What are you doing here?" I asked him as I settled into the empty seat he'd kicked out. The chair was broken and I had to position myself carefully to balance my bulk. All around us our classmates were griping and chortling into paper coffee cups as they waited for the teacher to appear by the blackboard. Everyone but me appeared to own a tarnished jacket or bent baseball cap advertising his fire company. I would have to go clothes shopping locally, it seemed, adopt the native dress if I wanted to walk the streets—hike the roads—without getting beat up for my lunch money. The previous morning I'd bought my first pair of boots at the near-defunct clothing store in town. From here I was looking at substantial investment in the denim and flannel sector.

"I'm here same as you." Sully scratched a sideburn, embarrassed. "Never passed this thing."

"Didn't you have to?"

"Supposed to. Hell yes. Lot of these guys"—he gestured with his ample eyebrows around the room—"were supposed to pass. But I've been at the firehouse since I was six. My old man was a firefighter. His dad was chief. Got two brothers who are pros in the city. Tommy's not gonna keep me off calls." Concern created horizontal lines all the way up his forehead and back to where his hair started, more or less above his ears. "Took the test three years ago and blew it. Year after that I wasn't close." He nodded at a guy across our table. "*Mis*-ter Hansen," Sully addressed him. Then he lowered his voice. "Next year they're changing the course. Nationwide. Making it harder. Ninety hours of training. Three-day practical test.

Screw that, I say. It's this year or never." He was slugged on the shoulder by a man passing behind him. "*Mis*-ter Richter," he said, turning to look up.

"Back for more, Sullivan?" asked Richter, a jowly man in his fifties who came, according to the frayed embroidery on his jacket, from Dovertown.

"Screw you."

Richter acknowledged someone else with an index finger and looked back down. "Didn't see you out on that gas spill Saturday."

"Didn't get the call," said Sully. "Wheaton Valley and D-Town got the call. You there?"

"Better believe I was there."

"Messy, I heard."

"Four hours of mop-up. Gas got belowground, into the drainage pipes. Emptying all the way down by the lake by the time we got there."

"There's a good time."

"Oh yeah."

I chuckled, for practice. *Fucking drainpipes,* I almost said.

Our instructor was a bald gentleman in an official fire-service uniform and clip-on tie who hailed, at full voice, from the State Academy of Fire Science in Montour Falls. He wrote his name in capitals, CAPTAIN STANLEY KRAKOWSKI, on the blackboard and then rapped on it with a knuckle, smudging a K. He handed out thick spiral-bound copies of our Firefighting Essentials workbook and instructed the class to turn off their pagers. Amid the subsequent rustle of sleeves and jeans I pantomimed compliance, fiddling with my empty belt. Then he gave what he called an "overall sum-up" of the fourteen-week course. He was immediately sweating in visible beads on his head. *Yous* was his term for the second-person plural. In return, he said, we were to call him Captain.

"Now I am a-*ware,*" said the captain, tilting forward with each stressed syllable, "that a *lot* of yous have been with your *fire* companies for a lot of *years.*" He slid a hand back over his head. "But I want yous to understand that, far as *I'm* concerned, far as this *class* is concerned"—he shot a bulldog look at the nearest table—"you're all probies."

There were moans and snarls at this.

"Captain Stan!" came a holler from the back of the room. "When do we get to put the wet stuff on the hot stuff?"

"Fire it up!" shouted someone else.

"Take an ax to some shit," suggested a third.

"If yous are so interested in using *tools,*" said the captain over the growing noise, "then I got some good news. I got a tool for yous right here."

"I got a tool for yous right *here,*" said a man at our table with a hand to his crotch. There was a spatter of laughter. Captain Stan lifted a fire extinguisher onto his desk.

"One of the most important tools we're gonna get to know about," he proclaimed. "Before we learn something about *combating* a full-scale fire, we're gonna learn something about *preventing* it. What do we call this."

"A waste of time."

"A dildo."

"Fire extinguisher," I called out.

Sully looked at me sideways.

"Thank you." Captain Stan lifted the extinguisher with one

hand and crashed it down again on the metal desk. "Yous are one kind of fire extinguisher. This is another. What can anyone tell me about this kind."

I flopped open my workbook to the index at the back. Lesson one was called "The Fire Triangle." Portable fire extinguishers were on page eleven. "They're identified by a letter-number rating system," I read.

"Everyone hear that?" Captain Stan turned to write it on the board. He had already sweated through his blue fire-captain's shirt, the round stains in the armpits climbing toward his epaulets.

"Class A, class B, class C, and class D," I recited.

"Easy, big fella," grumbled the crotch grabber across our table.

Sully leaned toward me. "That's in there?"

"Sure. Right here. Top of eleven. Page eleven."

He pushed back without looking. "Long as it's in there," he said.

I took a pen from my jacket pocket. I wrote in the margins what Captain Stan was block-lettering in chalk on the board. *Class A extinguishers.* I drew the letter A and labeled it green. *For wood, paper, plastic. Quenching-cooling effect.* Then: *Class B extinguishers.* I drew my B in a square marked "red." That should be easy to remember: Red Square, B for Bolshevik. *Flammable liquids, gas, grease. Flame-interruption effect.* There were two kinds of extinguisher in common use; I had seen them, I faintly recalled, by the stairwell of my office building: a fat silver can of pressurized water—class A—and a thinner red can of foam covering classes A, B, and C. There was a new "K-type" extinguisher, something involving gel and recommended for kitchen areas; but according to Captain Stan, it was *expensive* as all *hell* and a *mother* to clean up.

My hand started to hurt, unaccustomed to the strain of manual penmanship. My mind, however, had whacked into gear. There are some who are propelled upward in life, and certainly in investment banks, by the sheer force of charisma, by their lightning grins and bolts of luck. I had gotten there by soldiering quietly forward, armed with statistics and earnings ratios; by pressing my belly to the desk until long after midnight, every night, while the custodians zoomed past with their vacuums and the rest of the city finally went quiet enough for me to think. I had learned it, I suppose, from my father. *Knuckle down,* he used to tell me on the rare occasions during my childhood that he summoned the energy to tell me something. It was an expression he'd apparently learned from his tired father before him. It was the sum total of what I'd taken from my flagging dad. The never-ending need to work harder. The honor of bulling ahead. We were beasts of burden, my father and I, hard headed snorters from the same stock. The difference was that when he died, his much touted stocks had merely broken even. That I managed to plow forward, beyond and away from him, to greater success.

I bent into my note taking. Underlined *Aim at the base of the fire* and looked around. Not one other inhabitant of the room had moved to take down any of lesson one. I was flushed, once again, with the pleasure of accumulated knowledge, as treasured and intoxicating as wine. There was no glad-handing here, no empty art of the schmooze, none of the all-night strip-club outings and languid lying over thousand-dollar sushi lunches that were once how to get ahead, and that were the end of my liking my job. I brandished my pen, flexed my cramped fingers. Someone at a nearby table was actually snoring. These were not New Yorkers. These were men with no sense of urgency, of upward ascension, of the satisfaction—no, the cutthroat necessity—of coming out on top. I found myself in a dozing herd of buffoons, toying with mustaches and scratching at undershirts, daydreaming of tractor pulls and breakfasts of meat.

I patted the workbook and flashed Sully a smile. I would ace this class. He gave a last quizzical look at my pen before leaning back and folding his arms and appearing, with a quick squeeze of his upper face, to go to sleep.

I SAW HER AGAIN.

She materialized beside my woods like a reminder of something neglected: the ghost of options unpursued. The girl couldn't have been more than six or seven, I guessed. I had so little sense of ages that far beneath mine. We had never had children, Pippa and I. We had never thought of it. Although that's not exactly true. Pippa had raised the subject early on; but it was shushed and put to bed when I made vice president and, unlike a baby, wasn't heard from again. The truth is that the idea of having children didn't appeal to me. They were a project guaranteed to grow beyond one's control, a money loser from the start. The miraculous birth of a debt obligation. I had no natural affinity for youngsters, no knack for games of horsey or for earnest parental discussions of poop. I had my career. I had (had) a wife. My name was carved in removable plastic beside the door to an office and shared by a spouse who stood beside me, who snuck behind my back.

Starvation, whose onset was delayed by daily bags of Fritos and Doritos from the local gas mart and anesthetized by my near constant intake of gin and tonic, finally announced itself with a yodel from my gut. It only worsened with my opening and slamming shut every bare cupboard in the fucking house. Lack of food had emptied my head. I had no idea how to get to the tacky steakhouse or the faux-French restaurant where Pippa had driven us for dinners out here. There were no corner delis, no prayer of pad thai or take-out enchiladas in this unworldly stretch of the globe.

Yet the thick pot of Maxwell House that I'd been gulping all afternoon while stuffing clothes into closets had me feeling like my old self. I reached for my cell phone only to find myself lacking a suit jacket and its inside pocket. I descended to the kitchen and snatched the cordless off the wall to demand local information. It took some time to locate a restaurant, any restaurant, some goddamned food. "We don't work that way," the first and second operators informed me—I pictured ladies with beehive hairdos at a haywire switchboard—before the third dictated the number of a misspelled Italian place several towns away.

"O Sola Mio," piped a teenage voice.

"I'm going to need a pizza."

"Can you, um—okay."

"Large. Sausage and peppers. Fast as possible. How fast is that."

There was a delay. "Sausage and pepperoni, you said."

"Peppers. Jesus. Sausage and peppers," I said. "It's AmEx number 5307—"

"A card?"

"A credit card. A platinum card."

"Yeah," he said uncertainly. "Um, no."

"You don't take cards?" I asked, my voice rising. "You've got to be——fine. Okay. All right." I opened my wallet. "But you'd better tell your delivery boy to bring change, because I only have hundreds."

"There's no delivery boy."

"Girl, then."

"No deliveries."

"You don't deliver your pizza? What the Christ do you do with it?"

"We serve it," he said. "This is a restaurant."

"Good for you. And I am a customer. Who lives at——the fuck is it——Four Ridgepoint Circle. In Harristown. There's a dirt road, and it's the first driveway on it. Off it. Through the stone gate to the left. Are you writing this down? Tell me you're writing this down."

"No."

I let the phone drop. Brought it back to my ear. Three weeks ago my assistant would have handled this. I could have called the chairman and CEO of Pizza Hut and had the kid and his rinky-dink restaurant bought out and done away with in the course of an afternoon. "You're telling me you don't do deliveries."

"That's correct."

"So who does."

"Nobody." He seemed to be enjoying himself; a smile shaped his vowels.

"Somebody does," I said. I fingered my wallet, considering my offer. "And fifty bucks says it's you."

"No, it doesn't."

"Seventy-five."

"We don't deliver," he repeated. "We're too busy."

Silence then. No clang of a pot, not a peep from a coworker or the hiss of any stove.

"Tell you what, kid. A hundred."

"Sorry." He sounded on the brink of laughter. "But no."

I spun to shout out the kitchen window at the ridiculously yellow bushes: "I'm offering you a hundred American dollars to bring me my lunch. A fucking *pizza*. Let me tell you what I need, kid. You there? Terrific. Here's what I need. I need you. To walk. Holding my pizza. Over your goddamned head. Until you arrive at Ridgefield Circle. Ridgepoint Circle. And take a left at the first fucking shrub on your—"

But this wasn't the way. I should have learned it by now. I had never learned it, that smoothness, that chameleonic slickness, the ability to slip into another man's manner when he wasn't looking, to adopt his patter and in that way to talk a deal to bed.

"I'm sorry," I said. "You still there, pal? I apologize for that. I'm just hungry. Listen. Yo. Here's the thing." I slowed down and spoke more gently, adopting his rhythm. Rocking the deal to sleep. "I just need a pizza. Know what that's like? You're just hanging in your pad, and you need a pizza?"

"Um."

"Sure you do, buddy. No one's around. Nothing to do." Closing my eyes, I worked to imagine a teenager's existence. "No girls. Nothing on the tube. And you get the munchies. That's where I'm at," I said. "And shit."

"Uh-huh."

I smiled. I was doing it. I could do it now that I had to. The mission hadn't changed, only the setting. Life in the country was no different from life in the city. It was a series of confrontations, large and small, to be won by the hungrier man.

"Tell you what," I said to the kid on the phone. "I'm going to give you two hundred bucks. Could use it, right? Who couldn't. Buy some Rollerblades. Cigarettes. Twizzlers." I tried to think what else. "Electronic"—fuck were they—"games. Just to come over here with a pizza. Easiest money you've ever made, right? You dig? What do you say. Sausage and peppers, pal. Few minutes."

But by then he had hung up.

I WAS STABBED BY HUNGER.

I was being murdered by
my need for a meal. By the time I left the house I was physically
weak. The stomach pangs were crippling. I limped to the car, a
bear emerging from hibernation, to find food.

The pewter sky promised rain, threatened snow. The smell
of roasting leaf piles, far off and everywhere, burned a hollow
feeling into the gut. The car whizzed by sagging houses and the
neglected stretches of rock-hard field between them. I got on
the highway, roaring my engine and barely outgunning absolutely no one onto the entrance ramp. It was three exits
north that industry seemed to have taken root. The familiar
chain stores of my former clients had grown grotesque in an
area apparently selected for its accommodating bleakness. A
Toys "R" Us and a BJ's Wholesale sprawled beside each other
like twin cities. A Price Club hulked larger than any other club

on earth. With my vision stretched to such a scale, it took some time to find the somewhat more modest mega grocery store that had been recommended by my garbageman. I hooked a left turn across traffic, halting a pickup driver who screeched his brakes and actually shook a fist at me, the way folks in these parts still did.

None of the world-famous excesses of Manhattan, nothing I had witnessed in the skyscraping home of the larger than life could have prepared me for those endless aisles of tomato sauce by the gallon, for the sandbags of potato chips, hydrants of mayonnaise, packages of pork chops the size and weight of a pig. There, in that store, was the bulk of the country, the crates of corn dogs and Great Walls of Tang that health-conscious city dwellers would hardly believe, let alone buy. I cruised those aisles like a toddler at Disneyland, helpless before the merry appeal of Doo Dads and Snickers, the handy offerings of jarred lasagna and imitation fish. I was lost in the bright blur of all the crap I could consume. I had become one of the gullible all-American customers who used to plump up my stock charts, who fell into line with my earnings projections and followed me, without ever having heard of me, like sheep.

The Bull, they used to call me. I snorted and charged at the color green. Long before I was anointed managing director of the retail and restaurant group—back when I was merely an associate, one of the herd—I was already famed for my zeal: for my late nights at the office, my obsessive stick-to-itiveness, my attention to detail and my facility with transaction multiples and the elaborateness of the pie charts in my leveraged-buyout models. Even when I made VP, my talent remained largely numerical, my trusty Hewlett Packard 12C calculator rarely cooling from my grip. I was a mathematician at heart, a diligent trudger, more at home with accounting principles and valuation multiples than with human company of any kind. I lived in the nuts and bolts of the business, and I excelled at them like I'd never excelled at anything else. The eager-beaver associates who fill the trenches of an investment bank scramble to collect, of all things, transparent Lucite bricks framing the *Wall Street Journal* announcement of any deal they even remotely worked on. Atop the radiators and bookshelves of cramped offices throughout Midtown and downtown they are lined up as opalescent trophies, two or three in a row, sometimes eight or nine. The Bull had amassed a total of sixty-one Lucites. They stood like the tall wall of an igloo on their custom-built shelf before my window, making milky the light in my corner office, bathing my every activity with the glow of a winner.

But then, at an impressive thirty-four years of age, I was crowned with the kingly salary and ruthless power of managing director. After eight years at the company, I had been plucked from the cold callers, paper pushers, and spreadsheet monkeys to reign over the lot of them—with little desire, and no ability, to do so. I was not, as they say, a people person; yet I would be paid three and a half million dollars a year to woo and smooth-talk new clients. I would be the guy who brought in business, the man who kissed ass to kick ass. Already I was known as the Bull, thanks to my brisk earnings in a gung-ho market, to my ability to endure punishment, to gallop numbly forward, bellow and gore. But managing director was a nimbler position of social artistry, a mandate to romance CEOs and to sweep their companies gallantly under our wing. I would have to learn to talk golf, to cruise art-gallery openings, to lose weight. I would need more suits. I would collect more wine. I would be free from the drab productivity of days spent immersed in numbers. I was joining the ranks of the rainmakers, the market sages who suavely enthuse on cue on CNN. I had been elevated to the royalty of the tribe that had adopted me at the age of twenty-four. And I was lost.

I reached aisle 7 (frozen vegetables, ice cream) in a daze. High above me, godlike in the fluorescence, was the managing director of some investment bank or another, peering down to analyze a typical buyer of frozen foods. I took a moment, scratching my stomach, to consider the family-size bag of Tater Tots. I squinted up toward my hovering past. I sneered at what I had been, and, harder, at what I was now without it: at how far I'd fallen, and how surely I deserved that. I regretted it, then, the whole thing, if only for a frozen moment in the freezer aisle. Then I yanked open the nearest door and heaved the five-pound sack of potato product into my cart.

THE SECOND TRAINING SESSION

concerned the tapping of water sources and the connection of hoses. As we left to some final seal barks of wisdom from Captain Stan and headed across the parking lot toward our cars, the talk was of calls. I was relieved to be immersed in that chuckling dullness; preferring it, anyway, to the wrath that had surrounded me for the previous two hours. I had correctly identified FEMA as the Federal Emergency Management Agency to the low hisses of my classmates. I had promptly located the Office of Fire Prevention within the U.S. Department of State and been rewarded with the captain's bald nod and more angry stares. Now I smiled along with the rehash of local semi-emergencies. Dovertown Company had responded to a varsity football team bonfire that had spread, albeit briefly, to the edge of a neighbor's yard. Hempstead had gone out to the scene of a collapsed barn that had threatened, if momentarily, the well-being of a half dozen cows. This, it seemed, was life as a volunteer firefighter. Hoping for action; responding to mishaps; talking them up for weeks after the fact. No wonder my stove fire had made the front page of the paper. Thank God, for these restless meddlers, that I'd blundered into town and set it ablaze. I realized that I had quite possibly overestimated the danger of this job. I had intended to come face-to-face with what scared me. Instead I was trapped in a sort of mobile men's club, nodding at the tall tales of the otherwise bored.

We had stopped in the parking lot, halted before our cars. Grayville, someone was saying, had a one-car pileup on Sunday afternoon that required the help of the Jaws.

"Who's Jaws?" I asked Sully.

"Jaws of Life," he said. He lit the stub of a cigar, puffing hard to get it going. "The tool."

We stood in our circle like boys after a Little League game, hitching up our pants, not going home. I looked at my watch. "Well, gentlemen," I said, "I hate to—"

From somewhere nearby came a piercing *bip-bip-bip-bip* and I ducked. When I rose from my cringe Sully was looking down at his pager. The electric cacophony cut to static, then gave way to a robotic woman's voice.

"Sixty control Harristown: firefighters needed to respond to South Briar Lane for a PIAA, possible extrication. Repeat: sixty control Harristown, manpower needed at a PIAA on South Briar. Possible extrication."

"Never make the truck," challenged the burly man beside Sully.

Sully looked at me, a gleam in his beady eyes. "Bet we do."

"No fucking way!" said another of the guys. "Harristown's twenty minutes. Fifteen minutes easy."

We broke from the circle. Sully accelerated into a jog. I waddled to catch up, change jangling loudly in my pockets.

"Which is your car?" he asked.

"Right here. What's a PIA?"

But he had stopped, breathing hard. "That's yours?"

For a moment, then, the emergency was forgotten, the pager and the firemen behind us suddenly silent, the crackling inferno consuming South Briar Lane having simmered into the stares of my classmates. Mine was the only vehicle in the parking lot without four-wheel drive and crooked bumper stickers. It appeared naked among the mud flaps and gun racks of its neighbors. I had finally removed the sales sticker from the passenger-side window with the help of a sterling-silver butter knife; nonetheless, the car had the unmistakable gleam of brand-newness, its backside wide and smooth as the butt of the fat kid in the locker-room showers.

The bloop of my handheld unlocker mechanism broke the silence. I started up the car and pulled out behind Sully to a farewell round of kissy noises and shouts.

It wasn't until we were on the main road and I was struggling to follow the winking blue siren atop Sully's beat-up compact car that I realized two things. First: that driving over the speed limit was a skill wholly distinct from driving, and one I was unlikely to acquire in the next several minutes. Second: that should I somehow arrive bodily intact at the firehouse, I hadn't the slightest idea what to do. Nevertheless I gunned the gas, closed the gap with Sully. I was roaring to the rescue. Responding to the call. We were halfway there, by my blurry estimation, when I heard the faint whine of the firehouse siren. Sully slid a hard right before a plant nursery and lost me. I reversed, turned, firsted and seconded and thirded to catch up just as he screeched a left. I screeched one louder. We emerged on a familiar-looking road and were at the station a minute later.

A fire truck was idling in the station driveway. I parked next to Sully and opened and threw my door shut, stumbling after him and pulling up my pants. Panic sounded from the rooftop siren. I ran into the open bay. A man standing by the racks of gear windmilled an arm to hurry me up. Past him, halfway down the rack, I stopped looking for my gear with the realization that I didn't have any. The man helped me gather a helmet and gloves and heap of spare gear and I was standing beside the giant truck with it all sliding out of my arms.

"Put on your bunkers!" someone shouted.

I looked around for bunkers, for who the hell was yelling at me.

"Your pants, Probie!"

My heckler was the ax-sharpening fiend with the hooked nose and baseball cap who was pointing down at me, jeering at me, from the high passenger window of the truck. I was going to shout something back when the truck lurched forward, screaming now in a duet with the station siren, and the back door banged open and someone pulled me in.

I landed on a bench facing backward. I pushed myself off the lap of Pete Karl. A howling turn threw me again into my three fellow passengers, all dressed from head to toe in fire gear and wearing the same battle-ready scowls. Beside Pete Karl was a man with perfectly combed hair, helmet in hand. At the far window was the guy who worked the counter at the gas mart—I recognized him instantly—his chin showing the white remains of an unfinished shave.

"Suit up there, Will," Pete Karl advised me. He was fastening the last snaps at the top of his coat, pushing the hanging bush of his beard out of the way with the back of his hand as we went. He hadn't rubber-banded it this morning: he, too, apparently caught by surprise.

"Bill," I corrected him.

"Ought to take Pony Hill." He looked past me out my window. "Take Pony Hill!" he yelled over his shoulder at the Plexiglass that separated us from Sully, who was driving, and the tattooed jackass who called me names.

Sully spun the huge wheel to bear right. He gave a foghorn blast by pulling on a hammocked cord that hung from the ceiling. I stood, legs apart, wobbling slightly, to put on my gear. I steadied myself with a hand against the steel ceiling. I was in my suspenders and had nearly snapped closed my coat when Sully braked and I went down. He was honking and shrilling the siren, I saw when I stood to look, at a stopped flock of geese.

"Almost to South Briar," said Pete Karl. "I'd take a seat there, Will."

I sat. There were no seat belts. We were off again, sliding into each other as we careened toward the PIA.

"What's a PIA?" I asked them.

"PIAA," said the man with the well-combed hair. "Personal injury automobile accident. Gary."

I shook his offered glove with my bare hand. "Bill." Then I clutched the seat. I had only recently accustomed myself to the discipline of driving forward. Hurtling backward, and through hairpin turns, was a seasickness I'd never known. I needed air. I could see no handle for my window. Behind our heads, above our bench, portable oxygen tanks were fastened in a ready row with their shoulder straps facing out. I was thinking of sneaking a puff from the nearest swaying tube, if only I could guess how to turn the thing on, when we pulled halfway off the road and to a stop.

Sully cut the siren and spoke into a walkie-talkie. Mr. Gas Mart shoved open the far door and we all climbed down after him. I was handed a length of gleaming iron that was forked at the end like a can opener and weighed a ton. It wasn't easy to walk with that and with all my limbs quilted in fireproof canvas. Balancing the tool over my shoulder like a miner on his way to work, I swaggered unsteadily toward the accident.

A station wagon and a pickup truck had collided in the entrance to a garden store. In New York City, the drivers would have been shouting it out beside the crash. Here there was no argument, no arguers, only vehicles ticking loudly as if counting the seconds until help would arrive. The owner of the station wagon had pushed open his dented door and stood woozily by his vehicle. The driver of the crumpled pickup must have already left. We weren't alone on the scene. Along with the store owner and a few customers warily circling the wrecked cars, the Harristown Volunteer Ambulance Corps had arrived. There were three of them, two women and a man, all in red jackets with medical patches on the sleeve. A woman with thick glasses pulled out a stretcher from the back of the ambulance, clacked down its wheels and rolled it toward the dazed man beside the station wagon. In a moment the other medics—a frail-looking grandfatherly type and a younger woman with a mop of curly brown hair—had surrounded the guy as well. With a start, I realized that the curly woman was the same person who had slunk down the stairs of Henry's Place in her undies to greet me. Now she was beaming a penlight into the victim's pupils, taking his pulse and listening to his hunched complaints of a pain in his ribs.

Our chief pulled up, screeching his wheels, with a bugling from the top of his chief's car. This was a kind of remodeled sedan, painted cherry red and equipped with a full brass section of horns and sirens on its roof. It occurred to me to wonder what the Christ we were doing there. There was no sign of fire. Not a damned wisp of smoke. I dropped my giant metal tool with a clash and walked to where the onlookers had clustered around the pickup. I parted them to take a casual seat on the mashed hood. After a minute, the curly-haired woman hurried toward me. Apparently she had recognized me. But she hadn't: she was looking right past me and through the spiderwebbed windshield. I turned to see the spattered blood and the body. I scrambled off the hood and to my feet. "Holy fuck."

Bits of blood decorated the windshield. There was a person discarded across the seat, a large one, thrown sideways like a pile of laundry: a bloody head in a heap of clothes. Henry's curly girlfriend tugged at the near door handle to no avail. She walked around the truck and pulled at the other.

"Jammed shut?" I asked.

Her sideways look indicated the stupidity of my question. "Whole frame's out of whack," she said.

"So what do we do?" My voice rose higher than I would have liked.

She stared at me head-on. There was no memory, there, of me, nor any discernible trace of the slumber-party kitten from three weeks before. Only her rowdy loops of brown-black hair and her fierce eyes and this: "You should probably just stand here with your thumb up your ass." She smiled prettily. "Yep, perfect. Just like that."

Before I could respond, Pete Karl called me from around the corner of the truck. He and Gas Mart were on the ground, kneeling and grunting, working to wedge blocks of wood behind the wheels. "Lift the chassis for me right here, Will. Just quick. Here we go. Gotta chock your vehicle," he told me without looking up. "Keeps it from sliding or shifting around. Extricating a victim, you've gotta have chocks. And up." I turned and with a huffed breath managed to lift the body of the pickup ever so slightly—facing away from it, hands under the edge, heaving upward and feeling, despite the wariness expressed as a ping in my lower back, the miraculous lift of the impossible burden, the flexed triumph of Atlas—as Pete Karl pounded in the last chock with the hammerlike heel of his hand.

Now the jerk with the hooked nose approached us from the fire truck, armed with a handheld electric saw. He had traded his usual baseball cap for a helmet but hadn't bothered to put on a jacket. In defiance of the frigid breeze, his sleeveless gray T-shirt showed off his etchings of dragons and eagles and motorcycles and the naked women who ride them. The chief strode over to join us in rollicking slow-motion. Gas Mart had lit and dropped flares in an arc around the accident. They frothed red, roaring softly, stinking and smoking to high heaven. Gary held the nozzle of the hose that lay taut as a pipe along the street. He stood with it aimed forward, chin up, helmet crooked, pointless and proud as a Buckingham Palace guard.

Henry's girlfriend was back by my side. "Boys with toys," she muttered, maybe to me.

"Let's go," shouted the bespectacled medic. She had wheeled out a second stretcher, over which she called out: "Golden hour ticking away here."

"Get over here and back up Finelli," said the chief. He was pointing at me. "You. Big man. New guy."

"Probie," supplied Finelli. Given the size and shape of his nose, he may have been capable of nothing but that sneer.

As I moved reluctantly toward him, I felt—it couldn't be, and yet there was no denying the dull thump on the back of my fire pants—an encouraging butt slap from Henry's girlfriend. Somehow I kept from turning around. I stood, as ordered, at Finelli's back. I peered over his shoulder and through the red-splashed glass at the woman lying across the seat. She was a fat woman—enormous, actually—taking up virtually the whole cab. Half her face was visible where it wasn't covered by her flung arm. There was a round cut on her forehead, like a crushed strawberry, and what looked like a deeper gash under her chin. There was a generous crescent of flab where her sweater had pulled up at the waist. There was blood everywhere, her life having leaked out in all directions. No one else seemed to react to the fact that she was dead. Who the hell knew we would be dealing with dead bodies? There was ice in my stomach, a jellyish quality to my legs that made me think they might buckle completely, as they had once before.

"Just peel back the windshield while I saw it," Finelli turned to yell at me from inches away. He was holding the electric knife to the corner of the glass. "Think you can handle that, Probie? Put down your shield. God-*damn*."

I owned a shield? I did: a face shield. I slid down the clear plastic visor at the front of my helmet. The circle of spectators craned forward. Gary dragged his hose closer. He was beside the curly woman who had smacked my ass, whispering and nodding with her. Apparently she had secret, loving links to every man on our squad. The other two medics waited behind us with the stretcher. Sully, I noticed, stood all the way back at the fire truck before the shiny panel of dials and levers devoted to Gary's water pressure. He was clinging to his dials, staying a safe distance away. I didn't blame him. I envied him. The saw revved suddenly, an awful sound.

Finelli pushed the serrated blade into the crushed glass and sliced loudly downward. I held the sagging flap, leaning around him, until he had cut back along the bottom and top edges and I could peel the whole tinkling thing out of the way.

"Not in," Finelli complained. "Out. Keep the fucking glass— there you go. Come on, Probie. Keep the glass out of the car."

I was forced to look, once I'd pulled aside the heavy screen, at death itself. Death by car. The woman had been killed in the crash, bashed to death, heavy and gone. And with that, I was too. The road was rising to meet me. Again I was collapsing in the presence of a victim. But this time I didn't quite go down. From behind, someone prodded me back to full height: a miraculous laying on of latex gloves. Attached to the gloves, I saw when I turned, was the woman with curly hair. Good of her, I thought as I swooned once more and stabilized myself, setting my feet. She gave me another push, harder now. I realized she was trying to shove me out of the way.

I stumbled aside and stood between Finelli and the chief to watch the ambulance corps take over. The curly woman scampered up over the hood, through the empty windshield, and into the cab to talk to the dead. There was, after several sentences, a cough and a murmur in response. The elderly male medic climbed through the same windshield hole to help wrap the victim in a head bandage, chin bandage, neck brace, and oxygen mask. Soon the gigantic woman was strapped to a wooden board. She lay across the interior of her truck like a trophy fish. It was rapidly established, in mumbles and shouts, that she was too big to fit back out through the front. Finelli stormed back to the fire truck, issuing curses and instructions, pushing past Sully, banging open a compartment door and dragging out some tremendous tool. He returned, his arms all tendons and bulges and graffiti, with what looked like a beaked chain saw. The Jaws of Life.

The chief gave a husky update into his radio. Pete Karl, having retrieved the tool I'd dropped—a halligan, he called it—fit its sharp end into the front seam of the driver's-side door and rocked his whole little body back and forth until he'd wedged open a hole. He stood back and nodded at Finelli, who by then had finished connecting all the hydraulic hoses of the Jaws and stepped forward to insert its beak into the ragged gap. As he turned the handle, the beak separated into two heavy pincers that spread outward, mightily dividing the door from the frame. There was a low questioning sound, a rising moan from the vehicle. The woman with curly hair peered out from the other side of the window, talking into the ear of the victim on the board. Smushed tightly beside them, the elderly medic signaled to us with a twirling hand to hurry up.

The circle of civilians pressed forward. The chief scared them back. In the car, in anticipation, the curly woman draped her arms protectively over her patient. Then she was hurled aside. The victim was bucking her big legs. Her head lolled back and forth. The whole truck shook with her mighty frenzy as the medics tried to pin her down. Bits of blood flecked their faces. They shouted inaudibly along with the groan of the Jaws.

"Get 'em out! She's done in there!" screamed the medic with the thick glasses behind me.

"Let's move it!" boomed the chief.

Pete Karl and I grabbed the halligan at the same time and I wrenched it away. I jammed it in a few inches above the Jaws, finding a seam and working it, heaving back and forth. Gary dropped his hose and ran over. Gas Mart joined in, still holding an unlit flare, reaching around me to help push and pull at my halligan with his free hand. In the car, in the corner of my eye, the fat woman continued to flail. Finelli kept at it with the Jaws. His swollen biceps looked like they might burst. The straining of the hinge grew louder and higher.

Almost there, Finelli shouted. I, too, was there. Then there was a metallic squeal and a bang as the door jumped open and we were in.

THE DRIVE BACK WAS SIRENLESS.

Once in the station, at the rack beside the others, I peeled off my borrowed fire gear and hung it up on an open hook. Walking aimlessly around, I counted four posters advertising Freightliner trucks. I noticed at the back of the truck bay a wooden staircase leading up to some hidden headquarters or secret tree house. I wondered if the smell of gas was something you got used to, and whether you could breathe it long enough to establish some kind of semi-toxic equilibrium in your lungs. The rest of the squad, Finelli first, was headed for the staircase, and I was considering following along when Gary caught me, with a soft paw on my shoulder, from behind.

"Well, look whoosh here."

His outfit, now that he was wearing his own clothes, was an echelon above the fashion of the other locals. The arms of a lime green sweater were draped forward and knotted over a crisp-collared shirt. His hair was carefully smoothed into a sideways part and buzzed neatly over ears that, as a result, seemed jug-large. There was the gold watch, the khaki pants compliments of one of those catalogs whose cover photos inevitably incorporate a golden retriever. A local boy made good, or at least playing preppy dress up. All that was missing were the zipper-cased tennis racket and the unread issue of *Fortune*.

"Gary Dickershon," he said. "How've you been."

I accepted his hand for the second time that day. How had I been?

"Show," he said. "Hear you're one of ush now."

"Not quite," I said, glancing at his mouth—I couldn't help it—to discover the cause of his lisp. And there it was, in his half smile. The man had braces. "Apparently," I said, "I'm a pierogi."

"Shorry?"

"A prozie," I tried again.

His face trembled ever so slightly, holding off laughter. "Pro-bie," he said. Then: "How you holding up."

"Okay, thanks."

"Rough firsht call for you."

"Sure."

"Not pretty."

"No."

"Dush happen, though."

"Right."

"Dush happen." He had walked around me to block my way anywhere but into a conversation with him. "Got your pager yet?"

"Nope."

"Come on."

He led me through the firehouse. I followed casually, keeping my distance, reading the posted sign-up sheets as if I were actually considering taking part in a Sunday workshop on roof ventilation. Gary removed a clipboard from a nail in the wall and filled out the form with a fake-gold pen from his breast pocket. Together we lifted an ancient Xerox machine off a box in the radio room that didn't turn out to contain pagers.

"What's the golden hour?" I asked him as we relocated to a small supply closet. "Medic said something about the golden hour."

"Thatch your turnaround time," he said over his shoulder. "Time you got." He was reaching to rummage through a back shelf.

"What do you mean."

"One hour. Thatch ideal. Matchimum time it should take you to get your job done, get your victimsh into hoshpital care. Shixty minutesh, impact to ER. Thatch what you're after. Thatch golden." He turned with a pager in hand, a *ta-da!* look on his soft and merry face. Then he sobered to conclude: "Any longer and you're looking at a lot more fatalities."

He explained the functioning of the pager. Channel one was for our calls: Harristown calls. Channel two was for listening in to all area calls, neighboring fire companies included. The pager was to be clipped onto my belt or otherwise kept on my person at all times, stored in its charger (we'd have to find me a charger) at night. Jush be sure to keep it shomewhere—

"Somewhere I'll hear it," I finished for him.

Gary smiled his tender smile. "Oh, you'll hear it, all right."

A far-off cackle came from the direction of the wooden staircase across the bay.

"Show," Gary said. He had shut and leaned against the closet door. "Pete Karl tellsh me you're going through a divorshe."

"Jesus. He does? My garbageman?"

"Shorry to hear it," he said. "You know, we've been meaning to get you over for dinner." Slowly he reknotted the sweater arms at his chest. "Me and Maddy. Cook you a pot of my shtew."

"Huh."

"What do you do again, Bill. Shtocks?"

"Not much," I replied. "You?"

"I mean for work. I should know thish. Finansh."

I didn't know why Gary should know anything. "What about you."

"Real eshtate," he reported with some gravity. He was watching me, apparently to gauge whether I was impressed. "Shtill a broker. And how about you."

Screw it, I thought. "I was on the Street," I told him.

There was a moment of shock. Then a murmur of sympathy. The rustle of pocketed hands and shuffled loafers. "Thatch tough," he said. "Thatch no way to live."

"Telling me," I said. I fiddled with my pager. Then I looked up at him. "On Wall Street."

"Oh, heck. Wall Shtreet. Jeez." He gave a chuckle of relief. "Show—what. Early retirement?"

"Nah," I said. "Could be. Just taking some time." From the distant staircase came the sound of a man's belch. "What's up those stairs?" I asked Gary. "There a bar?"

"Make your money, though, that line of work." He had lowered his voice, ignoring my question, keeping things between us. He leaned closer. There were traces of a terrible cologne. "Dabble a bit myshelf."

"In investment banking?"

"No, no. Heck no. I jush mean the market."

I pictured his market: baskets of green beans, bushels of corn, a table of fresh-baked pies. "Good for you."

"Treasurer of the fire company, for one thing."

"Are you?"

"But you can't move much money with that. Not much money to move, between you and me. Company's pretty shtrapped."

"Uh-huh."

"Shtrapped financially, I mean."

"Got it," I said.

"Yep. Pretty bad shape." He smoothed his glossy hair. "Not enough money, not enough guys. The way Harrishtown's growing? Number of shummer residents? New homesh? Not a chance. Jush not enough volunteers."

I looked at the pager in my hand. I switched the tiny channel dial for practice. I hadn't thought to take off my wedding ring, I noticed. Did one remove the ring at this stage? Or does one wait until the thing is finalized, until the end is announced by a banged gavel, before yanking it off and flinging it upward with the glee of the graduate?

"You know," Gary said then, "your place is right next to my shishter's."

"Huh."

"Well, not far," he reconsidered. "Around the corner there. You met my shishter."

"I don't think so."

"Paula. With the ambulanshe corps."

"That's your sister? Henry's Paula?"

"Not Henry'sh. Not at all. Paula. My shishter Paula."

"I met her at Henry's." I probably shouldn't have said anything. Christ, I didn't care. "Few weeks ago. Early in the morning."

He smiled, then, which surprised me. "Well, Henry ownsh a bar. Thatch enough for Paula." Before I could say anything he went on: "Paula'sh PJ's mom."

"Who's PJ."

"PJ. My niche."

"Your niche?"

"Niche. Shister's kid. Your little neighbor over there."

"I don't have any little neighbors."

"Sure you do. Little girl."

"Oh, right. Maybe. I have seen a girl."

"Tough shituation there. Father up and bolted. Just took off one day. No note, no nothing. Heard he was shacking up with a girl in Claremont, but I never shaw her."

"Just disappeared," I heard myself say.

"Paula dush what she can. Lot of booze, though. You know. Worksh hard, don't get me wrong. Teaches pottery. Goesh out on the ambulanshe. But PJ gets kind of losht in the shuffle. Alone a lot of the time. Playing in her garage. A kid needs— heck, you know. More than that, anyway. A kid needs shomeone to be there. If you ashk me. All about family."

"Mm."

"All about the kind of shupport you get from a family. Mother and father." He spotted something on the hanging arm of his sweater and attempted to brush it off. "I'm not shaying that PJ needs a man around. Heck, I'm just shaying that she needs a bit of balance. Bit of authority, if you ashk me. *Attention*, for one thing. The kitch practically crying out for—"

People in the country create conversation the way chimneys create smoke. They contribute it to the open air, allowing it to pleasantly and meaninglessly evaporate overhead as a wafting sign of life, a symbol of warmth. I moved doggedly toward the door of the bay that led outside, the promise of freedom.

"Keep an eye out for her," he said finally. "If you would."

I startled at the request. "An eye out?"

"Time to time. You know."

I had no idea what the hell he was talking about. "Do you mean baby-sit?"

"I don't mean baby-shit," he hissed through his braces, apparently offended. "Be a neighbor. Shall I'm ashking."

"Sure," I said. I had no option there. "I'll be her neighbor," I agreed. "You bet."

IT WAS NOT IMMEDIATELY OBVIOUS,

sipping my awful coffee and looking out the kitchen window, gagging and sipping again to keep warm, then narrowing to a squint, that someone had kicked in the side of my car. But someone had. There were boot marks before the back wheel, a barrage of angry dents. There had been a midnight attack: an outburst of pure fury directed at the vehicle that had brought me to town. I stared at it, frightened by the depth of those dents, until my coffee was gone.

I picked up the phone and tried Mark again at the office. I had called him back three or four times, each time regretting it miserably but needing to ask (Christ, I might as well ask) for any more information he might have remembered about Pippa's date. But I could tell from Shelly's tone that she had ceased to give Mark my messages. I was out of the loop now. Irrelevant. Unemployed. Life was too short—those office days were too short—to accommodate any damned charity cases. I would never hear from him again.

I had studied all I could about knots in ropes: about the usefulness of the bowline, the half hitch, the clove hitch. I had quizzed myself on how to tie a becket bend and tow a victim with your basic figure eight. I smacked closed the workbook. It was freezing outside, the sky heavy lidded. It was dead cold again in the house. Three point three million dollars I'd paid for this arctic shack, this three-story iceberg. I stomped out of the piano room and upstairs to get a sweater. In an early-eighteenth-century Queen Anne walnut chest of drawers, I found the few of my clothes that Pippa had deposited—demoted, really, after years of my neglecting to wear them in the city. I pulled on a large-looking sweater decorated with snowflakes and had to force it over my gut. I tried another sweater I didn't remember, a purple one, with the same result. I wrestled it off and looked at it. I had never owned this sweater. I was not a purple person; nor was Pippa the type to buy me clothing on a whim. These were his sweaters, not mine. In my drawer. I clenched my teeth.

I pawed madly through the drawer. There were four of them, by my count, layered atop a white cable-knit job that I recognized as my own. I threw the offending items aside and yanked on the white one. I glared at them, my fallen enemies, as if I could decipher his identity from their sprawl. With a strange sound that seemed to break from my chest, I bent to grab and gather them up. I charged the window, flung it open, reared back, and hurled.

I expected they would sail a bit on the cold air, planing and fluttering in a graceful catharsis. Instead, they more or less plopped straight down. The other surprise, when I looked, was that they'd plopped on a little girl.

I jogged all the way downstairs and shoved open the front door. "You all right?"

She didn't hear me. She was returning from school, singing something as she crossed the grass, the heavenly bombardment forgotten. It was frigid enough, with my loafer bracing open the front door, to consider letting it go. The cluster of trees that once distinguished my yard were bare now, a clutch of dead arms and fingers.

I tried again: "Hello."

She only sang louder.

"Halt!"

This she did. Standing several yards away, in the middle of my lawn, was a gnarl of dirty blond hair around a dirtier face. Beneath her open pink parka, she wore overalls with a Superman patch at the chest. Her shoulders were pulled back by the pink straps of a book bag that was nearly her size. It wasn't dirt dotting her face, I could see now, but Magic Marker. "Who are you?" she said.

"Who am *I*?" I almost laughed. "I am the owner of this property."

Fists on hips. "The *oooo*-ner?"

"The owner, right. Which makes you a trespasser."

"I'm not a trepasher."

"Yes, you are. A trespasser. You are trespassing on my grounds."

"You own the ground?"

I descended the steps into the freezing breeze. "Come here." I beckoned with my hand and then my whole arm. "Come over here. Right now."

She shuffled forward with reluctance, evidently well trained in the rules regarding strangers and strange houses.

"This," I said when she stood waist high before me, "is my house. Which means that no one can come over if I don't say it's okay. Nobody. Ever. You, in other words. Are we clear on that?"

"But you told me to come over."

"No, I—right. Yes. I did. Just now. But not before. Not as a general policy."

"What's a gerenol po—"

"Not for keeps," I snapped, attempting a translation. "Not for keepsies."

She pointed. "That's my school." Her finger was painted a vibrant maroon. She was, all in all, the filthiest child I'd ever seen. "Past those trees."

"I understand. I don't care. What I'm telling you—what's your name again."

The colored finger moved toward me. "What's yours."

"Mine?" I had to think about it. "Mr. Schoenberg."

"Mr. *whaaaat?*"

"William. Bill. What's yours."

"*Wheel*-yum!" she burst out. "That's a funny name."

"No, it's not. Give me yours."

"*Guessss.*" She grinned with her *s* to show a set of mangled teeth.

"I'm not going to guess. You tell m—"

"Oooo, my arm. Ow. I pulled my muscle." She gripped her elbow. "Ow. *Owwww*. No, I'm okay. Whew." She shook out her arm. Then she remembered. "Hey. You haven't guessed my name."

"I'm not—"

"You have to guess! You *have* to."

I looked angrily at my watch. I was late for nothing. "Adelaide. Amy. Andrea. Anne. Antoinette."

"*Adelay!*" The girl clutched her stomach with both hands, opening her mouth in imitation of a laugh. "*Ya*-ha-ha-ha. Adelay! What a name!" She almost went over backward onto the hard grass, stepping back just before the book bag took her down. "Whoah." She giggled. "Did you see that?"

"You're going to have to find another way to walk to school," I said. "This is my lawn. These are my woods."

"Are those your *trees?*"

"That's right."

"Even that one?" She pointed, a jab of maroon.

"Yes. So good-bye."

"And *that* one?"

"Sure, that one. See you later."

"Even *thaaat* one?"

"Bye-b—"

"You're not looking where I'm looking," she complained. "I said *that* one." She was on her tiptoes, pointing up and past my log pile, the handsome wall of cross-stacked wood that had been transported and arranged for a mere eighty bucks by a toothless dump-truck driver named Lucky.

"Yes. Right. That's mine."

"But I wasn't pointing at a tree!" she shouted. "*Ya*-ha-ha-ha. That's a rock! You said you owned a *rock!*"

"I did. I do. I own every part of the—"

"Do you own *that?*"

"Absolutely. Whatever the fuck you're pointing at."

"I'm pointing at the *air!*" she crowed. "You can't own the air!" But she'd heard it. "Hey, you said a bad word."

"Yes, I did. I used a very bad word," I said slowly, instructively, "for a very bad girl."

"I'm not a berry bad—hey. I said *berry*. Did you hear that?"

"A girl who trespasses on property belonging to someone else. But I'll tell you what. If you leave now, and I do mean *now*, then I won't tell on you. Only you can't come back. That's the deal. Our deal. Just between you and me. Will you make that deal with me?"

I could hear my cell phone ringing in the backseat of the car. I ignored it, keeping my stern parental gaze on the girl.

"You had a *fire*," she said then.

I rocked back on my heels, continuing to glare at her.

She was stamping around on the lawn. "Know what?"

"What."

"My uncle?"

"What."

"My uncle is in the fire company."

"I knew that. Larry. Gary."

"Know what else?"

"What."

"My friend Jessie?"

"Jesus. What."

"Her father?"

I imagined washing her face, scrubbing it clean, bearing down with the stiffest washcloth I could find.

"Her father's in the fire company."

"Everybody is in the fire company," I said. "I have to go now. Actually, *you* have to go. Right now."

"Are *you* in the fire department?"

"Yes I am."

"But if you're in the fire department," she asked me very seriously, her small brow gathering all the divots it could, "then how can you have a fire?"

I put a hand to my temple. A mean ache pulsed behind my eyes. That was the question, wasn't it. How had I allowed it to happen? How does one drop his God-given defenses, abandon his husbandly duties in order to stand aside, lie down and let things go wrong in his home?

"Kid," I said softly. "We have to stop talking now."

She tilted her head. "But you just talked," she pointed out.

THE LEAVES HAD BEEN OFF

the trees for a couple weeks, carpeting the hard ground in scraps of brown. The giant sky gathered into layers. The river went black. And then, as if the cold itself were crumbling, it started to snow. I went out on the lawn to feel it. There were only flecks, and tiny ones, brushing the bare tops of my cheeks and catching in my beard. A look toward the trees along the river confirmed that the air had gone cotton white. In New York City the onset of winter meant the ornery clanking of radiators in apartments, the all-importance of finding a cab. Steam off the Central Park pretzel carts. Wild herds of fur-coated shoppers on Fifth. Holiday tips extorted by the doormen in their hokey wool-lined caps. Here winter was more delicate, ticking away. Building into the softest of downfalls. Faster now. And then fast.

With the snow, things slipped. Over the first few white days there was a one-car collision off North Fork Road (Dodge mini-van, row of oaks, two forty-five A.M.,) and the smash of a Toyota (*Japtrap,* Sully called it) into the posted fence before the tree nursery. I began, after several extrications, to think of cars as tin cans on wheels: easily crushed by accident, at the risk of their contents; openable with all kinds of tools in a jam. No wonder I'd never wanted to drive one. When I took the wheel now I drove more slowly, and only after pulling on the seat belt and double-checking its security with a quick couple yanks. But it wasn't just car accidents. Things went wrong all the time, and a battery of men enlisted to right them was in desperate demand. My life became charged with the expectation of alarm. The calls didn't come constantly, but over the course of a month they added up to a dozen sudden outings under red and white lights. A smoke detector malfunctioned at an office-furniture store near the highway. An automatic alarm went off twice at the post office. A backyard leaf burning scattered to bright ashes before we could arrive to scold the old lady with the rake. These were not death-defying rescue missions; and yet the silence of the days in between them throbbed as if about, any second, to burst into beeps.

I filled that charged time with workbook studying sessions and then, remarkably, exercise. I had resolved, with a last melo-dramatic swig of gin straight from the bottle, to shape up. I had no choice if I was going to try and keep up with those hose haulers down at the station: men who split felled lumber for sport, who erected toolsheds on the weekends, who shot turkey and wrestled deer in the dark daily hours before breakfast. I did sit-ups with my feet wedged under the dryer in the basement and my ass on an oriental rug I'd found in the attic and dragged (a sickening workout in itself) all the way down. My push-ups were abbreviated helpfully by the impact of my stomach. Chin-ups, with a grip on the wooden beam that ran below the base-ment ceiling, had thus far proved a nonstarter, hanging me to swivel like a side of aged beef. Always I feared and awaited the tones of the pager. I heard them in the squeak of the large tree at the corner of the house, in the weep of a passing bird.

Yet still it shocked me when the call came. The screaming tones, my stumbling to attention and taking off at a run through the house and through the nausea of adrenaline. *Brush fire,* an-nounced the robotic woman who sat in the county-wide control room and dispatched us from her perch on my waist. I snapped my pager off my belt to hear better as I ran out the front door and down the fuzzy white steps. I crossed the lawn in a powdery downpour. *Brush fire,* it was repeated, *at the Reyfeldt Farm, Rural Route 8.*

I was late to the station, as usual, but had learned to dress more quickly in the swerving backward cabin. Sully, as always, was in the driver's seat. Pete Karl hadn't made the truck. Finelli, I was sorry to see through the Plexiglass, had. Each call meant a new combination of local personalities. We were a rotating social group, a kaleidoscope of jerks. This evening we numbered— with Gary and Henry—five.

"Sheinberg," Gary greeted me. He had forgotten half his gear: below his turnout coat he wore khaki pants with hiking boots. Henry, too, was pantless, wearing only jeans.

"So how can you have a brush fire," I asked them as I twanged up my suspenders and snapped my jacket, "with all the snow?"

"Burnsh under the ground."

"Under the what? The ground?"

"Can burn for weeksh like that," Gary said. "Munch. Yearsh. Catches way down in the peat. Can't shee it, can't touch it. We had a call here at the Reyfeldtsh' in July. I'd bet the shucker never went out. Jusht come up through a new hole."

I looked at him and Henry. "You're telling me the ground catches fire."

"Hell," said Henry. "Everything catches fire."

We entered the gates of the farm, rambled past a red barn and empty chicken coop and sped across a field, bumping over gopher holes and stray livestock. Sully flipped to a different siren of deep whoops and jammed on the brakes. He cut the noise, left the lights, announced our arrival over his shoulder, and we all emptied out. I clambered stiffly as an astronaut in my knee-high boots. And then I stopped. The smell hit first—then the sight of the roasting woods. Before us, all around us, an entire forest crackled and fumed. There were real flames, the occasional flicker, a few scraps of orange dancing on branches behind the spreading haze and beneath the falling snow. Black smoke built upward, erasing the afternoon sky. There was growling and snapping in all directions. Everything had caught fire.

The chief pulled up behind us, slammed the door of his Chiefmobile, and passed me with his seesaw walk. He yelled to Sully to charge the one and a half. The one-and-a-half-inch hose was one size more serious than the booster line, which was the option of smallest diameter—something like a rubber garden hose—when it came to brush fires. I suppose I should have taken some comfort in the fact that the chief hadn't ordered the one and three quarters or the two-incher. But I couldn't move.

"Better take off those bunkers." The chief was pointing at my legs. "Got no mobility in bunkers."

"Yo, Probie," shouted Finelli. "Gotta be able to run if you want to fight a brush fire."

I sat down, right there in the field, on a hard plate of ice. I didn't actually want to fight a brush fire. I took off the jacket, yanked down the suspenders, ripped apart the Velcro fly and wrestled off the fireproof pants over my boots. I was wearing, to my dismay, the slacks to a pin-striped charcoal suit. I re-snapped my jacket and clomped over, wincing in the snowfall, to join the rest of the squad at the edge of the crackling woods. We were too close. That's what I was thinking. I could feel the heat of the thing on my face. My stomach was sprinting back-ward, dragging me away. Sully, standing alone by the truck, had the right idea. Yet tools were being passed out. Finelli got an ax. Gary took the chain saw. Henry dragged forward the hose. I was afraid to take my eyes from the smokescape before us. There were more and more flames by the minute. Sully handed me something hard and light. When I could look away from the chuckling smoke and the deadly bits of red, I saw that I held a rake. Apparently I was to sweep up afterward. I'd been de-moted to company custodian. I stabbed down the rake as if dis-appointed, awash in relief.

The chief loomed beside me. "Make us a fuel break," he commanded. "Know how to do that, right? Fuel break?"

Where I was from, a fuel break meant drinks at Moran's or the Crane Club. I looked behind me at the fire truck; at Sully, who delivered a far-off nod; and back to the high-helmeted face of the chief. "When you say fuel—"

"Fuel's what's feeding your fire." He pointed at the ground.

"Dead wood. Dry leaves. Bark. Moss. *Fuel*. You follow? We need a fire line around the area. Nice clean circle around the periphery. Stop the spread before the fire gets out of control. Can someone explain to the new g—"

"Got it," I said. "Rake a break. Right now?"

"Right fucking *now*," piped in Finelli. He brandished his ax, marching forward. "Let's go."

I walked behind him toward the seething trees. Facing the fire. Entering the cackling forest armed only with a goddamned rake. The snow was a gentle blessing, ticking off my helmet, a benediction of last rites on my cheeks and jacket.

"Henry's on the hose," came the voice of the chief behind me, the last human sound I would hear before the fizzing woods took me in. "All right, Gary, get in there. Get the saw going. How's our pressure, Sully?"

The pressure was mine. I was on the brink, only steps from the inferno. And then I was in. I passed the first smoking tree. I stepped over a flaming patch of leaves. I was advancing by layers and degrees—it was already hot—into the fire. The smoke was sour in my nose. I breathed through my mouth. The woods were enormous, sulphurous, and I combustible in them. I hopped several flames and dodged the curtains of smoke in search of the far edge, the end, where the trees and branches would be quiet. Soon the air pushed cooler against my face. The black ground, with its red licks and worms, returned to snow. I crunched a dozen more steps. I breathed, able to breathe now. I dropped the rake to the ground and began.

I forked aside the layer of snow and clawed at the heavy leaves until there was nothing but the combed earth, a bare moat that couldn't be crossed. Panic had settled in my chest and served as a reservoir of energy, quickening the numb activity of my arms. It was a job, that was all. This was my job. My job had always been to put out fires, I thought. Although this was the first one that might kill me.

I moved counterclockwise, choosing my path between the trees, scraping hard at the ground around the shouts of the other guys and the faint shush of water and all the smoke and scattered flags of fire. Despite the cold, I sweated beneath my heavy coat and Paul Stuart shirt and in drops down my face. My back was miraculously painless. I had no time for its gripes. The snapping of leaves and wood grew more distinct, coming closer and louder. I spun around, terrified. I raked faster and faster. I'd begun to perfect a brisk system of rake and shuffle, rake and shuffle, and my path was beginning to curl around the fire when a twig cracked and scared me to death.

"Jesus, Henry."

"Coming through." He was advancing with the hose, spraying the trail I'd cleared. "Gotta soak the break." He peered down over his big mustache at my work. "Wider," he judged.

"Oh yeah?"

He pointed with a glove. There was indeed a narrow stretch that I supposed a flaming branch could fall across, igniting the chance of a runaway fire. I doubled back and scraped the break wider. I had to work harder to stay ahead of Henry. The fire appeared to be creeping, bush after tree, toward the dark section of the woods a hundred yards ahead. I'd have to hurry to get there first. Henry straightened up to eyeball it and, without a word, agreed. He opened up the hose in that direction, shooting it over the fire, raining it down in advance of the flickers and smoke. "Never get there," he grumbled. "Let's go."

So we ran. I could run faster than he could, as he had to lug the hose. I held my rake like a javelin, taking the lead, humping it through the woods, overweight by the usual seventy pounds and almost coming out of my boots, but moving, pumping my jacketed arms, racing to meet the danger and quash it. It is hard to describe the primal importance of that rush, the terror of it, the thrill of it, the bringing of equipment and muscle mass to bear, the concentration of all one's efforts, the mounting speed and determination, the absence of petty second thoughts in the rash embrace of danger. The answering of a call.

I got there—having stomped on an actual flame, ignored the smoke—and raked like hell. From here I could watch the fire come, lapping and prickling, as I worked. It didn't spill recklessly forward so much as pulse with evil life, glow and settle on each new shrub or inch of woodland consumed. The flames had climbed into the branches of trees, lighting their tops like candles. Henry's beam of water arrived before he did, fizzing more smoke to my left, halting the spread. In a few minutes I'd dug out a wide enough arc. Henry soaked the break until it was mud. Then he began to douse the whole woods one square foot at a time. He hit the trees and extinguished them, turning their long trunks to pillars of smoke. I reconnected with my first stretch of break and worked to make it wider. I was a fucking samurai with that rake. Darkness had fallen sometime in the last hour. The snowfall was invisible, barely trickling through the trees. My breath was less ragged now. My back killed.

On Henry's cue we headed back through the soggy black forest and the reek of wood smoke, following the hose line, to where the chief stood directing the others as they cut things down and finished them off. Finelli was laboring to fell scorched trees one chop at a time. Gary was chain-sawing them faster, louder, toppling and dissecting them into parts that poured smoke until Henry doused them. Sully could be seen through the woods, still safely back at the truck, seated on the back bumper like a woodland gnome. In the night air, the glow of his puffed cigar highlighted his features—club nose, Harley-Davidson sideburns—in a jack-o'-lantern effect that lasted the duration of each inhale.

"Pick it up, there, Gary," said Finelli between chops. "Don't got all night."

Gary was red-faced either with the effort or the criticism. The chain saw looked heavy for him. He gritted his teeth, jowls shaking, and roared the saw louder. I leaned on my rake, standing beside the chief. Meanwhile Henry soaked everything in sight. He stuck the nozzle of the hose into stump hollows, jabbed it into the very earth. And as I watched him work, it occurred to me that the man I was looking for (without bothering to look for him—because what was the point?) was Henry.

He was handsome in a way that I could never be. He had been carved by rough experience, his smile lines scrimshawed by the wind, his eyes burnished to their blue twinkle by the rub of seasons past. He spoke, when he could finally be roused from his cranky silence, as if he were a hundred years old; and yet his movements were spry, his body trim and potent. He redirected that hose as easily as I might wield a stretch of dental floss. There was a grouchy mischief to Henry, the crafty old coot.

With that sterling-silver mustache and youthful torso, he could have been anything from fifty to seventy; and with those years had come a certain prowess, an elderly machismo that I, among so many other things, entirely lacked. If he wasn't dating the floozy Paula, as Gary had insisted, then he was free to take a stray from the city into his bed.

It made a kind of creeping sense. Henry had been huffy and silent with me from the start. Could the sardonic glint in his eyes actually be an awkwardness in my presence, a wariness of just how much I knew? He ran the town bar, the only vaguely social establishment for miles; naturally he'd be among the first men she'd have met on her forays into town. After all, he'd been the first one I'd met. First day. What do you know: I'd found the guy right off the bat. The answer had been there, hidden only by a mustache, all along. The mustache must have been an acquired taste for pearl-skinned Pippa. Her sparrow accent would have been foreign to him. But as we all know—as she and I proved—it's not just birds of a feather who flock together. It's the plump and the svelte from different countries; or else the wife and the fireman from different counties. A woman in search of ageless manhood to replace the forty-something fat guy she too quickly took on.

I watched Henry tap-tap the nozzle of the hose on a perfectly healthy-looking tree. We all stood back as Gary cut it down with a scream of the saw. Sure enough, smoke spouted from its insides, blossomed into flames. Gary buzz-cut the thing into logs that Henry drowned.

"How about I take a turn on the hose," I said to Henry then.

He turned his back to rocket the water at a pair of burned trees.

"Yo, Henry."

"Hm."

"I'm thinking I ought to learn to handle the water." *Hosework,* Captain Stan would have called it. "Do some hosework," I said.

"Why do *you* got to learn *hosework?*" sniped Finelli. He halted with his ax in a tree, the latest bang still an echo around us. Spoiling for a fight. "Why are you fucking *here?*"

The chief didn't intervene. I lifted the handle of my rake toward Henry: an offer to trade. After a second, he shrugged and took it, dropped the hose in a hill of snow. I dug out the heavy brass nozzle with both gloves. "So, just, what. Press this? Or pull it. Got it. It's a pull."

The spray began as a wide umbrella and narrowed, as I pulled back the throttle, to a powerful beam. I pegged the trunk of a tree, tunneled into the ground. Obliterated all snowflakes that dared to wander my way. Finelli looked skeptically at everyone in turn, distributing ill will, before returning to his swings and chops. Henry raked at embers. Gaining control, I managed to extinguish a smoking shrub. I walked wide of the group until I spotted a clutch of leaves on fire and turned the beam on them, left them in a lake. I tried Henry's sprinkler technique, aiming into the air to drop a steady rain over a wider area, but the hose was too heavy to keep it up for long. Exhausted, then, I turned to redirect and stumbled on a sawed-off trunk and went down. Somehow I managed to keep the hose up and going, though wildly off-kilter, and when I looked up from my knees I was blasting Finelli dead in the back.

He was shouting, spinning in the woods, losing his baseball cap, bawling like an animal, pegged by the beam that I lifted up and off him only to have it hit branches and ricochet sloppily down. When I finally shut off the water, he stood for a long moment with his jacket shedding streams, hair slicked back, nose crooked, his face a picture of wet rage. I had the momentary urge to turn the water on him again. Then came the yells of laughter. My unacknowledged apology. The spooky woodland shiver of retribution to come.

I HAD BEEN LIVING

with my mistake. Breathing it all day long. I could smell the barbecued den from where I sat, studying my workbook, at the hexagonal Frank Lloyd Wright table in the reading room on the second floor. I had taken pains to avoid reentering the room, cowed by the tenacious smell of burnt wood and cooked paint. I figured the house was big enough to allow several years to pass—the smell, too, to pass—before I would have to deal with the damage. But with the restless, endless bending of the bare trees out all the windows, and with the way the breeze that rattled their branches blew my thoughts back toward me, I realized, despite my efforts to stop realizing things, that I had never fixed anything in my life. I figured it was time to try.

The car door almost didn't close once I'd managed to tug it open. The savage boot blows had continued under cover of night. As I found my way onto the highway, my cell phone rang in the backseat and didn't stop ringing until I'd gotten off, as directed by Sully, at Exit 19. The megastore, when I got there, was vast as an airplane hangar. Shelves of furniture and construction materials rose several stories high. Far beneath the tall racks of boat trailers and wood chippers, employees and customers walked back and forth like ants. I watched someone drive a green forklift down aisle 3. Two men lugged the cross section of a tree toward register 6.

"Repair section?" I asked a passing employee.

Tied into a green Tool Depot smock and plagued by acne, she nonetheless exuded an air of superiority. *"Repair,"* she repeated. "Would that be car repair or home repair?"

"That'd be home," I said in my deepest voice. "Home repair."

"What kind."

"Hand. By hand. Hand repair."

She sighed and tightened her apron. "Better follow me."

Together we walked through a maze of Peg-Board, down long aisles of gleaming weaponry of all shapes and functions. Circular saws were displayed as proudly as platinum albums. There were infinite types and sizes of hammer, thousands of numbered bins of nails, advertised specials on hex nuts and eye bolts and headless brads. Bent riffler files and shoe rasps, plunge routers and base routers, knobs and pulls pushed and tugged at my peripheral vision as I hurried to keep up with the girl. It was the scale of things that was flabbergasting. The store sold not only firewood but entire fireplaces, whole stone chimneys. Gazebos and carports were posed in formation like oversize chess pieces. I expected to turn a corner and see a floor display of price-tagged mansions like mine.

Pippa had probably come to this store, it occurred to me; unless old Henry went for her, the romantic devil, her handyman at heart. Certainly he had spent enough secret time in our house to know the hardware necessary. That might have been their pillow talk, sweet whisperings of light fixtures and upstairs faucet options: the high-pitched designer and the heavy-limbed workhorse, fitting together like nut and bolt. Meanwhile I worked away, with my uncalloused hands, on my air-conditioned ass, in the city. Sensing the worst. Hoping for the best. Sticking to the game plan. Losing bad.

I suppose, looking back, that I stuck with Pippa because I'd never met anyone like her. The Manhattan girls I had striven to date in my youth had been stony and polished. Pippa, however, possessed a far subtler gift for absorption. She swallowed things: common lies, at first, the sooty myths of New York City, and soon more useful lessons that she incorporated with startling ease. The wielding of irony. The deft release of friendships. The importance of indifference. The definition of *arugula*. By the end of our first semester of business school she had stopped asking absolutely everybody how they were, *hi?* Over the course of that spring she'd cut back severely on her smiles. Even her body grew more rigid, dieted down, as she shed the extra layer of health that used to give erotically beneath my fingers when I kneaded her back in the throes of our amateur passion. She had arrived in this country wearing shapeless jerseys of unfashionable colors that she'd knit herself, the hobby of a homebody. By second year she was a cult follower of the glossy fashion magazines that she had never seen on the newsstands of Cape Town. She began to speak less of the equality of the races and the core principles of democracy, more of the flea markets in Chelsea and the sloth of the Mexican kid who belatedly delivered our Chinese food. Shortly before our graduation, when she announced that her life's calling had shifted from African urban planning to American interior design, I wasn't surprised. As an only male child, as her boyfriend and soon fiancé, I tracked her changes with genuine curiosity. This, it seemed, was how girls grew up. They learned to act like men: toughening their skins, armoring for battle. Not knowing that many of us men, when faced with an actual battle, run away.

Our wedding was a harried affair, neither Christian nor Jewish, that Pippa arranged to take place in a Unitarian church on the Lower East Side that would have us. There was the ushering of Pippa's parents, who were as skittishly out of place, out of Africa, as a couple of giraffes. There was the somber hand shaking with my dead father's friends. (He had been gone for a year, having quietly crashed to the carpeted floor of his bedroom, his heart and his lower back exhausted, plumb out of gas.) There were the enthusiastic comments and loud dress of my mother (who seemed to have been freed by my father's death, her incompetence no longer required in the kitchen, liberated to wear flounced skirts and absurd earrings and to dine with elderly bachelors and to pay less attention, from that dark year onward, to me). The honeymoon took place on an island of Pippa's selection whose remoteness made it a celebrity destination, whose beaches gave me second-degree belly burns, and whose overpriced cabanas housed the slidings and grapplings that ended in my new wife's patented high-pitched gasp.

And then the gradual falling apart, the slipped knot of our marriage. We had precious little time together: too little, really, to be precious at all. I spent weekends at the office, she at one client's apartment or another as her business grew, as our home life shrank, as we turned away from each other to administer to things that bore greater reward. Gradually we lost the klutzy back and forth that had bound us. I used to love our differences, the mismatch of her *lift* and *boot* with my *elevator* and *trunk,* her naughty words in Afrikaans, my groping inability to explain the appeal of Yankee baseball, our ongoing argument over her muddled pronunciation of *milk.* We had nothing in common, all the more to share. Yet these cheerful clashes became, over time, merely clashes. Our sexy miscommunications gradually lost their sexiness, grew irritating and became some of the gaps through which we were drained.

Just as romances begin with conversation, they end with the lack thereof. Our phone calls during the day grew blunter until they were nothing but spoken grocery lists, voice-mailed reminders to leave a check for the maid. Eventually we used objects in place of statements. A Canyon Ranch pamphlet, splayed repeatedly atop my dresser, represented her desire to be sent for a long weekend to a spa. I accused her not by confronting her vocally but by sticking the eleven-thousand-dollar Barney's bill into her endive salad in the fridge. Then came the notices of her need for expansion. She circled nine-bedroom estates in sandy Long Island and leafy Pennsylvania and taped the pages to the Italian coffee machine so that I'd be sure to see them at five A.M. Underlined notices of country manors for sale in New Jersey. Beach houses with boat landings for only six million bucks. When I made director, we shifted a few blocks uptown into an eleven-room condo in the East Eighties that made our previous luxury apartment look like a shed. Still her newsprint insistence on more space continued. It was the plea of the suffocating, a scrabble for dear life. She was trapped in our cavernous apartment, in her marriage, and wanted out.

And what, I wondered now, looking back, did I want? I wanted her still. I loved her, unfortunately. I needed to understand what I could have done wrong. I had made the money, made good, sprung her from her old world into the New World with cash to spend, caring husband and (sure, yes, fine) country house: the works. I had given her everything she said she wanted, including—as she had vowed for all to hear at our wedding—me. But she had reevaluated her options. She estimated, accurately, that she could do better. She was an interior designer who had renovated herself spectacularly. She was beautiful, blond, and rich, now, in the United States of America. She could have whatever mustachioed man she wanted in her bed.

"Plaster," I read aloud off the tubs of plaster where the salesgirl had stopped us. "There you go."

"Knocking down a wall?" she asked. "Or just redecorating."

"I had a fire."

"Okeydokey." It was not the response I would have expected. "What's your damage."

I looked past her shoulder. A man was pushing a wheelchair loaded with a fat woman near the end of our aisle. He leaned forward to hear her—no, to kiss her cheek—before shoving onward. Passing a rack of preposterous-looking gas masks, he sneakily reached to pluck and pull one quickly over his head. He waited for the woman to crane her neck and catch him. When she did, heaving her big body and lifeless legs around to see, they collapsed forward to laugh together, still rolling, veering haphazardly now, laughing some more.

"Damage," my salesperson repeated more loudly. "What are we talking."

The couple reached the end of the aisle and turned the corner, the guy leaning hard left to maneuver the heavy chair, and in that passing moment, from the side view, just before she rolled out of sight, I recognized her. She was the victim of my first PIAA: the beached and broken whale I'd helped to pull from her pickup truck. That was her damage. That had to be her husband. Her marriage, for that matter. I watched them wheel away.

The girl was handing me something that looked like a clothes iron with sandpaper. "Sander," she said. "What else are we talking. What's your floor, maple? Oak? Pine?"

"We're talking tile."

"Linoleum or stone."

"Um, Mexican."

She drew a labored breath, expanding and contracting the pocks on her face. "They glazed?"

"Hard to tell," I admitted.

"Might just need to clean them. Some muriatic acid will do that."

"Right-o."

We located a green cart, deposited our plaster, and rolled along to the acid section of the store. From a nearby aisle I could hear the hearty laughter of the hefty woman in the chair, the accompanying chuck-chuck-chuckling of her husband. I couldn't imagine what those days must have been like, that masculine manual labor, the pushing and hauling forward of a loved one, the being behind her all day long. I couldn't quite picture that successful a marriage. To be crippled. Obese. To be that lucky as hell.

We paused by the grout-residue removers, looked over the porous stone sealers and brick and block cleaners before locating the right shelf. I fit my fingers through the handle of the nearest plastic jug to grip its sloshing weight.

"That's sulfuric," she pointed out.

"All righty."

"You don't want that. Stuff is way too strong. Sufuric acid will dissolve a penny. Eat your hands off. This is what you want right here. Muriatic."

"Don't tell me what I want," I said as I lifted one jug and then the other into my cart and, with one wheel squeaking, steered righteously away.

I SMEARED ON THE PLASTER

with my plaster knife. Let a bit off it drop onto my drop cloth. Kneeling in the ruined den, somewhere near midnight, I labored to smooth and erase the grooves that the flames had browned into the wall. In the morning I would sand the area, match the paint, roll it on. The next day I'd add another coat. Touch it up the day after that. The burning could still be smelled in the wall as I pressed forward to paste over it, ignoring the stronger smell of rotten eggs behind me. These were the fizzing sounds of liquid destruction. This was the way things were fixed.

The grizzled face that moved in the window bore a warrior stripe of soot from the hour I'd spent scouring the stove. I wiped away the sweat that hung on my brow, adding a white slash of plaster to my forehead. From the bucket behind me came the stench of the sulfuric acid, pops and whispers from the cell phone sunk in its depths. I breathed the odors of ruin and repair. Exhaled. Inhaled. Leaned back into my work.

MY NEXT-DOOR NEIGHBORS

had come to the country for the weekend. Some momentous event could be discerned through the windows of their redbrick mansion. The wife (had to be) puttered about the visible square of her kitchen before vanishing out of frame. A moment later she was back: a fading beauty, Grecian nose, long body in a black dress, her hair turbaned in a towel. A stocky woman in an apron rushed by. I deduced a dinner party: the ordering of a caterer to and fro. My eyes drifted upward to survey the rest of the place through its openings. There was a green-walled billiards room, a Far Eastern tapestry on a hallway wall, a satellite dish craning skyward off the near corner of the house that suggested—given the right peeping angle on the right window—I might be able to watch TV from here. A white-fenced balcony, floored with white snow, jutted out from a master bedroom. The husband was missing. Husbands were always missing. I beat my head softly against the pane of the picture window before heading downstairs to answer the phone.

It was Gary, whose lisp was static on the line. He was calling to offer a third invitation to dinner at his place in as many weeks. I saw no way around it. I could claim to be kosher; but with my luck, and his social ferocity, he'd find a way to cook matzo ball soup on the grill. Gary and his wife lived on Sparrow: a nearby street, lane, lake, or possibly farm that I'd never heard of. Dinnertime was set, outrageously, for five.

After hanging up, I passed the dining room table on the hunt for my firefighting workbook and stopped cold. There, carved deeply and sloppily into the satinwood, was the word. The top of the C, in fact, was so badly hacked by a large knife—possibly an ax—that it looked like TOWARD. But that would make no sense. No, the term was correct. Whoever had come into my house and chopped it into my table was not wrong. I nodded, found my workbook on the third step of the staircase and went up.

I GOT TO GARY'S

good-size colonial house at five-thirty, a half hour late and still a dinnertime for eighty-year-olds and toddlers. In a panic, then, leaving the car, I wondered if they could have toddlers. I slogged through the wet snow across the ample yard before pulling out and letting bang a knocker shaped like the head of a dog. A stout woman swung open the door with gusto. She clasped her hands under her chin and said over them: "Bill."

"You must be Ms. Dickers—"

"Madeleine."

"Madeleine. Good to—"

"Gaaaary!" she screeched at me, but with her eyes bulging sideways to indicate she was in fact shrieking at her husband. "Come in, Bill. Come in out of the cold. The Stranger—no, no, The Spy—Who Came in out of the Cold. Remember that one?

I'm crazy for the movies. Don't get me started. Give me your coat. Aw, that's a beauty. That's shearling. Gimme gimme gimme. Yay, you brought wine. Yummy. Gaaaary!"

Although she was far from pretty, she had trussed herself up for the occasion with a fervency that was difficult to ignore. I found myself staring as she dusted the snow off my coat with her pink-painted fingertips and turned in a rainbow blur of ceramic parrot earrings to lead me through the house. A spangled silver dress was stretched mercilessly over her body. She might have been going to the Oscars. She had the frame of a professional football player, arms a lot like mine. Her short black hair was plastered to her head in the style of Josephine Baker but with no discernible grace, a shellacked helmet that she double-checked with her free palm every few steps.

"So finally," she announced to no one in particular, "we got Bill." She thudded past a standing cuckoo clock over the wall-to-wall shag carpeting of the living room. "You've been keeping to yourself. House on the hill. Talk of the town. Aw, 'Talk of the Town'! *The New Yorker!*" She stopped walking to bend suddenly over my folded coat as if she'd been punched in the gut. She turned to face me. *"The New Yorker,"* she insisted. "The magazine. You read it, Bill. You read it every week."

"I don't, no."

"Sure you do. *The New Yorker.*"

"I know it. I just don't—"

"You probably write it."

"I certainly don't wri—"

"Bill readsh the *Journal,*" came Gary's voice from what must have been the dining room. He emerged from the relative darkness of that chamber to stand before us. He wore an apron. "Readsh the *Wall Shtreet Journal* and thatch it. Maybe *Barronsh*. All you have to know. Tell me I'm right."

"Right you are," I said as loudly as I could bear.

He stepped aside to usher us in. His wife brushed past with my unwieldy coat, forcing him to shuffle back another few steps. The dining room was set as if an entire Middle Eastern sultanate were expected. The chandelier was draped with vines and hanging clusters of red winter berries. At the center of the table, bright tropical fruit cascading from a wicker basket revealed itself, as my eyes adjusted to the dimness, to be plastic. The tablecloth was actually two or three quilts, their clashing patchwork almost covered by the four pottery plates allotted to each of the three of us. Gary must have caught me counting the plates.

"Polish handiwork there," he said.

"I'm sorry?"

"Paula. My shister. I mentioned she's a potter. Platesh are her specialty. Platesh and bowls. Right from the kiln. Thrown by hand."

I pictured, for a quick moment, throwing those blobby brown plates by hand, imagined the dull shatter of their landing.

"What'd the market do today?" he asked me then.

"The stock market? No idea."

"What'd the Nasdaq do yesterday?"

"I don't know."

"Me neither," he admitted. "Not much, I gesh." He stared down at his apron, spattered with what looked like mud. He threw a thumb over his shoulder. "Working my magic in the kitchen," he bragged.

"How about working on finding a place for Bill's *coat,*" snapped Madeleine. She leaned close on her perilously high heels to tell me, as if in confidence, "I married a man who thinks closets are for storing tools."

Gary and I frowned at each other, a secret handshake of eyebrows, the national allegiance of husbands who just want to jigsaw and solder in peace. The wine, a 1985 Lynch-Bages, was removed from my hands and placed with some ceremony beside the false cornucopia. In truth, it was the cheapest bottle out of the wine closet by the maid's room that I'd finally bothered to stock the week before. Gary went so far as to dust off its label with a clean edge of his apron.

"That's a pretty good Bordeaux," I told them. "You might want to let that breathe."

"You heard him, Gar. Give it some room," said Madeleine with a shooing motion. It was hard to tell if she was kidding. "I'll be showing our guest around." She hurled my coat across a chair in the corner and snatched my hand. Her hand was burly and firm as a foot. No one had held my hand for years. I was oddly aware, once again, of my wedding ring as she dragged me off. "And by the time we get back downstairs," she called up at the ceiling as we went, "that soup better be done. Chop-chop. You're dealing with New Yorkers here."

"Shtew," Gary called. "Shtew, Maddie. I'm making my shtew."

She towed me through every room and then upstairs, making the very most of what little there was to show. The house, I suppose, was fancy for these parts. Deep white carpeting covered every inch of the floor, deadening the sounds of our plodding progress. Photos along the wall displayed their two daughters in various stages of growth before they vanished at the end of the hallway, I was told, to cities and husbands in Canada and the Southwest. There was a rocking chair that had belonged to Madeleine's great-grandfather in which I was forced to sit, rock once, and smile. The master bedroom was a menagerie of carefully placed pillows and vases, porcelain animals on the dresser, two matching bedside tables of gold-rimmed glass that contained yet more framed snapshots. I took a good look at one of Gary, pre-braces—and was startled, I have to say, by his Aryan handsomeness, his preppy and pristine good looks. There were several of PJ, their only niece, looking triumphant in her defeat of semiannual attempts to clean her face for photos. In one she gave a messy smile beneath the duck-faced hood of a yellow raincoat. In another she gave her barbarian grin, eyes clenched shut, as the blurry figure of Paula attempted to hold her still from behind.

"*Rooo*-ma," sang Madeleine. She was holding on to one of the bedposts with both hands, swinging back and forth like King Kong. Over the headboard hung a chintzy poster of Rome in a thick gilt frame. "You know, Bill, what they say about Roma. You of all people."

"Built in a day," I guessed. "Not built in a day."

She gave a dramatic shake of her head and bent forward, still hanging onto the bed, so that her silver dress fell away from her bare chest and my eyes jumped elsewhere. It occurred to me to wonder what Pippa would have done with the room. Perhaps, on Gary's request, she could have underscored the theme of money: dollar-green drapes, nickel fixtures, a headboard replica of the Big Board at the New York Stock Exchange. Or else a Manhattan motif for the missus: the skyline ghosted in metallic paint across the closets, bed of brushed steel, oversize images of Frank Sinatra and Liza Minnelli silk-screened on the walls.

"You speak Italian," Madeleine told me.

"I don't, no."

"French, though."

"Not a word."

"But you've been there on business trips. Jetting off to Europe. It's probably boring for you by now. All those countries, those trips."

"Not me," I said. My flights, in reality, had been to conferences in Phoenix and conventions in Key Largo and Vegas to check out the heating speed of industrial microwaves, the latest flavors of Slurpees, the newest blend of polyester for counter-worker uniforms.

"One lifetime," Madeleine pronounced, "is not enough."

"For what."

"For Roma. Rome. That's the saying. In Italian. It takes more than a lifetime to know the city."

"Ah."

"And Bill, I got news for you. For us." She pointed back and forth to her and me, her and me. "We only get one lifetime."

"Right."

"You know what I'm saying."

"Not exac—"

"This is my lifetime." She released the poor bedpost. "This. Here. In Harristown. *This* is where I'm spending it. My *life*. I mean, Bill, I used to live on Columbus Avenue. Heart of Manhattan. And look at me."

I looked at her. I thought of pointing out that, culturally and geographically, Columbus was hardly the heart of Manhattan. I was dying for a drink. When Gary hadn't offered me one, I should have opened the Lynch-Bages myself, glugged it straight from the bottle to gird myself for the tour. It was strange to be deposited in the middle of someone's home, to be roaming their privacy, loafing in their bedroom, perusing their stuff. Did people really do this—make an acquaintance and invite him over to see all they owned, to listen to their wives? This, I took it, was dinner with friends. These were the rules. I had opened my mouth to respond, faintly recalling that she'd said something requiring a response, when dinnertime was hollered, thank God, from the kitchen.

I was seated at the head of the table over a bowl of stew, a plate of salad, one slice of buttered bread, and a single cracker decorated with processed cheese and topped with a canned olive. Gary had removed his apron and was wearing one of those button-down shirts that appear to have been stitched together from a random selection of Brooks Brothers shirts of the season before. My glass of red wine (they had put out white-wine glasses) was filled to the very top as if with soda.

"So tell me," Madeleine said as we all started in. Gary watched me eat, inspecting my reaction and awaiting my shouts of delight. Awaiting some more. "How's the city?"

"City's fine."

"Ohhhh," she moaned into her soup, her stew, her brown slop with its slight aftertaste of cinnamon, of all things, which must have been the so-called magic. "Macy's!"

"Still there," I reported.

She lifted her spoon toward me. "Zabar's. God, Zabar's!"

"Yep."

"What I wouldn't do for a pound of that smoked salmon from Zabar's. That's heaven, if you ask me. That's my idea of heaven, that smoked salmon. I'd like to curl up on a bed of that salmon. Yummy. I'd like to make a coat of it. Wear it around. We don't get fish like that here."

"Not out of the Hudshon," said Gary. "How's your shtew, there, Bill."

"You can fish the Hudson," Madeleine argued between sips of wine. "Henry fishes the river every weekend. Said he caught a brookie the other day that weighed six pounds."

"So Henry," I said—hell, I was just going to say it—"doesn't date Paula."

"Henry?" Madeleine snorted, almost expelling wine. "No. Henry doesn't date. Henry's a pal. Henry lets Paula sleep over. Puts PJ to bed in the guest room and opens up the bar for her mom. That way Paula can crash when she's too schnockered to drive home."

"Maddy," warned her husband.

"Does he date *anyone?*" I asked. "Henry? He's single, I take it."

They both watched me dig into my stew.

"No," Madeleine answered after a curious pause and a quick look between them. "Henry's not a dater." She popped in her cracker and cheese and said as she chewed: "Equipment doesn't work."

"Come on, Maddy," Gary began. "You can't go—"

"What? It's a fact. It's a biological fact." She looked at me merrily. "The man's a veteran of foreign wars. His hose is no longer connected to the truck."

"Madeleine," Gary snapped.

We ate for a minute, clanking metal against ceramic and drinking as fast as we could. So Henry was not a contender. I would have to take him off my list of suspects. To stop giving him fierce looks whenever we met in the firehouse, sat half on each other's laps in the truck.

"Let me get you some more there," Gary offered. He scooted back from the table. "Seemsh to have gone down pretty quick." Nobody spoke till he came back, at which point, driven to desperation, he asked point-blank what I thought of the stew.

"Good."

"Good, right."

I allowed a nod.

"See, the tricksh to brown your meat. Little flour. Little black pepper. Tellicherry peppercornsh: besht in the world. Then by the time you throw in your onionsh you've got a ni—"

"So you're in real estate," I shot at him, puncturing the speech.

He tapped his fingers on the tablecloth, itching to go on. "Thatch right."

"Good times for the business," I gave him. At that he perked right back up. What followed was a long, lispy sermon on his success in the swelling local housing market. It seemed that as property value had increased in the area, so had the size of the structures. A new one-family home in 1999, according to Gary, was ten percent bigger than ten years before. Meanwhile, the average backyard had shrunk by fifteen percent. After a minute of this talk, and several more glasses of my Bordeaux and the corky Merlot that followed, Madeleine fell back from the table like a tranquilized bear.

"Like the houshe I sold you," I thought Gary said.

"What?"

"Your houshe. The Collinsh houshe. The castle."

"What about it."

"Eight thousand shquare feet. Didn't take me long to move that. Week and a half. Two weeksh, maybe. Sent the notice to Pippa the day it went on the market. Put the lishting in the *Gazette* and boom. There you were."

Her name, from Gary's mouth, was the jab of a stick. "You sold us the house?" I asked him. I fought to clear the lintlike residue of wine from my brain. "That agent? That was you?"

He gave a slow grin of metal. "Who'd you think?"

I thought nothing. I had erased the guy from my past peripheral vision. In fact, I had never noticed him in the first place.

"Pippa and I had looked at a good ten or twelve lishtings," he went on. "But that was the one. No question. You remember, Bill. She jusht walked in and: 'Shold.' "

"Uh-huh," I said. But I was thinking of a question. Then I asked it. "When did you get your braces?"

This froze the table. I must have asked it with some anger. Or else no one had asked it of him, most people knowing better, and he had come to think of them as invisible.

"Few monthsh ago," he said. "Why?"

"Huh. And before that, no braces. Before, say, September. All clean."

"Bill," Madeleine said, stirring from her stupor.

"I'm just wondering. About the timeline here. You got your braces in, what, September."

"Augusht."

"And you met Pippa, what would you say, a year ago."

"Little more than that. She shtarted coming out to look—"

"Got it." I was thinking of the photo of him upstairs. Sandy haired, pink cheeked, and bright toothed, he could have been South African. He certainly was her type, with his soft-shoe posing and laughable striving—and with his dumpy spouse, his too, who might be as easily left in the lurch as me. I had another question then. "Just one more question," I told him.

"Sure, Bill. Shoot."

Madeleine was watching me. I kept my eyes on Gary. I was on target; I was sure of it. "You been to Lincoln Center recently?"

But I could tell by the ignorant sag of his face that I was out of luck.

PEOPLE SPEAK OF CRIME

in New York City as if it's un-avoidable, even asked for; as if even the law-abiding people senseless enough to live in that place are guilty of a brutal recklessness of their own. And while this is untrue, there is something to it. There's something in the flare of Manhattan delicatessen-line rage, in the white-hot hatred directed at slow-walking tourists, in the moments of true cruelty, the knifelike sarcasm, the bloody ambition, that infects you day by day, that debases you over the years until it's hard to distinguish your screaming about the idiocy of your cab driver or the missing edamame in your take-out sushi from the crimes of the killers you pass on the street.

That evening, what happened in our apartment, was not my fault. Nor was it (despite her customary meanness and ferocious materialism and the tired old saw about chickens coming home to roost) my wife's. The Incident, as my lawyer termed it, was simply what happens from time to time in New York when the underlying anger crackles up, without warning, through an un-minded hole.

I replayed the events yet again. I was chauffeured home from the airport, roiling in the backseat of the limo, shouting into my cell phone as was customary in the business. The Atlanta meeting had been rescheduled at the last minute. Stretched before me, along with the parting sea of gray and brown apartment buildings, was the glorious vision of a full evening at home. I resolved that I wouldn't go back to the office. That I would plunk my keys into the antique brass spittoon by my doorway, drop my briefcase onto the foyer table of hammered Inca gold, kick off my shoes and—fuck it—watch the game. I would catch the Yankees, for once in my life, without having to tape and watch them on fast-forward at one-thirty in the morning. I would lie on my sofa, TV remote on my belly, triple gin and tonic, the works. Pippa wouldn't be there, as usual. Her work to assemble the house upstate, if that's what you choose to believe, would keep her late, poor dear, only to return the next morning with tousled hair and a suspiciously rosy complexion and little to say.

I barked at the driver for not having filled out the voucher by the time he curbed the limo before our wrought-iron gate. The doormen withered as I strode past them. The elevator operator gingerly wished me good night. I grumbled and got off and was watching the horror movie for the hundredth time (Pippa in the chair, the men in the apartment) when there was the noise of ringing.

I was lying on my bed. It was ten-fifteen in the morning. I

had never been in bed that late in my life. A second ring came from the direction of the staircase. After jogging down and down and down to answer the phone in the kitchen, I was too winded to speak.

"Bill?"

"Yes," I managed. "Mark?"

"It's Leonard," said my lawyer. "Is that you? Bill?"

"Right."

"Who's Mark? Where have you been? I've been trying to get in contact with you for two months now. Does your cell phone not work? A hundred times I must have called your cell phone."

"Huh."

"For two months I've tried."

"That's strange." I sat on a stool at the counter. He was flustered, almost angry. He had never dared to take this tone with me. I was mildly impressed.

"Anyway," he said. "So you're in the Harristown house."

His accuracy, too, came as a surprise. "Correct."

"And everything's fine."

"Is it?"

"That was a question, Bill. You're feeling okay about all this."

These were his questions. "If you say so."

"And no talks with Pippa."

"Not a word."

"No urge to call."

"None."

"That's good. I'd say that's probably best." He cleared his throat softly, gathering his strength. "I've been talking to her people."

"The South African people?" I looked out the window to the white world: the brightly loaded trees, the silver ribbon of river, the salt-and-pepper hills. Leonard had wanted me to stay in the city, to face facts. He had whimpered as much to my assistant and home answering machine and cell phone voice mail at the time.

"Her attorneys, Bill. Pippa's attorneys. Do you want me to call you back? It's been months now that I've been trying to get you on the phone."

"I don't want you to call back."

"All right then. Can I ask you to listen for a minute? I just have to tell you—you really have to know how things are going to proceed from here."

"Fine."

He struggled for a deep breath. "Now then." He was scared of me, unfortunately. I outweighed him in every way. He handled me, always had, with the skittish technique of a lion tamer: backing away in terror, employing a soothing voice; determined, nonetheless, to make me dance. "She has filed her complaint," he said. "I have the documentation right there in front of me. I'll get it to you right away. Just give me your address up there. Is it Ridgemont? Your street?"

Damned close. I left it at that.

"You should really look at this, Bill. This is your summons. We have to file an answer to this."

"My answer is yes."

"Well, then, I can file that." He turned a trembling page. "But I want to let you know, Bill, before I do—well, just what I've said already. That I have serious reservations about representing you on this one."

"So you said."

"I think it's probably best—and I regret having to say this—if I were to just, you know, step aside on this one. I do."

"Yeah," I said. "No."

There came a shaky swallow from Leonard. "Bill. You have to—I'm not a divorce attorney, Bill. That's not my area of expertise. As you know. And I think you would be better served by a divorce attorney. For one thing. A divorce attorney would point out, for instance, that you may have some wiggle room here. That you probably ought to pursue—"

"I don't want any wiggle room," I said. "I'm not planning to wiggle, Leonard. *You* fucking wiggle."

"You've—yes. You've said that. I know. I've heard you, Bill." There was a slight echo in the background: he may have been cowering under his desk. "But I am obligated to remind you, if you'll just, you know, it's my *job* to remind you that you have rights here."

"I realize that."

"Well"—and here he lost his nerve, his voice gone wobbly—"you're not exercising them."

"You know what, Leonard?" I boomed. In my anger I switched hands for a better grip on the phone and almost dropped it. "I'm exercising my right to get this done. To give Pippa what she wants and move the hell on. And you know what your job is? I'll tell you what your job is, Leonard. Your job is to tell me which papers I have to sign to make that happen."

"Okay, Bill. All right. Let me just—let me inform you of the charges. She's claiming abandonment."

"What?"

"There are five legally recognized grounds for divorce in

New York State. All right? Abandonment is one of them. They have claimed—she has claimed—abandonment. But I have to point out that this was not abandonment. Abandonment entails a period of voluntary and nonconsensual absence for one or more years. One or more *years*. You understand the point I'm making."

"I do," I said. "You're telling me that Pippa's the one who's guilty of abandonment."

"Pippa? No, Bill, I'm jus—"

"Because she's the one who's been having an affair, Leonard. That's your point."

"That's not my point. That's not my point at all. That's not actually—"

"She's abandoned *me*. I get it, Leonard. I see where you're going with this. But I'm not going there with you. Thanks anyhow. What's next."

A high sound escaped him. "Bill, you don't have any proof of—well, fine. I'm not—all right. Fine." He cleared his throat. "The next step will be pretrial orders, filed by her attorneys. And here we will get into some of the financial matters we've discussed. There may be disputes."

"I don't think so."

"Right. Well. If there should arise any discrepancy—I'll use the word *discrepancy*—there may be a deposition. In which case we'll have to review the Incident. On the fourteenth. I'm sorry, but—and you know this, Bill—there's just no way around it. As we discussed back in October."

"I don't want a way around it."

"I know that. I just don't think . . ." His voice trailed off.

Then it was back. He had taken a deep breath, perhaps a shot of whiskey, and was speaking as fast as he could. "I don't think I should be your lawyer on this, Bill. I just don't feel that I'm your best representative. I can certainly enter a plea of no contest, if you'd like, when it comes to the incident itself. But I should recommend a colleague for these proceedings. I have to step aside and do that. There are some top-notch divorce attorneys at the firm. Some of the best in the country. I'd like to step aside, Bill. Remove myself at this point. I can't represent you, Bill."

He waited for my response. But I hadn't heard a word he'd said. I was thinking of the paralyzed woman and her husband, the fatty and her pusher, whom I'd glimpsed that day at the tool store. I was thinking of his having to somehow lift and bathe her. I was wondering, frankly, how he got her into bed. I was realizing, as I listened to my marriage being broken down to its final and laughable elements—to signatures on papers, to the feeble angling and babbling of our representatives—that we had never been behind each other, not for a moment that fully with each other, and that we never would be no matter what. I had seen my wife trapped in a chair—me, too, as it happened. I had beheld her suffering. And it had knocked me to the ground. We all make it through danger, endure breakage, accept it as a duty: we all have to. The difference is that some of us lie down on the job.

I RODE WITH MY ELBOW

out the window, beard trembling in the cold wind. It had been our third false automatic alarm of the week ("smells and bells," the guys angrily called them), and I had come almost to enjoy the shivering ride home. I watched the passing farmhouses and trailer homes, squinting at all the white roofs and white yards with their white lumps of trash. The high hills behind them were sugared as well. As a child in the city, I was under the impression that snow naturally turns brown when left out, like sliced apples. Here I could marvel at its unwreckable brightness.

I crossed the cement with the others, pulled off and threw up my gear. It was eleven-fifteen in the morning. I felt like I'd been awake for a month. "How about a brew," said Sully with a slap, an actual irritating slap, on my back.

"Better go home."

"Aw, c'mon." He was drifting across the bay toward the mysterious wooden staircase. "It's Saturday."

"Is it?" I hung up my helmet. "Well, what the fuck."

"There you go."

I followed him to the base of the stairs—where we were halted by an armful of tattoos.

"*Mis*-ter Finelli," Sully sang to him.

Wordless, charmless, Finelli let down his arm and moved in front of us to take the stairs first. I had the urge to ask him why he'd missed the call, and then the almost insurmountable desire to reach forward and trip him as we banged up single file. He had never said anything to me about my hosing him down in the woods. Instead that tension seethed between us, whittled sharper by his eyes, kept alive and unmentioned, it seemed, by choice.

It turned out that the staircase led to a kind of homemade clubhouse above the truck bay, although its cheerful colors and boyish spirit had been steadily drained by time. The carpet was worn flat, the Ping-Pong table folded into a broken wooden sandwich against the wall. A poster of a buxom barmaid lifting mugs of St. Paulie Girl beer had faded to a benign pink. The chipped Miller High Life mirror reflected a parade of middle-aged men, me last. Sprawled around the room on a ragged sofa and folding chairs were a dozen men, scratching their crotches and slurping their cups. Gary stood in an argyle sweater at the bar. I eyed the sweater closely. It looked to be thinner—he was clearly a smaller size—than the ones I'd discovered in my drawer.

"What's on tap?" I asked him.

Gary looked from the handle of the beer spigot back to me. "Beer."

"Ah," I said. "My favorite kind."

"Nushing bottled. Nushing imported. Me, I'm a fan of the Europeansh. You?"

"Whatever you got there."

He clunked open the spigot over a plastic cup.

"Belgium makesh a good beer. Germany. Can't beat the German beersh. England. Holland." As he handed over the full cup, he said: "How goesh the training."

"The fire training? Not bad. Test in a few weeks."

"Few weeks already? Heck, that went fast. You ready?"

"I don't know. Sully, you ready?"

"I'm ready," he said beside me, indicating the beer spigot. "I'm ready for a brewski. There you go. Hit me, Gar."

I sipped the beer: thin as water, pleasantly cold, with an aftertaste of something like egg. Sully raised his woolly eyebrows at me in a kind of cheers before he gulped. We stood with our backs to the bar. Around the room the men seemed to be debating the best way to handle wildfires. Finelli, perched hawklike on a metal stool, opined that small woodland flare-ups are better left to burn longer. They create more space between trees, went his theory, and your pines and maples are going to get more light, more moisture, be less susceptible to diseases that are passed root to root. A man in a camouflage hunting jacket added his contention that leached chemicals from the ashes stimulate acorns' growth into oaks. The chief, who hadn't bothered to show for the automatic alarm, now occupied the room's only easy chair as his rightful throne. With a scritch-scritch of his beard, he ended the argument with the slow proclamation that our job, pure and simple, was to knock down fires. To this there were nods and hums across the room.

Someone announced that Wheaton Valley Company had bought a $6,000 power spreader, and the men of Harristown buzzed at the treachery. Someone else joked about the upcoming town bake sale that was scheduled to take place in the station driveway, and I made the mistake of mocking that too loudly.

"What you got against bake sales?" Finelli turned to me with a squeak of his stool. "Fire company is the heart of this town. You wouldn't know that, Probie. But we keep this town alive. Bake sales, tag sales, live auctions, Christmas parades." In fact, the firehouse had hosted a Christmas parade a few weeks before, which I had opted to skip without reservation, preferring to spend my holiday gargling carols with a quart of gin. "Summer fair," Finelli went on. He tugged down his Harristown Fire cap into even tighter alignment with the curve of his nose. "We're looking out for this town. Because it's our town. Maybe that's the difference."

I tried a sardonic smile. Sipped my beer. The room still appeared to be staring at me. Sully fidgeted with his cup. He was trying to think of something to say. And then he appeared, in the corner of my eye, to have come up with it.

"So that's about it," he sighed loudly into his beer, "for the grilling season."

Which was all it took.

"Hell no," someone said.

"Not for me," offered Gary.

"I'm grilling," said Finelli. "I'm grilling yearlong. I've grilled in the rain. Grilled in ice storms." His stool croaked again as he shifted his weight. "I'm doing chorizo. Doing linguica. Just last night I did a tuna steak that I got from Surfside in Hagersville." He slung his arm across his body and outward as if throwing a Frisbee. His hand remained before his eyes, thumb and forefinger a distance apart. "Thing had to be three inches thick."

"I'm doing ribs," offered another man. He swigged from his beer. It was the dimwit from the gas mart, wearing a cracked leather jacket.

"How you doing them, Boo," someone asked.

"Thing about ribs—"

"Shut up, Finelli. How you doing them."

Grateful for the encouragement, Boo sat up straighter on the couch. "Make your fire with hardwood, right. First things first. No *briquettes.*"

The use of the word—French, no less—brought derisive laughter.

"Take you a couple hours to cook it into coals. Oak or hickory. Burns cleaner and hotter than anything you can buy in a bag."

"Nothing wrong with a gas grill," objected an older man with gray teeth. "One of the new Webers will do you fine. Weber Genesis. Silver model. Propane burns plenty clean."

"Mr. Bowman there," Sully told me under his breath—I had to stoop to hear him—"sells outdoor equipment."

"Grills," I guessed.

"Bin-go."

We shared the quick smirk of schoolkids in the library.

"So I take my ribs," Boo resumed.

"What sort."

The question, grumbled from the easy chair, froze the room.

Boo turned to face the chief. "Pork. Pork ribs. Nothing but the bes—"

"What *sort*," the chief said again. He was toying with his prey. "Because there's two kinds of pork ribs. As you may know. Maybe not. There's your spare ribs."

"Here we go," Sully whispered into his cup.

"What, is the chief a butcher?" I asked.

"Naw."

"What does he do?"

"Who, Tommy? Guy can talk about anything."

"And your back ribs," the chief droned on. "Spareribs, I will tell you, would be my first choice for the grill."

"These were spareribs," said Boo. "So I marin—"

"And I'll tell you why." The chief was unhurried. The copper hair bristled on his arms. He recrossed his big boots. "Spareribs are from the pork belly, with belly fat that's going to baste your meat for you as it cooks. Bigger meal than your back ribs. Eleven ribs in all. Only eight on the back side. Get yourself a St. Louis cut: sternum section out, cartilage trimmed off. That's what I'd get for the grill. A nice St. Louie. Baby backs are tender, sure, but they're not going to give you the same kind of taste. Not close."

His conclusion hung in the air. Someone poured another beer with the chug of the pulled spigot, an overflow of foam, and a pronouncement of *fuck* into the quiet.

"You know who dush a good plate of ribs," ventured Gary. He had moved out from behind the bar and stood over by the dilapidated Ping-Pong table with his cup of beer. "The Rivershide. Route five. Right before Hagershville. Portions you can't believe. Rack of ribsh wider than your plate."

"Who the hell goes out for ribs?" sniped Finelli. "You don't go to a restaurant for ribs. You grill your own ribs." He glared around the room, rallying the opposition. "You want to spend thirty bucks for ribs you can make at home, that's your problem."

Gary wilted back against the wall. Sipped his beer.

"Tell you what I do with my ribs," said someone else. "I do a marinade. Little paprika. Onions. Little honey. Fresh orange juice."

"Do some corn with that." At the far wall, a guy in a camouflage hunting jacket spoke up. "Corn on the cob. Grilled right in the husk," he said. "Silk and all."

"You're going to be eating *char*," said Finelli, "if you don't soak the husk." He aimed the brim of his cap back and forth, daring any objection. "Soak your husk in water or it'll burn to a crisp."

I was back to watching the downward sift of the snow across the street. I checked my watch. Hitched up my pants. I was willing to stand here, I really was, if that's what was called for, amid the fucking parliamentary debate about ways to cook corn.

"What does Finelli do?" I mumbled to Sully.

"Pest control."

"Perfect."

"Hell no," the man in the hunting jacket was saying. "Won't burn on you. Not my way. Peel off the outer layers of husk. Put your ears right on the fire. Five minutes. Peel back the rest of the husk to brown the kernels. One minute. Done." He drank his beer, wiped his mouth. "You go and soak your husks, you're going to lose your smoky flavor."

"Cut off those kernels," another man offered, "and fold them into a polenta."

"Put them in your salsa," said someone else.

"I do corn in pasta," announced a man seated on the floor. "Little fusilli with sausage. Onions, garlic. Corn. Mustard greens."

"Corn's a starch," Finelli told him. "You don't do a starch with a starch."

"I'm not doing a starch with a starch. Where's the other starch?"

"Your goddamned pasta."

"Corn's not a starch, Finelli. Listen to Finelli. *Corn's a starch!* Hell do you know?"

"I know what's a starch and what's not a fucking starch."

"I grill fruit."

I was the first in the room to turn to Sully. "You do?" I heard myself ask.

"Shit yeah." He was boldly addressing the entire bar. The tension of the moment had squeezed his mole eyes even closer together. "Grill it for dessert. Cook it with meat on kabobs. Fruit's gotta be just barely ripe. Not overripe. Soft fruit's gonna turn to mush on you. Gotta still be crisp, but with enough sugar for carm—"

"Caramelization," someone jumped in. "You bet."

"What kind of fruit?" I demanded. I was striving for the throaty damnation of the chief's *Whut sort?* "Because a lot's going to depend on the type of fruit that you—"

"Anything. Don't matter. Pears, mangoes. Grapes go good with pork." Sully lifted his cup of beer in some kind of benediction. "Nectarines dipped in butter."

"Mmmm," I said. I looked around.

"Fruit works," decided the chief. "Little brown sugar. Cinnamon. Pinch of nutmeg."

That put an end to it. Sully, victorious, rocked back and forth on his heels.

Finelli creaked forward on his stool. "Thing about cooking fruit—"

"Shut the fuck up, Finelli," I said, and to the wary moans and whistles of the fire company I downed the rest of my beer.

AND THEN I KNEW.

It's hard to tell when it dawned on me: most likely at some point mid-exercise, in the throes of a nauseous push-up or sit-up, as the heaving around of my body prompted greater circulation of blood and the less agreeable swirl of thought. I hadn't thought of the most obvious. I knew who it was. It was Tom. Chief Thomas Moore. Big Tom. Big cheese. The chief.

Pippa would have gone for the top of the heap, the tallest and toughest among them, the manliest of men she could find in these parts. She had been taught this by her adoptive country: that rank and status are everything, that a girl is best off grabbing the biggest of us with both hands. Over the years she had come to appreciate the value of, well, value, the need to pluck items and people from the highest echelon and make them her own. She had learned from her marriage the lousy sense of settling for less. Of taking the bad with the good, of my high-net-worth contacts and low self-esteem, my boringness, my boorishness, the unimaginative sex and stultifying life of the just-rich-enough man.

She wanted more, I realized. Chief Tom Moore.

THERE ARE THREE STAGES

in the life of a fire. The first
is called the incipient phase, and requires enough oxygen to get
the flame going, the room superheating, the smoke collecting
under the ceiling and mounting downward toward the floor. In
the next phase, the free-burning phase, the fire consumes its
surroundings while the accompanying fumes erase the last bottom inches of air. The blaze slumbers angrily then, unable to
breathe. Welcome to the smoldering phase: seething embers,
sucking black walls, no space for fire or firefighters in a room so
tightly packed with acrid smoke and pressurized gases. Open a
door or smash a window and you're only delivering the missing
ingredient: fresh air. The beast will thank you with a roar before
flaring to life and devouring everything and everyone it can.

To combat these events, three types of hose stream are used:
solid, broken, and fog. A solid stream provides maximum pene-

tration when time and volume are of the essence. A broken stream, created by two guys colliding their beams, throws coarser droplets, helpful in the protection of walls and exposures. Fogging——twisting the nozzle to spread your water wide——is best for heat absorption, as the process of turning those tiny water beads to steam effectively saps the fire of temperature. For instance, to heat one gallon of water one degree Fahrenheit takes 8.3 BTUs; but to convert a gallon of water to steam takes over 8,000 BTUs in the same amou——

"Whatcha writing?"

I paused my pen. "What he said. About lowering fire temp."

Collapsed forward on his elbows, Sully picked something from one of his sideburns. At the blackboard, Captain Stan was going full tilt into his lecture on water physics, wiping his wet head and raising his unraisable voice. Around the room, grown men flicked doughnut crumbs at each other and slept in their chairs. And then we were adjourned. There was the yowl of slid-back chairs and the babble of students, over which Captain Stan shouted a promise that we'd be doing ladder work next week. There were noises of halfhearted approval as we moved toward the doors.

Crossing the parking lot and halting in our usual cluster, I was now better able to take part. One of my tablemates told of an overturned van in Grayville on Wednesday, and I chimed in with suggestions on chocking a sideways vehicle. A yard fire in Freemont had rekindled twice overnight, and I told our colleague from Freemont that if they'd doused it properly the first time they might have gotten some sleep. I clicked my pager back on before the others had thought to do so. At which point the guy next to Sully pointed at my car.

"Been playing bumper cars, big fella?"

We all looked over. It was true, my car was badly beaten. Marauding birds had targeted the sunroof. The branches of Ridgepoint Circle, like roadside fans at the Tour de France, were forever leaning in to rake my paint job as I passed. But the worst were the divots on both the driver's and passenger's sides where my car had been purposefully kicked in.

"Trashed to shit," the guy was saying. "Shame to treat a car like that. Wouldn't you say, Sully? To trash a Beamer? You tell me. You're the expert."

Sully was looking for his stub of a cigar in a pocket. "Shut up, Wikowsky."

"Aaah, Sully could bang out those dents," said another guy. "Right, Sully? Couple days in the shop and it'll be like new. Right?"

It occurred to me that I didn't know what Sully did for a living. I had never asked him. I had wondered, I suppose, as I had wondered about the chief: what career, lumberjacking aside, could logically contain that grouchy giant? I suppose I didn't particularly want to know these people well. I would be leaving Harristown shortly. I hadn't meant to be here this long. Months had gone by. Already it was January. I had filled the weeks with idle activities, with rereadings of the local paper, with my exercises, my studying, my elaborate lunch preparations and occasional walks, my life as a loafer interrupted only occasionally by a terrifying call to action.

"You in automotive repair?" I asked Sully now.

"Listen to this guy," said Wikowsky. "*Automotive repair.* He's got a chop shop, big fella. Same chop shop for thirty years. Since we were kids. Used to fix our bikes. Remember that, Francis?"

I looked around for Francis. Sully was eyeing the pad of snow beneath our feet.

"Skateboards, roller skates. Anything with wheels. Am I right, Bennie? Guy was a master. So how's it going over there, anyway. You employee of the month again, Francis?" He coughed out a laugh and spat a gob of phlegm behind him. "Employee of the month. Thirty years running. Guy's something else."

"Least I'm on my own payroll," said Sully. "Least I don't have to punch the clock at some—"

"And how's that payroll."

Sully had dug out a dark inch of cigar from his pocket and was examining its end. "Not bad."

"Because you got a woman to support."

"That's right I do."

"Fine woman." Wikowsky was openly sneering now. "Older woman."

"Well," I said loudly, "looks like I'm going to have to make a contribution to that payroll."

Sully looked up. "How's that."

"How's what? Look at my car."

He did. "It's a BMW."

"*Was* a BMW. Now's it's a fucking disaster. Got to have you look it over," I said. "Kick the tires a bit."

"Little late to kick the tires," offered Wikowsky.

I ignored him, gave Sully a nod as if we had long been in discussions on the matter and this settled it. "I'll bring it by," I said.

Wikowsky glanced from one of us to the other. "Bring your roller skates while you're at it," he said as I turned and blooped open the car.

SULLY'S CAR SHOP,
hung with no sign, could be identified
only by the large and small car parts that spilled from inside the
dark shed beside his house. The main house surprised me: a
brightly painted doily of a cottage with scalloped trim and
cheerful curtains, perched like a confection and frosted with
snow. A mat out front, complete with pine-tree motif, offered a
cursive *Welcome*. I scuffed my boots on its surface and punched
the door once. Twice.

"Right here," came his voice behind me. "Out here. Don't
knock on that."

I crossed the corner of lawn to the shed. I stepped on a tire
and over a crowbar on my way in. A single clip-on lightbulb in a
casing of orange plastic kept the place from utter blackness. My
eyes adjusted and the afternoon light seeped in to reveal Sully
with a wrench, dressed in a fully soiled jumpsuit and stepping
out from behind the upraised hood of a car.

"*Mis*-ter Showberg," he said. "Find the place okay?"

"Perfect directions. Excellent, Sully, thanks. Vivid detail."

"Got lost."

"I'd have to be a fucking Mohawk Indian to follow those clues."

He twirled the wrench neatly on his palm. He twirled it again, wanting me to notice.

"So this," I said grandly, "is where it all happens."

"This is it." He snarled one of his smiles. "Shit yeah."

It looked as if a traffic jam had exploded on the premises. Chains and belts covered the floor like a den of snakes. Sprockets (if that was the word) and metal doodads were everywhere. There was only the one full vehicle to be seen, a battered sports car covered with blotches of rust and lacking a windshield. An engine, too, I saw when I walked around to the hood and peered into the cavity.

"So there she is," Sully said. He was squinting out into the light of day, beady eyes aimed at my car.

I followed him out from the shed. There was a shadow in the window of his house, through the curtain—I was sure of it— that passed away as we neared. "Is there someone in your house?"

"Nobody." He reached my car and laid his hand on the roof, a healing gesture. "Just my mom," he said then. He circled the car, fingering its dings and divots, shaking his head and clucking in his cheek as he sized things up.

"You live with your mom."

"My mom," he said over his shoulder, "lives with me."

"That's big of you."

"Way it goes." He made no effort to keep his voice down. "Nothing to do about that. Dad dies, brothers take off for the city, that's what you got. They're pros. Told you that. Full-time firefighters. She's not going to live with them. So that's that. That's what I got." He was speaking too loudly. Across the brief front lawn, a few yards from the car, the old crab might have been crouching at a window to hear. "Figure someone's got to take care of her." He flicked something, maybe bird shit, off the back window of my car. Rubbed at the spot where it had been. "No choice, really. Pretty much a catch-twenty-two."

"It's not really a catch—well, whatever." I'd been about to correct him. "I'm sure you had a choice."

He said nothing to that. His hands rested on the edge of the roof of my car. I couldn't see, but his eyes might have been closed. He gave a sudden shove, rocked the vehicle three or four times, and stepped back as it settled. I had the feeling I was being put on.

"Want to kick the tires?" I asked. "You haven't kicked the tires."

He moved to the front of the car. He considered the hood. He lifted his boot onto the front-left fender, leaned on it hard, jumped off, and watched the ensuing jiggle. He did the same thing on the right side, leaving two matching snow prints of mud. "This car," he pronounced finally, "has taken a toll."

"I don't think that's what you mea—"

"Suspension's shot. Look at that."

"The suspension? No, it isn't."

"Look right there. Shit yes. Shocks, maybe. How many miles on this thing?"

"I don't know. A dozen. A hundred. The suspension's fine, Sully." I talked to his reflection in the window as he peered into the driver's side to read the miles. "Car's brand new."

"Ought to be looking at a hundred thousand miles easy, maybe one-fifty," he said, "before the suspension goes."

"That's what I'm saying."

"You haven't even cracked five thousand."

"That's my point. So why don't we cut the——"

"You have a wreck?"

"What?"

"You crash this thing? That'd explain your suspension problem. Look at the back."

"No."

"Looks like you crashed this thing. Backed into something."

"I didn't."

"Well, then, shit," he said. "You've driven this thing into the ground." He looked up at me with a kind of admiration, his feral face illuminated by a grin. "Dirt roads around here don't help any. Give you that. Apple Hill is no, um, you know."

"Autobahn."

"Picnic. Still, that's some driving. Hoo-boy."

"Thanks a lot."

"You're going to have to get this baby fixed. I can try and bang out some of those dents—but suspension problem's pretty serious. Can't drive it like this."

"Oh, I can drive it like this."

"Don't think so," he said. "Might have trouble controlling the car. I'll fix it for you."

He was startlingly assertive. I hadn't seen this side of Sully. I found it irritating. "I'll bring it back next week."

"Don't think so," he said again. "Won't take long. Won't charge you. Been a while since I've done a suspension job. Not sure I've got the tools, to tell you the truth."

"Suspension tools?"

"Metric tools. BMW's a foreign car. Metric measurements." He walked briskly across the lawn and into the shed. It was quicker than I'd ever seen him move. He was energized by the task ahead, possessed by the springy sort of confidence that marks those who host shows on cable TV. He disappeared behind his practice car and rattled around. After a few seconds he poked up, holding aloft what looked like a black lunch pail.

"Those your metrics?"

"There you go."

He instructed me to back my car into the shed, the *shop,* and as I did he marched behind me, walking steadily toward my windshield, crowding my progress and performing a series of arm gestures meant to convey left and right, stop and go slowly, halt. From there it took him thirty minutes to jack up the car. He slid rusty safety stands under the wheels, located a half-rotted dolly, and began to dismantle my vehicle from beneath. I sat on a rickety workbench to watch. In the corner, a square space heater with hazardously glowing coils stirred and warmed the air just enough to keep it from turning to ice. Sully removed the stabilizer-bar brackets, narrating as he slid the metal parts out and onto the floor beside his wiggling legs. The rubber mountings for the stabilizer bar, called bushings, were tossed out as well, bumping over the dirt floor toward my boots. I was asked to retrieve a box of replacement bushings from a cobwebbed shelf and pushed them under the car. I was told to get him a towel. Remarkably, I complied. Then I was asked if I wanted to slide under myself.

"What?"

"You should get down here and see this."

"No thanks."

"Come on." Sully's voice, funneled through the parts and plates and pipes of the undercar, was deepened.

"There's only one dolly."

"Grab one of those carpets."

The carpets were squarish scraps of rug stacked knee high by the door and decorated with droppings of oil. Beneath the vehicle with Sullivan, I felt that I was on a strange date. Our faces were inches away from each other, car at our noses. I was fighting acute claustrophobia, trying to ignore the touch of my stomach to the warm underbelly of the car. We lay side by side like teenagers watching the stars.

"See that?"

"See what. I don't know what the fuck I'm looking at here."

"There's your suspension system. Shock absorber, coil spring, strut. The strut is what combines the shock and your spring. Right in front of you here. There you go. Now, our job——"

"Your job."

"——is to replace these parts. One by one. Play it safe. Whole new suspension system. Slide me those bushings."

I didn't like the new Francis Sullivan——I suppose the old Francis Sullivan——who gave orders and held his own, who knew his way blind around the maze at the bottom of cars, who talked lug nuts and leaf springs, told me what to do. However, truth be told, it was interesting, the messy science of making cars go. I was taught to trace the fuel-injection process. I asked about the oil and was shown the bas-relief outline of the pan. These were the straight facts, the nuts-and-bolts operations, that I'd drifted away from over the past decade as I had learned to pose and posture, to go uninvited to heat-lamp expos and flirt with the presidents of chicken-and-ribs joints, to crash the shareholders meetings of fish-'n'-chips franchises and entice the CFO with my improvised opinions on deep frying. *Like the story,* I told the founder of a taco chain, sitting ringside at a boxing match that I thought he might enjoy. *Stock's getting some traction,* I complimented the owner of a seafood empire while taking him tarpon fishing on a rented flatboat, reeling him in as we cast. I was made to become a mimic, a professional escort, a cufflinked whore. Even worse, I was never particularly good at it. Nuts and bolts, however, were me.

"Shit," said Sully then. "Test is next Saturday."

I made no effort not to gloat. "I'm not too worried."

"There you go."

I had an itch on my stomach. I rubbed it against the lower surface of the car, back and forth, like a grizzly. "How about you."

"Uh-huh."

"You been studying the workbook?"

"Nah."

"Why not? You've got to look at the workbook. It's all in there, Sully. Just give it a read."

"I don't know." He pushed a finger between two coils of a thick spring to touch the cylinder housed within. "There's your shock."

"Shock absorber."

"Take this. Yeah. Take it off. There we go."

"You know what I think, Sully?"

"What's that."

"I think you don't want to pass this test."

His arms' activity didn't slow. "What's that mean."

"You tell me."

"I don't know," he said. "Gotta remove these bolts here. See that? Top and bottom."

"I think you're a guy," I said, "who likes staying put."

I looked at his face then, contorted by his determination to twist off a bolt with his fingers. He was sweating profusely despite the cold that emanated upward through our backs, through our bones, from the dead core of the frozen earth. He gave up. "Need a special wrench for that."

"If you don't pass the test, you can't go interior. Right?"

"Get me that wrench over there. The one—yeah. Grab that."

"And if you don't go interior, nothing bad can happen."

I started to pass him the wrench, changed my mind, and fit it around the bolt myself.

"There you go," he said, pleased. "Take it home."

"But you know," I told him as I heaved and turned the bolt, "nothing good can happen either."

After a couple minutes of guiding me and my wrench work, he said, "I'll pass the test."

"Think so?"

"Shit yes. Chief was telling me a few things. Few pointers. Think I got it covered."

"Well, that'll help." I was tugging at the coil spring, as directed, with my fingers.

"Chief knows his stuff."

I couldn't help it. I said, "Bet he gets around, that guy."

"Who, Tommy? Bet he does."

"You do?" Then I said more calmly, "Think so, right?"

"Fuck yeah. The chief? I know so."

"Do you?" I had one shock removed, and when Sully didn't answer we scooted over together to administer to the next. "Bet he gets to the city from time to time."

"Sure."

"New York City, I mean."

"Could be."

I was off my rug now, flat against the frigid dirt floor, a fat tuna on a slab of ice. "Oh, he fucking gets around," I said, turning the wrench.

"Guy may be gay," Sully said then, "but he's a hell of a fire-fighter."

I rolled my head to look at him.

"You knew that," he said.

"No, I didn't. The chief is gay?"

"Shit yeah. Gay as they come. Guy's a bowl of fruit. Didn't know that? A fudge packer. Shirt lifter." The juvenile taunts and slurs came from Sully without a trace of humor, as if they were the Latin nomenclature for the species. "Pillow biter. What, you couldn't tell? Thought you were from Manhattan."

"I am. Jesus. I'm just surprised."

"It's a surprising thing," he said.

I pulled at the coil spring till it popped out. "What does he do again? Runs a store, right?"

"Runs a store." He watched me replace the second shock.

"Well, so much for that," I said eventually.

"Yep."

"Never know."

"That's the thing."

I repeated it, talking into the metal plate before my chin, putting forward another sentence as if to prop up the car and keep it from crushing us to death. "You never know."

THERE IS A CERTAIN SATISFACTION,
if you can be-
lieve this, in yard work. Here in the country, in the depths (in
the height, I should say) of winter, yard work meant shoveling
down to size the white hills and sparkling drifts that grew end-
lessly around the house, that speckled every tree, that mounted
overnight to a fresh level above the knees of my new jeans, as
noted every morning when I jumped off the steps to recarve the
path to my car. The solid work of chunk, lift, throw was not entirely unpleasurable. In fact, it took as much as ten minutes,
maybe twelve, to get old.

For the first weeks of the season, I hardly saw a neighbor.
The only arrival from out of town was snow dumped from
above. I gazed at the houses on either side, yards away, and I
grew friendly with the structures. I had come to feel the good-
will of the harbormaster toward the cavernous vessels,

unmanned and impressive, that leaned and creaked to our shared tide. I was almost disappointed, therefore, to glimpse their inhabitants as they began to come up for ski season. I wasn't sure I wanted to share our white seascape or the row of huge houses I had watched over alone.

They arrived on the Friday night, crashed about their garages for the sleds and snowshoes on Saturday morning, came and went until evening, departed the next day. Number 2 Ridgepoint Circle was commandeered by a portly swashbuckler with a voice that boomed throughout his house and mine. He was crisply dressed, the times I glimpsed him, with the brush cut and beard of a harried tycoon with no time for comb or razor. This, apparently, was the stubbly head of a television outfit in Albany; or so our real estate agent, Gary Dickerson, had bragged way back when. His wife would be the sour former beauty whom I'd spotted in her kitchen haranguing her caterer months before. Number 6, by contrast, was visited every couple weeks by a fierce woman in a sports-utility vehicle the size of a planet. Her house was the enormous Swiss-style chalet whose walls, narrowing as they ascended, produced the look of a multimillion-dollar teepee—one that was regularly invaded by a whooping and charging tribe of children, colorful plastic equipment, human limbs, squalling siblings, thirty or forty offspring in all (all right, three or four) trailed by a couple of pear-shaped nannies attempting to hold all their hands. The crowd would babble and fight its way into the house and out to the backyard until shouted back inside for dinner, screamed at to sit down, badgered to eat, forced to bathe, slammed into bed—our house-to-house acoustics really were crystal clear—and hauled away on Sunday in a cavalcade of tiny complaints.

With the disappearance of their tenants these homes seemed to gape and stare into space, exhausted. Slowly, then, they settled, the last human echoes dying down to leave us, me and the houses, with our sounds of snow, of wind and snow, of cars on ice, birds and snow, and the gossipy nods and clucks of the trees. I was listening to these, standing on my porch, when Pete Karl emerged loudly at the entrance of Ridgepoint Circle with a tremendous plow attached to the front of his garbage truck. I had been peering down the road at the house—number 5—that looked like the Death Star, its gray steel and smoked glass apparently soon to be replicated in another wing. One flank of the octagon was encased in electric blue plastic. I had never seen the people. For all I knew, they had never entered the house. They may well have operated the place by remote control from Albany or Syracuse, ordering hedges pruned and bedrooms expanded via fax and e-mail, tossing investment at the property and receiving occasional reports of its growth. They might return in the comfort of summer to meet with the architect, pay off the electrician. But by then I'd be gone.

Pete Karl's plow approached, smashing diagonally through the snow and pouring the lumpy avalanche aside. The result was the addition of an even deeper rumble to the usual cacophony of his job. He waved out his window as he passed.

"Hullo, Will!"

I raised my hand.

"Can't stop!" he hollered. "Stop now, I'm stuck!"

"Don't get stuck here!" I said.

"What's that?"

"Don't stop!" I yelled.

"Just clearing it off for you! Got to plow Ridgepoint, and

then I'm on to Apple Hill and Jayhawk and back down to Eight!"

"Going to charge me for this?"

"Can't have you stranded!" he yelled back. "Get a call, you'll never make it to the station! Another six inches coming! That's what I'm hearing! Six to eight tonight!"

He waved again into his tall side mirror as he rattled away. I started back inside, with a last look up at the sky, and caught sight of something odd. I stepped out onto the lawn. There, draped over the thickest branch of the tallest of my front-yard trees, was a shape that gradually revealed itself to be a sweater. I must not have noticed it after I'd hurled the whole pile of them out my bedroom window. I stared at it now. It occurred to me that I could retrieve it. All that it would require was a few sim-ple yards of vertical effort. I was fitter for the task than ever in my life, thanks to the cumulative hundreds of trembling push-ups and sit-ups and the half dozen times Captain Stan had forced us to rack and rerack hose on top of a truck. There was a ten-sion to my arms and chest, a dignity to them, that I'd never known. Actual muscles could be discerned, like turtles in a swamp, by pressing my gut in the right spots and at the right time of day.

I walked over across the snow, under the dark morning sky, to see about it. I stood at the base of the tree and reached up for the lowest branch, brushed off the snow, and grasped it with both hands. First came a scramble, boots kicking, against the bark of the trunk. It was the equivalent of a pull-up, only slop-pier, and I soon had wrestled myself onto the limb to sit in tri-umph. Then up and wobbling and steadying and pulling myself to the next one higher. A leap and a pull-up onto the next. And now just a sideways stretch of arm, hand, fingers and the sweater was mine. Or, rather, his. But in my grip. I threw it as far and hard as I could.

I had never climbed a tree. My upward mobility, though fiscally rewarded and ruthlessly envied, did not apply to the great outdoors. I'd ridden a bike a couple of times: once, anyway, that I remember, led by my breathless mother around and around a concrete courtyard on the Upper West Side. I had performed other pan-American rituals of childhood. Hot chocolate, for instance, was sold at the Rockefeller Center skating rink in the lit shadow of the tallest and most expensive Christmas tree in the world. But not this, not me, never seated with feet swinging on a branch, peering down from a good dizzy distance at the earth from whence I'd come.

"*Haaay!*"

I crossed my boots: Mr. Casual. "Hey yourself."

PJ had emerged from the woods, wearing a pink parka, to toddle under my branch. She bared her bad teeth, looking up. "You're in the tree."

"Damn right."

"Let me try."

"Suit yourself," I said to the charcoal sky. There was more snow coming. Pete Karl had it right. The unfallen flakes could be pre-felt in the face, their delicate blur almost visible if you closed your eyes. Behind my house there was a field that sloped downhill. Perfect, it occurred to me (and hopefully not to her) for sledding.

"Help me up."

"Nope."

"Help me!"

"That wouldn't be right."

"Why?"

"Nobody helped me up."

"Why?"

"Because I didn't need it."

"Why?"

Leaning back carefully into the crook of the branch where it met the trunk, I crossed my arms. This had been my pose of anger, when provoked, in the fourth-floor conference room at the office, a physical signal to my colleagues that I was displeased, that earnings charts would have to be rewritten overnight, dinner plans canceled, a battery of phone calls made and spread sheets urgently and more aggressively reworked. Glaring down at the girl, I noticed that she was carrying under the arm of her parka a yellow carton of M&M's. Peanut, they'd be.

"Want to buy some candy?"

Like the ruthless salesperson she was, she had noticed me noticing. I leaned forward too quickly, almost toppling with a half shout and grabbing the branch between my legs.

"Whoa!" from below. "That was *clooose*. You almost went—"

"I don't want any candy."

"But it's for school."

"That's your homework?" I asked. "To eat candy?"

"I have to sell M&M's. For school. It's to raise money."

"Selling often is."

"For the, um. What do you call it. Hold on. Wait."

The air was colder at this altitude, my altitude, a dozen feet higher than the level at which people lived. It turns out, further-more, that trees never stop moving. They sigh and shift in the winter wind, jiggle the nubs at the ends of their branches, crack their bare knuckles, stretch their legs, adjusting always to the movements of the earth.

"I don't actually care what you're raising money for, PJ. I'm not interested."

"Why?"

"I don't eat candy."

"You eat candy," she said slyly. "Why don't you eat candy?"

I ate approximately her weight in candy every day. "Don't like it. So where's your mom?"

"Working."

"At home?"

"Ummmmm." She moved the M&M's box to the other arm. Weakening beneath the burden. "Yeah. She's making pottery."

"Why don't you go help her."

"Because it's in the basement. I'm not allowed in the base-ment. That's where the *kill* is."

"Kiln," I corrected her. "Well, why don't you go play in the garage or something."

"Hayyyy." She smiled big at this. "How did you know I play in the garage?"

"My point is, PJ, that you should take your candy somewhere else. I'm not a buyer here. Try harassing the neighbors."

"The neighbors aren't there."

"Sure they are." I looked at the Georgian estate to my left. There is an instant sense, when looking at a house, of whether it's inhabited or empty. I had found this to be true over the past months of baby-sitting these abandoned homes. They swelled and glowed when pregnant with people, grew drawn and sharp-edged when not. "Try the other neighbors."

"I did. I knocked."

"Knock again. They're probably drunk." I looked upward for another branch. None was as sturdy or homey. I could climb from here, scale the thing bottom to top, only things got spindly fast.

"Come *onnnn*. They're M&M's."

I did, I realized as I shifted dangerously on the branch, have my wallet.

"It's only a dollar," she whined.

"Tell you what." I held my hand out over her, an arborial god calling for order. "I'm a buyer," I said, "at seventy-five cents."

She was struck dumb. She looked down at the box in her arms. Up at me blankly. "But they're a dollar."

"Not now they're not."

"But—why?"

"Because the closing price, my little friend, depends on the size of the deal."

"What?"

"Because I'm taking the whole carton."

Her eyes went wide. She gave a barracuda grin. "You *are?*"

"Wholesale discount. Buying in bulk," I said. "Seventy cents a pop. Times however many are in there. And with a cut of your future business."

"You said seventy-five before."

"No, I didn't. Seventy cents. Forget the future business. There's no future business. You want to unload the stuff or not?

Up to you." I dug into my pocket and pulled my wallet free, an effort that almost unhorsed me. I plucked out a twenty. "This ought to cover it."

"What's that."

Slowly I released the pinch of my thumb and forefinger to set the bill adrift on the air, seesawing unevenly downward, diving and spinning rapidly as if in a last-ditch attempt to impress the judges as it plummeted toward her. To watch that thin gray-green movement, that orchestral shimmy and fall, was strangely enjoyable enough that I did it again while she scurried to collect her prize from the snowbank at the edge of my yard. And again. And again. What lovely shedding: I would have thrown my wallet (calves' leather, Italian, $825) if I didn't think it might bonk her on the head. The fives and twenties were gone and there were only the hundreds I kept at the back. They fluttered like twenties, perhaps a bit more stiffly, pivoting for slightly longer in the air before landing around the girl who raced in circles with her arms outstretched to catch shreds of an easy miracle, my good riddance, bits and pieces of the old me.

WHOEVER HAD BEEN IN MY DEN

knew his way around a fire. It was easy enough to burn my antique Pig Stand menu (as evidenced by the single crisp corner of it that had drifted down to the tiles), but to stuff an entire Cracker Barrel apron and custom-made robe from the head corporate office of Banana Republic into a lit wood-burning stove takes real skill. All evidence of my decades of work had been incinerated. The culprit had no fear of making a fire in my house: of using the chimney, smoke-signaling his presence, and of taking his sweet time to torch my treasures. I supposed I could scatter the ashes, at least, for closure. Drop them in smudged handfuls out the back of a limo the next time I rolled past Wall Street. As if preparing for that ceremony, I fingered the soft pile of gray. It was still vaguely warm. Impossibly light. As soulless and weightless, in my palm, as it had always felt.

From upstairs, after my shower, I heard what I guessed was a woodpecker until it continued its rat-a-tat with an insistence that was uniquely and annoyingly human. Someone was rapping on my screen door.

"Yeah?"

Now the bangs came on the heavier main door. The handle rattled.

"Just a minute," I said. I was coming down the stairs in a towel. "Jesus. Hold on." As I passed the front closet I reached in and grabbed something, anything, to put over my gleaming wet belly: a raincoat. With that on top, and with a fist barely holding together the towel below, I pulled open the door to see Paula. "Hel—"

"What the fuck do you think you're doing?" She stormed right past me and into the kitchen, almost dislodging the towel.

"Can I help you?"

"Yeah, you can help me." She turned then, at the counter, her hair big and cinched into a frizzy ponytail. She appeared to be clad in seven layers of flannel shirts. She extended an open hand. "Do you think you could lend me, oh, I don't know. Twenty-two hundred bucks?"

"Okay. I see what you're—"

"What part of you thinks that's okay? Who the fuck gives a six-year-old two thousand dollars in cash? What"—she gesticulated wildly, and seemingly at my towel—"what *are* you?"

"Listen. I'm not a kid person."

"You're not a grown-up."

"Come on, Paula. At least I didn't stiff her."

"Please don't use the word *stiff* when you're naked and talking about my daughter."

"Wait a minute." I almost laughed.

"What. Okay. Fine. Call it bribery."

"I wasn't bribing her. What the hell would I have been——"

"Well, you were bribing someone."

"What? Who was I bribing? I was buying M&M's. I was buying something."

"Right. Buying your way in. As usual."

"Into what?"

"Oh, I don't know. Let's see, *Bill*." She said my name as if it were the punch line of a joke. "Into the community? Into the stupid newspaper? Where are you trying to get. Where does this end for you. In my pants?"

"What?" I looked—couldn't help it—at her pants, a snug pair of black jeans. "Don't flatter yourself, Paula."

"Why are you *here?*" she asked. "With all your money. With your big house. I mean, seriously, Bill. What's the point? Is it a dick thing?"

"A what?"

"Is it about the size of your dick? Because we could end that question right here. You could save yourself a lot of money. Cut down on the M&M's. Cut to the chase." She sat, then, on a stool at my kitchen counter and folded her hands. She was apparently prepared to be patient. "Why don't you take off your little towel there and we can be done with this."

"Funny." I found myself holding tighter to my towel. "You want a coffee or anything?" I tried to change the tone of this thing. I knew arguments. I had won arguments, and had sixty-one Lucite bricks to show for it. I could reverse this thing, spin her and sell her, anytime I wanted. "As long as you're here. Or a drink?"

"I would like a drink, yes, thank you," she said sweetly. "Just as soon as you take off that little towel, big guy."

"What do you want, Paula, an apology? Shit. An admission that I was too generous? You want me to take back the money? Fine. Give it back."

"I'm not giving it back. Hell, I've already spent it. That's rent, my friend. I'm just here to save my town a lot of grief. I'm doing this for Harristown. Let's see the size of your dick. Then, hey, mission accomplished. You can leave."

I went and poured her a gin on the rocks, using one hand. I crossed back in front of her to present it—this should help—and that's when she reached out, quicker than I could have expected, and snatched away the towel.

"Christ. No, Paula. Give the fuck—give me the towel."

"And there we have it."

"Paula. Fine. Right. Give it back." The raincoat wasn't long enough. I had let the glass of gin fall and smash. "Fuck, Paula."

She had whisked the towel behind her back and sat on it. "Not bad. I see your point."

"Give me the fucking thing." I grabbed for the towel. She kicked my arm with a vicious boot. I stepped back, wanting to lunge again, covering myself with both hands, lunging once more with no luck. I had flushed beet red, I could feel it. I wanted to smack her off the damned chair. But by the time I had mustered the strength for another stab she had quit, vanished with a door slam and a final threat thrown over her shoulder—"If I ever catch you anywhere near my daughter again, this towel is not going to be the only thing I rip off"—and I found myself half naked in my kitchen, alone.

IT WAS THREE-FIFTEEN

in the morning when I stood to a rage of beepings and almost fractured my ankle on a footstool from Napoleonic France. I limped across my bedroom and pulled on the shirt and pants and unlaced boots that I now laid out before going to sleep: a flat imprint of myself on the floor beside the dresser, roused and filled with life a few seconds after I was. At the station there were only three of them, four of us, croaking at each other with our hair in all directions. Downed power lines on Haymeadow. Fucking power lines. Windy fucking night.

After the ride, out of the truck, our job—until the lazy bastards from the power company showed—was to divert traffic from the stretch of Haymeadow Lane where the wires had fallen. A blossom of sparks came from the severed end of a cable and scattered with a brief sizzle across the street. Pete Karl showed up in his garbage truck and joined the team. Sully charged the hose. Gary held the nozzle. Henry lit flares and dropped them in a red arc around the danger. Pete Karl gave me a radio. Took one himself. I mentioned that the recommended perimeter for a wires call is at least five hundred yards from the wires. He nodded and stationed us at either end of the incident, then made sure of our connection.

"Hey, Will, you copy?"

"Bill copies."

"Copy me? Over."

"Copy. I'm copying you. Christ."

"Say over, there, Will."

"What?"

"Say over. Over."

"Right," I said. "Over."

For a minute there was radio silence.

"Windy night. Over."

"Copy," I said. "Over."

There was no traffic on Haymeadow Lane at three forty-five in the morning. There were no more sparks from the cables. The flares, reflected in red smudges off the snowdrifts, gave the roar of a television gone blank. There was nothing to do but tilt back my helmet to look up at the freezing-cold stars, at the blurry webs of them, at their pinprick sharpness, stamping my boots to keep warm.

Afterward we sat at the counter of Henry's Place. Usually after a call, we'd crash up the stairs to the station-house bar to enjoy a nice warm one amid the gripes of the other guys. This time, passing Henry's Place on the ride back, Sully braked and simply parked the truck out front. It didn't seem to me that fire-men in a fire truck should be able to do that. Still, there was no one around. No point going to sleep. Already the sky out the bar's window was purpling and loosening into daylight.

In the gray silence we stared at the shelves of bottles of liquor and mixers, the stacked pyramid of wine. Sully ran a stubby fin-ger over the variety, cruising the joint, waddling behind the counter. He got to the wine and got interested.

" 'Poo-ley Foo-see,' " he pronounced. "This any good, Henry? Your Pooley?"

Henry didn't answer. He was polishing the length of the bar with an unsanitary rag.

"Bet you've got yourshelf a nice shellar of wine," Gary told me.

I shrugged.

"You do, don't you. Bunch of good vintages tucked away. Thatch what I do. Put them away, forget all about them, and then—zam. You're in bishnesh."

Henry lifted his head, wiped his mustache. "Get us some beers, Gary."

Gary sprang off his stool like the kid on the bench who'd been chosen at last to go into the game.

"Bring out your imported shit if you want," Henry called af-ter him as he left for the storeroom.

" 'Porto'!" said Sully, reading the word on a bottle and pulling it off the shelf.

"That's port," I told him. "That one's from Portugal."

"Port from Portugal." Examining the label, he crinkled his half-bald head. "Makes sense."

"Is that a '94?" I asked, leaning forward to see. "Look at the date. On the label there."

"Bin-go. 1994. Nailed it."

"That's outstanding. Hey, Henry."

"Hm."

"You know what you should do?"

Gary emerged from the back with four beer bottles dangling from a hand and chiming against each other. He began to pop off the caps with an opener that was attached by an old string to the bar.

"Got some decent booze here," I told Henry. "Not a lot of space."

"Hm."

"Ought to merge with the dairy next door."

He straightened up from his labors, the rag at his side. "Merge?" He pronounced the word like the name of an ugly woman.

"That's right. With this place right next door. The egg place. Why not? Knock down the wall between you. Share assets. Pool your profits. Your wine, their cheese. And when you think wine and cheese, what do you think." I pointed a finger. "That's right. Author readings. Political fund-raisers. Art openings." The eyes above the mustache showed nothing but dungaree blue. "This place could be a goddamned cultural center. Local hotspot." I smoothed my beard: the prophet of retail and restaurant. "What do you think."

The three firemen looked at me blankly. Gary flicked the last beer cap onto the floor with a *tink*.

"Things like large-scale refrigeration are going to be a hell of a lot cheaper," I pressed on, "with two businesses kicking in capital. Whole back room could be a walk-in. Store your higher-priced cheeses, longer-term vintages." I leaned forward on my bar stool. Hitting my stride. "That's the beauty of a joint venture." The words and terms ran on like a tape on a loop. "Double your revenue streams." Behind my moving mouth, I felt dizzy. "Consolidate your assets. Rationalize some of your costs."

Henry said nothing. I was proud of him for holding out. I had no interest in the venture, no reason for the hard sell. The words seeped out of me like toxins. These were the last spasms of a waning disease, the flailing death of the investment banker who had lived in my blood.

"Fuck, forget it," I said.

At last Henry broke his stare to emit three words: "Forgot it already."

"Well, theeshe," Gary said, hoisting aloft two bottles in each hand, "are about the best beersh you're going to find in this town."

Wowee, I thought. I would have preferred to try the Portuguese port. But Sully had clunked it back onto the shelf and hurried over to be first in line. " 'Gubernator,' " he read off his bottle once Gary had handed it to him. He raised it toward us. "Got the Gubernator here."

"From the Ukraine," said Gary. "Russian beer. Shtrong shtuff."

"Shit yeah."

"And thish is from Belgium." He passed Henry a taller bottle of rose-tinted beer. "Belle-Vue Kriek. Made with fresh cherries."

"I know what it's made out of," Henry said in a low, warning voice. "I sell this crap."

"Ever drank it, though?" Gary quizzed him. "Ever tried it?"

"No."

"Well, you ought to. Sheriously. You should know your imports. Thatch lambic beer," he explained.

"It's pink beer," said Henry.

"Well, then, you can have a darned Rolling Rock," Gary snapped. "Thatch from a place called Europe. Don't know if you've heard of it."

"Sure," said Henry, unaffected by Gary's anger. "Same place you buy your fucking shoes."

I accepted the bottle Gary handed over. "Birkenhead," he told me. "From Shouth Africa."

I must have frowned.

"Shit," Sully consoled me, "at least it's not pink."

"Not a lot of microbrewsh in Shouth Africa," said Gary, pointing with his bottle to mine. "Don't know if you know anything about Shouth Africa, but I'll tell you thish: not a lot of microbrewing going on. Lot of *black* people. Angry blacks, too. Worsht kind."

This was unexpected, not just the clumsy bigotry, but the topic itself. Strange of Gary to have brought it up. Even, I'd have to say, suspicious. What the hell did he know about South Africa, anyway—and from whom? In arranging Pippa's real estate tours, he must have spoken to her often, met her all the time and at all hours. They could easily have ended up at a woodsy hotel on one of their early property hunts—or else tussled in the woods themselves, from which she'd returned wearing a leaf.

"Me," Gary said, "I'm drinking Hoegaarden. Called Hoegaarden Forbidden Fruit." He was leaning against the bar. "Nine perchent alcohol by volume. Shtuff will knock you on your ear."

We all watched him swig from his bottle as if, there before us, he might be knocked on his ear.

"Switch with you," I offered Henry, nudging him with my beer.

We traded bottles.

"If you want to know the truth," I said, resettling myself on my stool, "it's not the black people who are the problem. Over in South Africa. Blacks own the place. Ask me, they can do whatever the fuck they want. Lived there for thousands of years. It's the uninvited guests—the whites—who screwed things up. Jailed people. Killed people. Thousands of people. Women, children." I lifted my bottle. "Angry whites." I took a drink of the fruity Kriek. "Worst kind."

The sky out the window had thinned to a high blue. I had pulled countless all-nighters studying growth charts at the office, had skimmed pitch books and goggled at bad pay-per-view television straight through to morning in some of the very best hotel rooms in the crummiest cities in America; but I don't think I had ever actually watched night turn to day. It was not what I would have imagined. Daylight did not arrive with any weight or significance. It was darkness that held things, that kept and stirred them until it was taken slowly apart, its walls removed, its deep colors leaking and finally let go as it unfolded into the empty container of the day.

"Show," Gary said. "Your buddy Pete Karl told me"—and here he took a sip of his beer, fiddled with his pager, walked all the way to the pale window and looked at the other guys before he went on—"that the divorshe is going through."

I was in the middle of a swallow and almost coughed out my beer. "How the Christ would he know that?"

Sully smoothed a sideburn with his bottle. "Says you chucked your ring."

"Kind of incredible," said Gary pleasantly, looking out the window, "what you can learn from a man'sh garbage."

I had. It was true. I had thrown it away. I had stood over the trash in the kitchen, flexing my hand over and over, tugging it off and examining it, turning it in my fingers, listening to the carping of birds and the repeated query of a bare tree and thinking it over and letting it go.

To the surprise of everyone, then, Henry spoke up. "Been through that myself."

"Hm," I said after a silence.

"Twice. Matter of fact." Gently he patted the bar top as if it were one of his former spouses. Sully and Gary exchanged a look that suggested they had not heard this speech before. "Throws you for a loss," Henry went on. "Don't it. Feels like starting all over. Square one. And you can't fucking believe it. Five years, ten years, and nothing to show. Spend a few months taking it apart, looking at the pieces, and what do you got. Pieces. You got squat."

"Nineteen," I said. "Nineteen years."

"Makes no sense," he said loudly, mustache jumping, "that you could make a mistake like that. Because that's all it is: you made a mistake. Bet wrong. Guessed wrong. That's all that happened. Guessed wrong and then lived with it long as you could."

I tried to nod.

"But I'll tell you this. Piece of advice. From someone who's been there." I had never heard him speak for this long. He appeared to be wearying. "You don't just toss your ring. Not in the garbage," he said. "Not like that."

"Oh no?" I snapped. I bonked my beer down on the counter. "So what would you suggest? Swallow it? Frame it? Melt it down into a tiny golden dagger so I can jab it in my fucking eye once a d—"

"Give it back," Henry said calmly. He rapped on the counter beside his rag. "That's what you do. You return it."

"I bought that goddamn ring."

"She gave it to you. As part of the wedding. I take it you did have a wedding. You people do get *married*."

This, surely, was a Jewish slur. "Yeah, sure, we get married," I said. "The second we find someone else who has horns."

"Down there in the city," he finished absently, trailing off. He stopped his exhaled breath with a drink from his bottle.

We were quiet for a minute. To our left the store window was catching fire, its cracks and smears ignited by the first flare of the sun. Henry crouched to put away his rag. Then he appeared over the counter to give me one of his twinkly old looks.

"She sure fucked you up," he said.

Startled, I looked at him.

He stared back unapologetically. "Something bad. Real bad." He was amused. "What are we talking."

I drank the last of my beer. "Usual shit."

"I don't think so," he pressed. He wasn't letting this go. He gave a chuckle. "How bad."

"Pretty bad."

" 'Nother guy," he guessed.

Henry had stolen my line, leaving me only to echo it weakly: "Another guy."

Sully made a strange sound out of the side of his mouth. Gary whistled through his braces.

"You might know him," I said.

"From Harristown." Henry sounded pleased. "Who we got."

"Who is he?" Sully's voice was hushed and childish. Sully, certainly, would know him.

"I don't know."

"What do you mean?" Gary asked me.

"Don't know who he is. No idea. Not unless you guys know something."

They all stuck out their lower lips at once. There were shrugs, a cluck, the picking of an eyetooth. A few more sips, sorry eyes all around. We drank our beers, then, four men in Harristown sampling the world.

"So, then, hold on." Sully had missed something. "How do you know he's from out here?"

The leaf, I could have said. The leaf in her sweater didn't lie. Nor did the phone bills filled with the Harristown area code. The mugs in the den. The sighting by Pete Karl. The run-in with Mark. The sweaters in my drawer. They blurred together, these clues, all this evidence, until I couldn't see. Blind now, eyes closed, I sagged against the bar.

"You all right there, Bill?"

"Ho boy."

"You with us, buddy?"

I was.

SULLY'S MOTHER HAD THE SOFTLY

cheeping voice
of a shoreline bird. She had invited me to breakfast, or so Sully
said, nimbly slipping that information in between his instructions on the oil change as he performed it. I had asked for this—
the instructions, I mean, not the breakfast—out of curiosity. I
was interested, frankly, in cars, now, and willing to spend a Saturday morning back under my vehicle with Francis Sullivan in
order to learn something. Little did I know it would mean waffles with his chirping mom.

She appeared in the kitchen of the main house, when we
knocked and entered, with a puffy smile, stocky limbs, faded
flowery housedress, the works. She looked as if she were coated
with the faintest of powders, rolled in a fine flour. Her features,
however, were not delicate. They were those of a dockworker,
softened only slightly by age and by the 1950s tent dress that she

continually dusted off for no reason as she moved back and forth across the linoleum, retrieving the waffles from the freezer and inserting them in the toaster and scrambling eggs for her boy and his friend. We made coffee. We chomped down our waffles. As we ate, she asked me questions that Sully had to amplify out of the side of his mouth.

"Cheepity cheep."

"Right. Yes, ma'am. New York City. Right in it, yes. Right in the mess."

"Cheepa cheepa."

"Not me, no. No family, I'm afraid."

"Cheep cha-cheep."

"What did she—that's right. The castle. Well, someone has to."

Do we ever get better at this? Meeting the parents never changes. Generations never merge. My freshly fallen layer of gray hair and my St. Nicholas beard did nothing to unite me and this old biddy or make her any easier to hear. For Sully's sake I kept a smile stuck to my face. She teased him harshly for never having actually been in a fire. She reminded us both that Sully's father had been in the company, that her own father had been chief back when they still used buckets of sand. This last claim caused some factual argument, with Sully wagging his head and complaining, catching my eye and bad-mouthing her again. She pestered me some more about my history and plans. Encouraged me—with a long look at Sully as he translated—to do more than just drive the truck.

What I was thinking about was Finelli. There was no one else left, no other explanation for the glare that pulsed above his dilapidated nose, for the tension in his tattooed biceps, just itching to spring into a punch at my head. I had been fooled by the tattoos, thrown off his trail. He hated me for a reason. Since the moment I'd crossed the county border he had tried to pin me with his stare, dissecting me as if to discover what made me tick and what had made me and Pippa married. They'd be some matchup, Pippa and Finelli: a prizefight of scrappers, each of them hungry as hell. She probably hadn't met anyone with tattoos. She would have traced them with a finger in bed, treating them as noble wounds, asking their illustrated stories one by one.

Sully's mother ate only a piece of toast. Eggs, she said loudly enough for me to hear it the first time, gave her gas. Gas, Sully repeated as he got up to bring ketchup to the table. Gas, I reconfirmed. Eggs give her gas. Got it. Thanks. She spoke in bird language to her son about the heat in her room as he wolfed down his eggs. There was, for a time, a bright gash of ketchup below his lip. We spent a few minutes talking about the test that was only a week away. Sully predicted, perhaps for his mom's sake, that he'd pass. I fetched myself another cup of coffee. I offered one, unheard, to Mrs. Sullivan. I was leaning forward to inquire once again when both our pagers went off at once. The tones, a fraction of a second off from each other, blended to create from their usual bip-bip-bip an unbroken stereophonic beep.

"*Sixty control Harristown. Firefighters needed to respond to Hardy's Pier at the end of Carlson Lane. Possible incident on the ice.*"

"Well," I said, pushing away my paper plate, "we can't have incidents."

"*Repeat: sixty control Harristown. Manpower needed off Hardy's Pier for a possible incident.*"

"See you, Ma."

"Good-bye, Mrs. Sullivan."

I felt all the more valiant, every bit the public servant, for having an old lady there to receive my best wishes before we loped out her door to take arms against a sea of incidents.

"Where's my fucking car?"

It was still jacked up in the shed. We slammed into Sully's and took off for the station, spinning a bit on his snowy road. He was a damned good driver, to see it up close. His short limbs were custom-made for yanks of the gear shift and sideways jabs of the wheel. His weasel eyes darted precisely where they should a split second before his car darted there, too. He was out of the vehicle, keys stashed in his pants, before the rotors or whatever hummed beneath his hood had stopped. It took me some time to follow him into the bay, to reach the rack and pull on my bunkers and boots and carry my gloves and jacket, helmet almost tilting off my head, to the truck.

Pete Karl gave me a hand up. Beside him sat the dipstick from the gas mart. Finelli was up front next to Sully. Terrific. This time I was the first to glare. As usual, Pete Karl was looking back and forth out the windows, using his rubber-banded beard like a dowser as he judged the efficiency of our route.

What had happened became clear once we got there and stepped down from the truck and looked out over the lumpy and largely frozen Hudson River. A few of Harristown's teen-age homeboys—white of skin, baggy of jean, their hip-hop drawls learned from television and their gang-colored kerchiefs bought with their moms' credit cards at the Dovertown Mall— had driven their oversized go-cart, a Honda ATV, onto the river.

The legs of the pier were packed in the snow that encased the riverbank. The ice thinned to black water near the river's middle, and it was there that we saw the sinking ATV with its back tires submerged. A ski-hatted kid was still in the seat, afraid to move. He could barely respond with rigid nods to the counsel being yelled by his posse.

"Yo-yo, Freddy, man, don't move."

"Just chill. Just stay chill, ah-ite."

"That's it, baby. Awww yeah. Be fine, now."

The boys were taking this opportunity, slouching a safe distance from the ragged edge of the ice, to practice their lingo and perfect their accents—not at Freddy's expense, exactly, but rather in support of him, and undoubtedly in compensation for the less urbane squeals and sobs they had uttered at the moment of crisis. An ambassador from their group crossed the ice to tell us the situation and whatnot. He skated a bit as he did so, puffy jacket blowing open to reveal a T-shirt that read "Don't Ask Me 4 Shit."

I worked with the King of the Gas Mart to unload a collection of likely tools (an ax, a halligan, a long plucking thing) from the compartments of our truck. I noticed the ambulance parked farther down the river, looked for Paula and found her unrolling reflective blankets with the other medics. She might have seen me; her blowing hair obstructed her face. With no sign of the chief—where the hell was the chief?—Finelli had naturally taken over, shouting commands to all within earshot. "Get us a halligan, Sully. Do *something*. Need a hell of a lot more length than that, Pete. Give me more than three fucking feet." He had tossed the end of a thick rope over his shoulder and looped it around his neck, coil after coil, taking care not to dislodge his idiotic Harristown Fire cap. He charged onto the ice, slipping and running, his ungainly necklace attached to a rattling spool in the back compartment of the truck.

Reluctantly I followed Finelli and his skimming rope out, with careful steps, onto the ice. Gas Mart followed me. Little Pete Karl overtook both of us from behind, speed-walking past. Sully alone lingered on solid snowy ground, pacing with the radio back and forth before the truck. Evidence of Freddy's peel-outs and skidded doughnuts were all around us in a looping design that led to the cracked hole. The kids themselves hardly looked up as we slid past them. The ATV didn't appear to have sunk any farther. Nonetheless, Freddy's terror had risen.

"Help me. Get me off. Get me off this thing."

"Shut up," Finelli told him.

"Nice," I said.

"Don't talk," he told the kid. "Shut up now. Don't move. Just relax for me. Just close your eyes and relax."

I watched the boy try to close his eyes with a spasmodic series of blinks. "I can't. Just get me off." He jiggled a bit, gripping the handlebars.

"Don't fucking move!" I shouted at him.

Pete Karl was at my shoulder. He was banging his gloves together with such anxious force that I thought the vibrations might shudder open the ice.

"Where's the chief?" I asked him.

"Stuck at work," he said. "This is not good."

"What work? What's he do?"

"Not good," he was chanting softly through his beard. "This is not good."

We were probably thirty yards from Freddy and his slowly drowning vehicle. The watery crack beneath him had not widened, best I could tell. The front wheels were still balanced on the edge of the broken rink. But then, at that moment, they appeared to slip and to slide a few inches in reverse as the kid gave a loud moan. Yells spilled from the medics and from the kids on the ice. When the sliding stopped, Freddy's feet were dipped in the freezing water.

"Jesus—why aren't those wheels floating?" I asked Pete Karl.

"Too heavy," Finelli answered. He was uncoiling the rope over his head. "See, Probie, when things are heavy? They don't float."

"Really? That's interesting, Finelli. Fuck you very much."

One of the kids behind us heard this and laughed a manic laugh, the cackle of the wild hyena, but it wasn't picked up by the rest of the pack. I looked back and past them to see Gas Mart, fifty yards back, who had looped the rope snugly around his waist to serve as Finelli's anchor. He gave a ready nod. Swiftly Finelli tied what I had to admit was a magnificent chimney hitch.

"I'm going to throw this rope," he told Freddy, dangling the knotted lasso end toward the boy. "You just catch it."

Freddy leaned back a few centimeters, shivering visibly, readying himself to pry one of his hands from the handlebars. He hadn't pulled his feet from the water. They might, now that I looked, have sunk slightly deeper.

"Can you catch?" I called. This was meant to be encouraging. Kids can catch, I was thinking. They play baseball and football and basketball (don't they?) in backyards and school playgrounds; in leagues, for Christ's sake. The kid would do well, I thought, to remember the frolic of competitive sport. "You can get this, man. Make the catch," I said. "Pull it down." I knew my teenagers, more or less. I'd spent six months kissing up to the head of finance for Chuck E. Cheese. "Don't fuck this up, Freddy," I called. "All you."

Pete Karl had turned to stare at me. When Finelli looked around, his face tightly screwed, his nose had bent even larger and lower.

"C'mon Fred," I called past them. "C'mon Freddy now. Big catch here."

Eventually Finelli twirled the rope and loosed it high into the air. It went over Freddy's head, hit the back of the vehicle and slid off.

"Where were you there, Freddy?" I yelled.

"Shut *up,*" Finelli snapped. "Try again," he told the kid.

Freddy hardly flinched when the rope banged him in the thigh and slipped off into the water and back across the ice as Finelli reeled it back in.

"He's not going to catch that," I said. "Kid can't move."

"No time," muttered Pete Karl.

"Give me the rope." I stooped to retrieve it from the ice before Finelli.

"And what the fuck are *you*——"

"I'm going to hand it to him."

"Hand it to who?"

"I'm going to put it over the kid," I said, quickly changing my mind. "Loop it over him. Only way."

"No you're not."

"Will, that's not——"

But I was already stumbling and skating forward. Freddy and his farm equipment appeared to have retreated a mile away. I couldn't stop slipping on the ice. I half-fell and righted myself, retook the rope in both gloves. I walked more slowly now, bending my knees to lower my center of gravity. As I lifted my eyes to face the boy, I was crushed to the ice with someone's arms around my waist.

My helmet hit hard, spinning away as I slid with a guy on top of me. We sledded to a stop. Finelli was beside me on his knees, his hands still on my back. There was no way around it now. No way around him. I brought myself to a crouch as he did. Shakily we stood. For what seemed a long time we glared at each other, breath after breath, readying for battle. I balled up my gloved fingers for the punch. But when I lunged for him, I couldn't lift my arms.

"Hey—hold it. Easy does it. There you go, big boy," said a female voice in my ear. I was being held back by a woman. I could turn my head far enough to see it was Paula. "No time for this crap," she said.

With a burst I pulled my arms free of hers and spun around. The look on her face, dead set, stopped me cold. I turned back to Finelli. "Took my wife," I think I said. I was on the brink of tears, to tell you the truth, fat rolling tears, blubbering on the ice. If the kids hadn't been looking on in stunned silence, in a lengthy pause before the savage laughter and high-fives broke out, I might have cried. Instead I shouted loud enough to hear it again a second later off the trees: "My fucking *wife,* you *fuck!*"

He was still breathing hard. He had run to catch up with me. "I don't," he said, "know your wife."

"Pippa," I told him. "Pippa's my wife."

"Good for you."

"You know her."

"No."

"Yes, you do," I said, more quietly now. "It's you."

Slowly he bent to pick up the end of the rope from the ice. "No dice, Probie."

I looked back toward Paula. She was far away already, skating back toward the shore. "So why'd you tackle me?" I asked him.

"You were going through the fucking ice."

"Give me the rope."

"You're too much weight."

I was seized by pain with my first step toward him. My back was out again, clenched into a fist that wouldn't let go. "I won't go through."

"Going under, Schoenberg. No doubt about it. Bottom of the river."

He was right. "You're wrong." I looked at the kid, still sitting and sinking twenty yards away. Freddy appeared to have stopped trembling, having been captivated instead by the spectacle of two oldsters fighting on ice, the kind of pro-wrestling freak show that he and his buddies might have watched on pay-per-view. I realized, belatedly, that Finelli had used my last name, and correctly. "Could have made it," I told him.

"Not you," he said. "Not today." But there was something gone from his voice. The metal edge of it had been replaced by the cadence of our middle age, a natural up and down, our inevitable softness. "Pete Karl! Get over here. Front and center. Think you could get to the kid?"

Pete Karl scooted over to us. He was our very best scooter, it occurred to me, shortly after it had occurred to Finelli. He took the rope as requested. He touched the rubber band on his beard, perhaps for luck. Then he shrank down to all fours. The lasso went around his neck as he started toward the kid. Finelli and I stepped back a few paces to watch from there. He got lower as he went, ten feet away, eight, six, until he was snaking on his belly, plowing forward on his jacket, edging closer by fidgeting his elbows and with the smallest toe movements of his big boots. He excelled at the job. He must have weighed thirty-five goddamn pounds. Freddy was knee deep now in the killing cold of the water. There was a sharp crack, and even before it echoed back off the trees Pete Karl had splashed in.

"Jesus," I shouted. I lunged forward and stopped. He was out of the water already, scurrying backward, a jagged hole before him where the ice used to be. His beard was wet, his arm sopping as he waved to us and stayed where he was. He had dodged a drowning. Finelli had saved my life. We watched as Pete Karl turned resolutely back to the boy.

He was not more than six or seven feet from Freddy. He crawled slowly, almost too slowly to watch, around the new hole. Then he rose to one knee. He stretched up and just over the broken ice and the vehicle to let the rope fall in a circle over the kid's head. Freddy hesitated, frozen there, freezing for real. Then he delicately pulled the rope down over his shoulders and under his arms, not moving a centimeter more than necessary. Pete Karl slithered back, saying something, tugging the rope to give Freddy the idea. It was on the fifth or sixth tug, this one harder, that Freddy disengaged from the handlebars, leaned for a second over the water before clambering down, jumping head-first, splashing his legs and landing on the chiseled edge of the ice to be towed up and forward by Pete Karl with both hands and by Gas Mart with his whole backward-marching body until he had crawled clear of the wreck, gotten to his feet and freed himself from the rope and broke into a run, crying out loud—not to his friends, breaking through their ranks as they started to slang him and running faster, right past the medics, wailing at the dark forest and running faster and faster as if into all its frigid and open arms.

AT WORK THERE HAD ALWAYS

been a cutting significance in whether you bothered to lift the handset and speak directly and personally into the telephone or kept your caller on speaker, stammering into the void. There was the matter of how long you waited to pick up a call on hold, ending or prolonging someone's blinking desperation once your assistant patched him through. There was the opportunity, with speakerphone, to issue unheard comments while the caller was talking—comments like *Bright fucking idea* and *Junk bond, junk bond* and *Suckerrr*—for the benefit of the other yuk-yukking analysts in the room. There was an arsenal of defenses and smoke screens (*Could Mr. Schoenberg call you back after market hours?*) useful in the avoidance of any conversation anytime. Here, however, there was nothing to do but take my chances, walk to the phone and lift it off the wall.

"Yes," I said.

"Bill."

"Yes."

"Leonard."

"Leonard who?"

"Bill, please."

I sat back down on one of the kitchen stools. I had wondered, approaching the phone, if it might be Paula.

"I'm calling to check in, Bill. It's been a while. You know, things are moving forward here. I've been trying to keep you posted."

"You have."

"Yes, I have. You don't have voice mail. Were you aware of that? No answering machine. And your cell phone is useless up there."

"Is it?"

"All cell phones are useless up there. Your house is in a terrible spot."

This seemed an odd thing for him to say. "Is it?"

"But I have to tell you, Bill, let me just say up front that I have an associate on the other line."

"You want me to *hold?*"

"No, Bill. I want you to talk to him. His name is Scott Sanderson. He's a partner of the firm. An excellent litigator. He's been a divorce attorney for twenty years. If I can just put him through, you two should talk. Scott should be representing you. Not me. It's just not my—"

"What do I have to sign here," I cut in. I was bored. "What do I have to do. Just tell me, Leonard."

"Well," he ventured courageously, "for starters, Bill, you have to try to stay in better touch."

"I'll write."

"No, I don't believe that you will." This took more courage for poor Leonard, an out-loud contradiction of my statement, and for a few tremulous seconds he waited for me to reach through the phone and throttle him. "And I base that, frankly, Bill," he said, "on the fact that you have not gotten back to me about the division-of-property document that I sent you last month."

"Yes, I did. I sent you that. Two weeks ago, Leonard. I went to the post office myself."

"That was the verified complaint and summons that Pippa had filed. That's different, Bill. That has nothing to do with property. I think you know the document I'm talking about. It details the tangible assets and liabilities you and Pippa accumulated during your marriage. I have a copy right here."

"I can't see that from where I'm sitting, Leonard."

"Why don't you look at your copy. Do you have it? I'll hold on. Page eight."

I pouted for a minute. "Ah, here it is," I lied. "You know, Leonard, I get a lot of mail." I reached across the counter and pulled over the remaining half of my gin and tonic. "Right. Sure. Here's the monster."

"Terrific." He brightened. "Thank you. Why don't you turn to page eight."

"Page eight."

I took a sip. It was another radiant day, the third or fourth in a row, hard to look out the windows with eyes all the way open. Two squirrels faced off like boxers, fidgety bantam-weights, on the snowy lawn. They scurried together and away at the sound of a plane that, squint as I might at the brilliant blue, I couldn't see.

"You find it, Bill? Page eight."

"I don't see page eight." This was not a lie.

"You don't? In your packet there?"

"I don't have it. No page eight."

"Well, that's my fault, Bill. All the pages should be there. I'll rectify that. Forget page eight."

"I can't."

"Just turn to the assets and liabilities page that starts on thirteen. Page thirteen. Let me know when you're there."

"I'm—hold on, hold on." Big sip. Long swallow. "I'm there."

"You don't have to do this now, Bill, but what I'd like for you to do is look through all these items. See if there's anything that seems off base. Any inaccuracies. Because I'm getting the sense from the other camp, from Pippa's people, that she might make a grab for her things."

"A grab? What kind of grab? A legal grab?"

"She may just show up to take them. I'm quite serious, Bill. She may well come to the house. You may not want to be there."

"I'm supposed to leave my house?" I choked for a moment, the gin in my nose. "You're asking me to clear ou—"

"I'm only concerned," he whimpered, "about your emotions. I'm trying to make this easier, Bill. For you. Because she is claiming a lot. Let me be frank, Bill. I believe she wants every-thing in the house. All the Harristown assets. That's the sense I get. So whenever you can take a look at page thir—"

"I'm looking now."

"You don't have to look now. I just want, at some point, to ascertain——"

"I'm looking now, Leonard. Hell, I'm just doing it. Jumping right in. Reading, reading. Looking through. And . . . nope. Done. Perfect. No problem here."

"Why don't you take some time with this, Bill."

"Clean as a whistle, I'm afraid. On the money."

He gave a ragged sigh.

"Of course," I pointed out, "she's going to have to split all this with the new husband."

"The new——"

"The guy. The lover. Don't play dumb, Leonard. You're not dumb. You know him by now. You're a lawyer, for Chrissake. You don't have to tell me who he is—I really don't care—but please don't act stupid with me when I'm paying you to be smart."

"I don't actually know what——"

"Okay, Leonard. Forget it. Fuck it. You know what? I give up." In fact, I had officially given up several days before. I was no longer looking. I had come to terms with the fact that he was probably—obviously—one of her clients from the city, and I had wasted my time and efforts bothering to look anywhere else. It was the Soho job; or the Upper West Sider, that condo king; who cared. She had coupled with one of the paying husbands, men with too little time and too much money to lavish it all on just one woman. Men with country houses themselves, for that matter; who's to say they romped on all the beds and furniture at ours? She had disappeared for her leafy trysts together with an accomplice. She had escaped the city not alone, as I'd pictured, but along with a partner in crime.

"You know this," said Leonard. "About the lover. You can confirm this. Bill. That was a question."

"What?"

"You can confirm this."

"Forget it, Leonard. I told you. I'm done."

I could actually hear his spasmic breathing.

"Anything else?"

"No. Yes." He riffled some papers. Through the phone came the strained silence of Leonard Mankowitz Esquire gathering his strength. "Concerning the assets in the house," he got out. "I want to ask you about the personal property you would like to protect and retain."

I looked around to consider my personal property. I had already taken care of most items of any significance. I had hacked and marred the satinwood dining table that had been handed down by my parents. I had torched my corporate history, piece by piece, in the wood-burning stove. I had kicked the crap out of my car, assaulted it with my steel-toed boots, reversed it repeatedly into the front stoop, smashing backward, until the suspension was gone and my prissy, richie newness gone and a small fraction of my self-hatred gone too. I had preyed upon myself, loathed and menaced myself since my arrival. Punished myself—as if that might help. Hell, it *had* helped, in a way. I was scraping and denting myself down to size. I had no need, any longer, for excess furnishings. Or furniture, come to think of it.

"Bill? Are you there?"

"Right here," I told Leonard.

"We were discussing personal property."

"That's right," I said after a breath. "She can have it all."

"Well, I certainly don—"

"I mean it, Leonard. You can tell her that. Take it away."

I THOUGHT OF GOING TO HER HOUSE.

Surely I could
find it. I could easily imagine her sagging front porch, thought of
us downing vodka-and-instant-lemonades from her hand-potted
mugs as PJ ran back and forth skinning her knees and tugging the
wings off flies. But there was no point. No time, in any case. It
was test day. And I was as focused as I'd ever been.

Sully, for his part, was nervous enough to have called me four
times in the previous twenty-four hours. It was just like high
school: that semicasual prying over the phone for extra advice, a
couple of tips, any gleaned bits of wisdom that I could provide to
the schlub who hadn't studied. I had offered him a few words
about hose diameters and fusible-link sprinkler heads, quizzed
him on fire-ground safety regulations and nationwide auto-
accident stats. Now we rode together to the test. He had picked
me up at my house in the spirit of camaraderie and in order to

brag about a couple repairs he'd performed on a Toyota Camry two days before.

Birds yakked in the woods as we got out at the training station. There was a tattered rug of snow on the ground but a warmth in the air like a breeze from the future, friendly notice that we were on our way slowly out of the season. I shrugged off my jacket and left it on the seat. Grabbed my gear bag. Led the way.

A firefighter in formal blue uniform directed us upstairs, where the written half of the test would be conducted. A canvas curtain had been pulled across the truck bay to hide the practical test to come. I walked into our classroom on the second floor, nodding at classmates, settling into my customary seat and dropping my gear bag, as usual, with a bang. Sully sat, too, looking—now that I got a good look at him in the fluorescent lights—as if he'd pulled a month of all-nighters. His monkey hair had been worked upward by the pulling of fists. His denim shirt was buttoned lopsided, and there was a sheen on his face that suggested a previous lather.

"*Mis*-ter Wikowsky," he greeted Wikowsky, seated at our table.

"Where's your gear," I asked Sully.

"Left it in the car. Written's first. I'll get it before the practical." He scooted his chair in. "Practical's going to be tough. Last year it was an obstacle course. Bet you it's the same thing."

"That's what I heard," said Wikowsky.

"Full turnout gear the whole time," Sully said. "Thirty, forty pounds of gear. Guy last year had Kodiak arrest."

"What?"

"Heart attack. Right there. That guy Gannon, from Mills Falls. Middle of the course. Overheated or something."

"People don't overheat," said Wikowsky. "Cars overheat, Francis."

Arson, I was thinking, is covered by section 150 of penal law and punishable by twenty-five years in jail. The annual pressure test to be conducted on hoses is the maintenance of 250 pounds per square inch for a minimum of five minutes. I wanted these idiots to shut the hell up and leave me to shuffle and count my knowledge. There were two kinds of rope: your basic twisted rope, made of fibers collected into strands, and your kernmantle rope, where the yarn was braided (that was the mantle) over a rubber core (or kern).

"Gotta fart. Watch out, boys. Fire in the hole." Wikowsky released it. "There we go."

"Damn, Wikowsky."

"You're a fucking pig."

There were four hose rolls to remember: single donut roll, double donut, twin donut, and self-locking. Self-locking I'd never done. How had we forgotten to do the self-locking? Sully and I had partnered for the rolls, unloading the hoses from the top of the truck and stooping and shoving them into heavy spirals, racing the two guys next to us, hauling each completed coil to where Captain Stan had stood with his goddamned timer. Double donut, I remember, had been harder than it looked in the book.

"Aw, jeez!" a tablemate shouted, covering his nose. "It's a bad one."

"Shut your face," said Wikowsky. "Grin and bear it."

Captain Stan was flanked by two associates, their hands behind their uniformed backs, one on either side and a respectful step behind him. The men were clearly from some elite oversight committee of former firefighters, with their well-earned potbellies, professional bowler mustaches, hard-chewed gum and dignity. Encouraged by their backup, Captain Stan addressed us even more loudly than usual.

"All right," came the yell. "Test time, people." He fingered his clip-on tie, slicked back his head. "This here's the *end,* right here, of the probationary period of your firefighting *careers.* Not that it's a career for *yous.* It's a career for *us.* Yous don't get paid much of *anything.* I may have mentioned that. Bit of a *pension,* if you're in it that long." He glanced sideways at one of his men. "Not that *we* get paid much either, by the way."

Perfectly synchronized, as if a puppet master above them had dropped both sets of strings, Captain Stan's rigid helpers collapsed in laughter.

"Naw, but *seriously.* Getting *serious.*"

They snapped back to position.

"Yous should all be proud of what yous have *learned* here over the past few months. Proud to be *firefighters.*" He was launching into a speech, of all things, a commencement address, the preparation for which entailed a quick couple of head swipes and a resetting of his bulldog stance, a lifting of his double chin to let fly the blessing. " 'Cause yous don't make any *money* at it. Like I said. But yous make something *else.* Something *better.* You make people *safe.* And that's not gonna make you rich. But it's gonna make yous important. And I don't know about you, but I'd rather be important than rich." His pitch dwindled: "Well,

I'd rather be *both*." The big-bellied marionettes fell floorward again. "But so be it. You do things well, you do things by the book, and you'll do some good. That's all I got to tell yous. By the *book*." This apparently was our motto, our dull mantra. "By the *book* now. Let's get *going* here. All right, people. Everybody gets a test."

The uniformed duo split up to distribute the exams around the room. The cover contained references to various governmental offices and codes as well as the signatures of the secretary of state, the state fire administrator, and New York State's governor George E. Pataki. Pencils were passed out. Captain Stan stood as tall as he could before us, glanced down at his watch, and barked go.

The test, all told, took approximately a third of the allotted hour and a half to complete. It was basically a cinch. Anyone who'd bothered to memorize anything could get nine-tenths of the questions; anyone with any brains could polish off the rest. These two criteria, however—based on the heavy sighs and muttered *fucks* around me—seemed to exclude a majority of my classmates; unless, like early American locomotives, that was simply the noisy way they worked. Sully's pencil kept moving, I was relieved to see in my surreptitious glances. Clawing at his hair, his eraser drumming a sideburn, he kept at it until Captain Stan hollered *Pencils down*.

Then we were guided from the room and down the reverberating iron stairs, humping our bags (everyone but Sully) and reassembling at the edge of the truck bay. What we had here, Captain Stan explained, was our practical. The doors of the truck bay were wide open now, the curtain raised on what was indeed an obstacle course. Benches and chairs were arranged in clusters. Thick spiderwebs of hose had been tied from wall to wall and purposely tangled. We were to navigate this cluttered imaginary structure, get through the free-standing wooden door in the middle of the room, locate the crash-test dummy dressed in a Freemont Fire Company shirt and lying on the cement floor and hurry to carry him out.

"Only *catch,* now, people," Captain Stan pointed out, "is that yous aren't gonna be able to *see.*"

"What d'you mean," said Wikowsky on the class's behalf.

"Can't see in a structure fire," said one of the captain's henchmen. "Can't count on visibility. Use everything but your eyes. Sound, strength, feel."

"So yous aren't going to see in *here,*" finished the captain as I tried to remember whether strength was actually one of our five senses. He was holding up the kind of black blindfold they used to give out on planes.

"Naw."

"Shit."

"C'mon, Cap."

"Just remember what you've *learned* in here," he assured the troops. "Remember your search and rescue. Don't *need* your eyes. Because like Officer Karnofsky here told you, you might not *have* your eyes. So play it *smart.* By the *book.* All *right* now. First up is Picardi. Picardi A. Who's that."

By the time Picardi was standing at the ready, gear bag unzipped beside him, air pack behind him, Sully had retrieved his gear from the car and nudged up next to me.

"Shit yeah," he whispered unconvincingly. "Here we go."

On the captain's word, Picardi scrambled to get himself into his boots and bunkers, air pack on, mask fitted, helmet in hand and running to Officer Karnofsky, who stretched the black blinder over his head with an elastic snap and pushed him toward the course, his helmet jammed on. He hit the bench shin first.

"Hands and knees!" called Captain Stan.

He sank to the floor, felt the bench with his gloves, and climbed over. We could hear the rasp of his breathing, heavy already—although everyone sounded asthmatic when pulling in doses of that canned air. The captain walked to the end of the course and, with a pompous smirk at the class, snuck the dummy to a new location, slumping it behind a rake against the far wall. Picardi conked his helmet on the low coffee table in his way.

"What do we do when we *hit* something?" yelled Captain Stan. "We *feel* it, right. Figure it out. And we stay *low,* people. If you gotta choose between over and under, yous always go *under.* Where's your heat. Your heat's *up,* right. Gases go to the *ceiling,* build their way *down.* So you stay *down.* Could be a thousand-degree difference between the temp at the *ceiling* and the temp at the *floor.* Let's see it now. Losing some time here, guy. Hustle it up."

The guy went low, as directed, pushing forward on his padded belly, scraping his tank on the underside of the table but pulling through. His breathing was alarmingly loud and fast. He crawled his way around the chairs, clanging one with his tank and knocking it over. He made his way under all the hose. By the time he hit the door, he appeared to be exhausted.

"What do yous do with a door. First thing, people."

"See if it's locked," I said.

"Feel if it's hot," the captain corrected me.

Picardi yanked off one glove and reached up to slap the door, which trembled at the impact.

"*Now* see if it's locked."

He stretched upward again to rattle the handle. He turned it farther and it creaked open.

"Awright. Now go find your victim."

He kneed his way into the make-believe room. Getting to the dummy took longer than you'd guess. Eventually he bumped into it, heaved it up and into a decent firefighter's carry, sideways across his shoulders with an arm and leg dangling front and back. He jogged with his man through the doorway and straight into the tangle of hose.

The laughter died down and Picardi made his way out, dumping the dummy and pulling off his mask, shining with sweat, hands on hips, glancing between attempts to catch his breath at Captain Stan, who wrote down the clocked time on a clipboard. For a minute Stan consulted with his lieutenants. "And . . . McGuire," he announced then. "McGuire T. Hagersville Company. There you are. Let's hop to it. Sergeant Melito here will replace the dummy once you're blind."

We settled into a loud and jittery spectatorship. We applauded the occasional heroics of a hurdled bench or lucky guess on the victim's location. We hooted at the missteps and crashes to the cement. With the completion of every course, Sully tensed by my side, sucking in his bad breath until his name wasn't called. Richter from Dovertown got his air tank caught in the hose and lost a full minute. A man named Georgie got turned around and actually crawled elbow over elbow out the bay door and into the parking lot before he was catcalled back. Wikowsky, then, had to stop halfway through, snapping off his mask and throwing off the blindfold to sit and clutch his massive chest, flabby sides heaving, a man of my size. One of Captain Stan's blue-suited disciples hustled over with a med kit. The crowd kept quiet. The crisis appeared to pass when Wikowsky's face unpurpled and Captain Stan instructed him, over his clipboard, that he could either go again or fail. He was helped to sit on a folding chair behind us. And then—with a *Schoenberg W*—it was me.

There I was, shrugging off Sully's last whispers and walking tall, walking fat, to the start of the course while wondering if my gear bag actually contained all my gear. I cast a look toward the dummy, my victim, who would soon be moved to the opposite side of the room. I had the familiar feeling of being tested in a real way, a dangerous way, and of sprawling headlong before the challenge. It all came back: fear, yes, and worse than fear. Dismay. This advance inkling of failure was replaced by the certainty of it the moment I got the captain's *And . . . go.*

I WAS ANGRY AT THE ABRUPT

rescheduling of my trip. The trip was to meet with the heads of the largest clothing stores in Atlanta, and while I hadn't been looking forward to the usual debates over foot-traffic flow and fall style launches, I hated to get mixed signals, preferring to give them myself. I spent the limo ride home venting my bile by cellular telephone. And then, somewhere around Fifty-ninth Street, I began not to mind. By the time the elevator had deposited me on our penthouse floor, I was actually looking forward to my lonely night watching the Yanks. I luxuriated in the rich, rare thought of a full evening with the knock and catch and drowsy pauses of baseball. I remember leaving the elevator. I remember the sound of my keys, the brief song of them—a New York anthem—as I shook them out and lifted them toward the lock that was, I saw then, unbolted. My keys hung useless in the air. The door gaped open.

This was wrong, I was thinking. My apartment door was always locked. Unless someone—for some reason—unlocked it.

Which was when I pulled it another inch open to see. I don't remember dropping my briefcase. Could I have been so careful, so cold, as to bother and place it quietly down? I do recall dropping myself onto the cool marble, as if all the tendons in my body had been severed by the same weapon that they had used to threaten my wife.

And there she was, terror itself, wild-eyed in her good silk kimono and seated in one of the straight-backed Amish chairs from the kitchen. Only she wasn't in the kitchen. And she wasn't sitting so much as bound. Our apartment was such that one could see from the opening foyer straight through the large living room and between the kitchen and dining rooms to the back windows overlooking Lexington; and that's where they had put her, out of their way. The sight of a blond woman tied into a chair is a classic, let's admit it, roundly celebrated in uncountable movies and shows: so many, frankly, that it almost fails to alarm. There was the sense, God help me, that every good-looking blonde ends up strapped to a seat and humming through duct tape for a savior, kicking her long legs and banging around. Staring at her husband. Pleading silently for help.

I FUMBLED AT FIRST

with my snaps and lost a few seconds misfitting the mask. There was the momentary lack of air, the settling knowledge that I couldn't breathe before the pop of the opened seal, the rattling breath, the subsiding horror of death by asphyxiation. The blindfold was twanged and snapped behind my ears and I was off to the races, absolutely lost, crawling like a baby. My breaths were deafening. I mounted the bench and banged my elbow on the concrete floor coming down. The world gets big when you can't see it, every inch a dark mile. I plowed my helmet into the table and went lower, keeping the imaginary gases and Picardi's mistakes in mind. Face to the floor, I budged forward. I couldn't move. Faintly I heard the taunts of the crowd.

"When we get stuck, what do we do," came the carnival bark of Captain Stan. "We *unstick* ourselves, right. We address the *problem*."

I tried to shove backward. I was pinned by the low table. Trapped for good—I felt the panic of Wikowsky—before I thought to roll sideways and loosen the straps of my air tank.

"There we go," from the captain.

My breath was a chainsaw in my ears. I shrugged out of one strap and the tank dislodged itself from where it had hooked against the tabletop. I shimmied forward, hugging the metal weight of the tank, hauling it along. Once out the other side, I knelt and pulled it back on. At which point I had no conception of which way to go. I swept my arms outward until I tapped a chair leg and crawled that way, butted into a second chair, bulled through *(Go, Bull)* and remembered to duck the network of hose. I took a moment to wonder at the time I'd consumed—it felt like forty-five minutes had passed since I'd entered this sightless claustrophobia—and whether I would be failed for exceeding one hour. I wrestled with a sudden length of obstructing hose that one of the mustached meddlers must have dropped on me, threw it aside and found myself in the clearing before the door.

And there, in that black silence, it caught up to me. I huddled at the edge of a doorway yet again. History was repeating itself: I, horribly, was repeating myself, crouched there on the threshold of sickening disaster once more. I managed to bare my hand and rest a palm against the wood, pretending to feel for the make-believe heat; but I was deeply in trouble, reeling backward in time, sinking fast under the weight of what I'd carried for a country winter and could no longer bear. Someone yelled to hustle it up. But I was useless. Motionless. Trapped and pinned not by any two-bit card table or dangled hose but by the events, as Leonard would say, of the night in question.

HELP WAS NOT POSSIBLE.

                       Not from where I lay, as yet unnoticed by anyone but Pippa, partially hidden by the half-open door. Not when there were men in my house—two, by my count—and one knife. I saw the knife after a minute, a brownish bit of metal in the hand of the guy who rushed all of a sudden past my captive wife. Not when she was having an affair.

There was nothing between us. She had made sure of that, chosen that by choosing someone else. She had abandoned our marriage; and while I had no evil intention to punish her, I couldn't quite muster the chivalrous impulse to save her either. She had elected to look to someone else for love and protection. She hadn't spent an evening home in a month. For years she had ignored and pointedly avoided me—which made it awfully hard to act like her knight in extra-large armor now. I was invisible to her, and thus irrelevant to this scene, a mere onlooker as the drama unfolded before me with all the televisual shallowness of events not my own.

Her eyes were more murderous than the thieves in our bedroom. By this point, in fact, the men might have advanced into her study. I wasn't meant to be here in the first place; I thought again, with sudden longing, of Atlanta. There was blood, I noticed then, on Pippa's kimono. There was spilled tea a couple of feet before my face, a beige puddle—and, there, the scattered pieces of cup—that answered the question of how they'd gotten in. She must have opened the door. Why would she open the door in a skimpy silk robe for an unknown intruder, a muffled voice and bing-bonged doorbell in mid-evening in the middle of New York? She wouldn't. That was the answer. She would open only for someone she knew. She'd been expecting him, and not expecting me home until tomorrow. I thought it through, unable to stop thinking, unable to act. The black bloodstain on her lapel, I saw as she stared at me, had come from her nose. She must have pulled the door open, tried to push it back, and gotten belted in the face as the fuckers with the knife stormed in.

And never looked back. The men didn't pause to double-check the doorway or bother to cast a single glance toward me. There was no other apartment on the penthouse floor; they obviously knew that. No reason to fear any sudden interruption. They had clearly cased the place long enough to know my customary midnight arrival. They couldn't have come up on the elevator, not with snoopy Rico or Nico, whatever his name was, on the lever. Eventually I would learn from the local precinct that they had gained entry from the neighboring building, leaped the narrow air shaft, landed on the generous sill outside the hallway window and jimmied it open. They had a smooth interior system as well, as I would later report to the authorities. They collected all valuable electronics first, assembling our wide-screen TV (so much for the Yankees) and stereo and DVD player and her laptop computer into a kind of miniature Manhattan skyscape across the living room. Her jewelry was piled in a surprisingly small heap on the sofa, topped off by my watches. As they gathered our CDs and DVDs, I got a good look. The guy stuffing the pillowcase was not what you'd expect: grizzled, yes, and tired looking, a man on the lam, but Germanic and well cheek boned, more of an exiled politician than common crook. His accomplice was younger, darker skinned and dressed in a jogging suit that swished to warn me each time he came back. I would have to identify these faces, these two people, to the police. I was cleverly taking mental snapshots—that's it, yes, that was my reason—rather than blundering into danger or taking a futile stab at help.

But the truth was that I had no idea how to proceed. How do you defend with your life a woman who no longer cared for that life? How to stand up for someone who can't stand you? She was bleeding, for Chrissake. She was scared into wide-eyed shock. She was my wife, loving and faithful or not, and I owed her my wholehearted defense. But it didn't come. It was as if my limbs had been quietly removed. I still felt them, with the well-known delusion of the amputee; but I could no sooner move them than I could simply call back the elevator and shout at Paco or Pico to call the cops. Pippa ought to have invited her lover if she wanted such manly decisiveness. She had, in fact, invited him. He ought to have been on time.

The worst was the exit. After watching the selection and organization of our belongings, I realized with a cold shock that the guys were on their way toward me. I could have run if I had limbs. I would have tried to stop them if I had it in me. I looked over my shoulder toward the open hallway window and looked back just as the head thug, the chiseled white guy, lifted our TV set and his gaze. He halted there, seeing me for the first time, wavering with his load. He hissed something to his comrade. They glared at the intruder on their doorstep. Then they approached me, one after the other, with my television and stereo, the German and the guy in the zip-zipping sweatshirt with the knife. This was when they would stab me. I was a material witness, a gawker at what they'd done. The television set loomed large, then larger, rising slightly, and I realized I was about to be crushed. *Right on my bad back,* I had time to think before the television set was brought down hard. But only an inch. It must have slipped. The guy simply carried the television past.

It was the first of five trips to the window and out to the neighboring roof and calmly back. I watched them come and go. They hardly watched me, couldn't be bothered to stomp my hand or kick a parting field goal with a boot to my ribs. How I longed for that boot. I lay at the mouth of my apartment like a broken lawn jockey, a man with no point. I had no home, now that it had been emptied. No wife: that was certain. No longer was I linked to the woman crying and kicking in the chair. I would have to get up, go look for scissors in the pantry, find them in the kitchen, and cut her out. I watched her straining against the duct tape that held and hurt her hands, wanting only the freedom to cover her face and sob.

We would live through this. We would live together, technically, for another few days. But just then there was only us in our binds. The untangling to do. All the ripping apart.

I LAUNCHED MYSELF
from the floor. I had to move on, to
move. I barreled through the door and was on my hands and
knees, hunting for the victim, finding it behind what felt like an
iron grate. On my way out I got a leg caught in a loop of hose
but shook it off without losing more than a second. By the time
I hurdled the bench and smacked down the dummy, I was tired
enough to accept Sully's help in shutting off my air. I received
the news from Captain Stan, after an examination of his timer
and a sliding pass of his hand on his head, that I had the best time
yet. Two minutes twenty-one seconds. Approval came from my
classmates as a couple of scattered claps.

"All *right*, then. Who we got *now*. Sullivan F."

Sullivan F. looked like he might vomit. I leaned over to him
and muttered: "Eight crawls from the bench to the table."

His expression didn't change, and his lips didn't move as he
muttered back, "Eight?"

I barely nodded and stepped back.

When he got the green light, he dressed at a good pace. He had the air and mask on, got his blinder, and cleared the bench with a little jump, even, his heavy boots actually leaving the earth. He hit the ground and crawled elbow over elbow eight times and ducked in perfect time to finesse the bench. A hanging bridge of hose caught him up for half a minute, and the dummy proved elusive; nonetheless, he was back to Captain Stan in under five. Breathing hard, he turned to me once I'd shut off his air for him and gave me a hangdog look that I interpreted— correctly, it turned out—as gratitude.

Wikowsky took his second turn and triumphed over his girth and shortness of breath to barrel back with his victim through the hose, under the table and over the bench, collapsing like a fullback in the end zone with the dummy in a hug. I clapped my gloves, thonking applause, and then I stepped forward to help him up.

WE WENT WITH OUR SIGNED,
stamped, and frameable
training certificates, like overproud adolescents, to show the
chief. I myself would have come straight home; but as Sully had
driven us, I had no choice but to mandate ten minutes tops and
go along for the ride. Tom's store, it turned out, was an antiques
store, one I'd driven past a hundred times without catching sight
of the big guy himself. When we entered the front door, I saw
why. The place was an impenetrable wreck.

There is a fine line, of course, between an eclectic assem-
blage of valuables and a heap of total crap. In the chief's inven-
tory, that line appeared to be unnecessary, as there was nothing
of any notable origin or worth to be found. There were boxes
of cassette tapes. Bookshelves of moldy paperbacks. A footstool; a stuffed Barney; a ragtag army of mismatched shoes. The
pièce de résistance appeared to be a basketball hoop with a

cracked backboard. Could that be considered, old as it was, an antique? Sully dinged a brass bell (the brass bell, perhaps, counted) and there was a groan and a *Comin'* from the back. He jackknifed himself through a small doorway and straightened before us.

"Tom-*may*," Sully greeted him.

"There they are." He gave us a slow-motion smile. I could almost hear the crinkle of his beard. "Flying colors, right. Tell me now, boys. Flying colors."

Sully waved his certificate and nodded. He had actually brought it with him from the car. "We're official."

"Good," grumbled the chief. " 'Bout time, Sullivan. Congratulations," he told me, having quite possibly forgotten my name. "Calls for beers. Come on in."

I had thought we were in already. We followed him back through the doorway and into an inner sanctum that turned out to be the heart of the store. Here were the strikingly handsome French Provincial dining room chairs, a perfect set of six. Along the interior wall was a medieval trestle table of well-worn pine, above it a beaded mirror that looked nineteenth century. The effect of passing into that large room was like going from the Salvation Army to a Parisian salon. With a gesture he invited us to perch on a couple of chaise longues while he fetched us our Buds. Then he himself sat on a steamer trunk and, after a *cheers* of banged cans, launched in.

His treatise was nostalgic in tone, almost moving, or at least moved, and clearly inspired by our graduation. He leisurely recalled his own first ride out on a call with his uncle in nearby Claremont. He growled on about the changes in our fire zone, the multiplying of houses and the stripping of ground cover and the sucking dry of water sources into which you used to be able to just jam a hose and go. There was the loss of volunteers to higher-paying office jobs, tourist jobs, that they couldn't just up and leave on a call.

"Seventy-five percent of all firefighters in America are volunteers. You know that? Talking about a hundred thousand people. In New York alone you're looking at around two thousand fire companies that are all-volunteer. Not for long, though. Tell you that. Soon you're looking at paid firefighters in volunteer companies. Forty-odd mixed companies already in the state. More on the way. Pine Valley's already got two career guys." He took a deep breath and let it ceremoniously out. "We'd be next."

We all drank to that.

"Talking about the end of a long tradition." He was honing his lecture, as he turned his attention, to me. "Don't know if you know that."

I tried to cut it off: "I do, actually. Sure. Damned straight."

"One of the oldest traditions this country's got. Know where it started?"

I couldn't hazard a guess.

He pointed with his can to the certificate Sully still clutched in his hand. "Philadelphia. 1736. Birth of the damned nation."

"Technically," I pointed out, "that was before the birth of the na—"

"And know who started it?" he steamrolled on. He was staring at me, bearing down on me. "Might have heard of him. Guy named Benjamin Franklin."

"How about that."

"George Washington. Thomas Jefferson. John Hancock. Paul Revere. All those guys were volunteer firefighters. Don't believe me, look it up."

I didn't actually believe him. Then again, I didn't particularly care.

"What we need now," the chief said, "if we want to stay in business, is more money from the county. But that means petitioning the county commissioners and creating a special taxation district, all of which adds up to a major pain in the ass."

"Taxation districts aren't too hard to rejigger," I said. "But you should go for state money. Cleaner that way. Private money would be even better. You should think about that. Little private outreach."

This caused a rare silence from Tom. He considered the matter as Sully looked from one of our faces to the other and back.

"You're a guy who knows his way around a company," the chief finally bestowed upon me.

"I suppose."

"You want to handle our finances? Company finances. Keep our doors open. Keep the pros away."

"Well, I'm not much of—"

"Gary's been looking to get out of that job for a year now. Not to mention that he sucks."

"Shit yeah," Sully seconded.

"Maybe you could give us some of that private money you've been talking about," the chief joked slowly. He chuckled and slurped at his can.

"Maybe I could." I lay all the way back on my chaise longue, stretching like a fat cat, like Louis the Fourteenth, careful to keep my beer upright. "Maybe you could pay me in ottomans."

"Already have."

I looked at him over my stomach. "What do you mean."

"You got my ottomans. Three of them, I think. She never picked up the fourth."

"Who didn't."

He put down his can on an Italian tiled table. "The missus. Your old lady. Never heard from her. Five times a day she'd call me. Nonstop on the weekend. Had my delivery truck bringing pieces to your place twice a week. Figured she was selling my stuff in the city. Fair enough by me. Held on for a while to a wrought-iron day bed and an ottoman she'd asked for. Sold them when I didn't hear a peep. I'd put it at, say, September. Not a peep. That about when you took over the house?"

I had sat straight up. "What's your number here, Tom? 355-something?"

He nodded slowly, thinking of something else. "I think you do owe me some private money," he said with a red-bristled smile. "Come to think of it."

I lay back down. I placed my can on the floor. Fit my hands behind my head. "I'd bet I do."

It was only a matter of time,

of approximately
six months, until I spoke to one of my neighbors. Following our
first full week of temperatures in the fifties (a statistic that
earned a banner headline on the front page of the *Harristown
Reporter-Gazette*), the big houses shook off their snow, dropping
it in wet thumps, and stirred to life. The romper room to my
east became animated every weekend with the merry sounds of
childhood and the shriller noises of one adult's attempts to
quash it. Across the street, in that oversize igloo of white
stucco, the orange-vested man of the house set out every Saturday morning with his trusty dog and terrifying gun. Three
cars—a Porsche convertible, an Audi sedan, and a Mercedes
SUV—were parked at his place, glinting in the brand-new sun,
arranged according to size from left to right like the automo-
biles of the three bears. Yet I had counted only two people in

the house. This was enough of a brainteaser to compel me into an idle round of SAT-style problem solving. If the husband drove out for the weekend in his own car, the wife separately in hers, he could have gone back by train—maybe she stayed the week—and returned in a third vehicle the following Friday. Except that that would have left a car at the station. Unless she had driven him to the train.

After pouring a juice from the fridge, I turned to glimpse, through a den window, the gray truck that was parked on my neighbor's lawn. I walked to the window. I peered across the lawn and through the bushes, increasingly green, that served to divide us. "Finelli Pest Control" was stenciled in black on the side of the truck. Beneath that, it seemed, was a dyslexic sketch of a mouse. Kneeling on the ground behind the truck, sure enough, was Finelli. Above him stood a man in a cardigan sweater gripping a fly-fishing rod. This would be the television-station owner, I figured, with his shorn silver hair, stubbled silver beard, all the follicles on his head and face more or less of uniform length. He whipped the long fishing rod back and forth, back and forth, filleting the air. As I watched, Finelli rose from his knees as if he'd been knighted. His tattoos were cloaked for the occasion by a canvas work shirt.

"What you have," he whined, adjusting the brim of his cap, "is not a pest problem. What you have are deer. Whitetail deer."

I was surprised to hear his nasal voice until I saw that my window was open. That voice could pierce wood and glass, in any case, with no problem.

"Tell it's whitetails because of the prints. See this here? With your four little indents here? Two long ones and two dots? That tells you it's a whitetail. Blacktail hooves leave cleaner prints. No heel mark. Same with mule deer. Don't know if you've ever seen a mule deer. Probably not. Now, you said something about rodents. See, these aren't rodents. Thing about rodents is they leave paw prints: fingers and claws and all. Same with your skunks and weasels. You know what a claw prin—"

"Hey hey *hey!*" the man cut him off. "Time out." He looked, rod poised, like he might be about to behead him. "Just get rid of them. That's what you *do,* I take it. That's why I *called.*"

I could hear them better when I pushed open my front door. My stone stoop had cracked off at the corner, a victim of an intentional automobile accident, and I stepped over this to get down to the lawn.

"What I'm saying," Finelli was saying, "is that you don't have pests."

"Yes, I do. I damn well do. Tell you what. Let's put it this way. I have animals that enter my yard, that *destroy* my wife's garden, that *tramp around* on our *patio.* Those animals, whatever *species* they may be, are pests. They are pestering me."

I knew, as I looked over, that Finelli was snickering without moving the pointy features of his face. "I'm with you," he said.

The guy's rod sprang angrily back and forth. He had been practicing his casting in the yard. His agitations with the bare rod—he hadn't yet bought a reel, it appeared, or invested in any line—brought him around to face Finelli from the other side. He was in plain sight of me now. He didn't seem to notice. He was an athletic sort, thin waisted; a jogger, if I wasn't mistaken. A taker of swims and vitamins, several rubdowns a week at the club. "I want them gone by next weekend."

"I'll tell you this," Finelli announced. "Your basic top-grade coyote urine will keep away most types of deer."

"Coyote urine?"

"Sure. Pour it around your perimeter. Mark the territory. I can get you some ur——"

"What, at the *urine* store? I'm not paying you to purchase *urine*. I'm telling you to do what I ask. Get rid of my problem. I don't give a crap how. Or else you don't get paid."

Finelli yanked down his cap as if to better absorb the blows. "See, I don't exactly have deer traps. You want your deer problem taken care of, I could round up a couple of hunter friends who'd be willing to sit up nights and take their shots. But I'm not sure you want——"

"Holy mackerel!" the man exploded. His fly rod was waggling back and forth, now, like a monitor attached to his pulse. "Just do what you're told! What part of this don't you understand? Do you speak English? *Off* the *deer!*"

"Hullo!" I called. I bounded down the steps, almost tripping at the bottom, and commenced a jaunty approach across the wet grass and soft scraps of snow. "*Mis*-ter Finelli. How's it going."

They both watched my approach with what might have been horror.

"Bill Schoenberg," I told the guy. I wiped my palms on my flannel shirt and pumped his free hand. "Finelli and I are over at the firehouse together. Volunteer company. Harristown Fire."

"Um," started the man, getting his bearings, gesturing toward Finelli, "we're in the middle of——"

"A heat wave. Got that right," I said. I looked straight up. "What a day. Days like this you can't complain about." I thumped him on the back. I actually thumped the guy. "You got a view of the river from your place?" I squinted at the brick colossus, the red-and-white universe of a house. Someone passed by a second-floor window, whisked into the next window, and appeared in the next. His wife, of course: black dress, as usual; her head dropping from view as she must have descended some stairs.

"Of course I have a view of the river."

"Me too. And days like this—well, it's something, isn't it? You should see it, Finelli. In fact, you should see it right now. Do you mind if he goes up? Just for a quick look. Do you have a third floor? Get as high as you can, Finelli. Take two minutes. Just a peek. It's worth it. I'm sure Mr., what—"

"Hey buddy," said my new buddy. He looked hard at my lumberjack shirt, my new favorite jeans, my boots, and back up to my beard to decide, quite understandably, that I was an illegal squatter in the mansion next door. The boiler repairman, maybe. Deliverer of venison. Caulker of the sink. "I don't want to be rude," he said firmly, "but him and me—"

"He and I," I corrected, nodding intently.

"—were in a kind of private discussion. Before you interrupted. This being my front lawn."

"Right," I said. I stretched my arm behind me. "That's mine."

"And my wife and I are actually having guests in a few minutes. So we're not inviting anyone over to see the freaking view. Not Ferrelli here—"

"Finelli," I said.

"—and not you. So I guess what I'm saying is that our business is done here." This last remark was not addressed to me.

Finelli swiveled the twin beaks of his nose and cap to face the man. He took a moment to respond. "You got it," he said. "You just let me know what you'd like to have done."

"Maybe I will."

"How much does he owe you," I asked Finelli.

Finelli's head jerked to me.

"For the house call, I mean. For your diagnosis."

"Diagnosis?" asked the man. "What freaking diagnosis. This is not a doctor. This is not an appointment, friend. I think I said our business is done." He turned to march toward his house, the rod giving a farewell wiggle over his shoulder. As we watched him I could see his wife in the kitchen window now, to the right of the front door, in her customary pre-party bustle. Again the stately nose, the air of panic, the stumpy caterer—there she was—running laps around her.

"We aren't done," I said loudly, "until Finelli here gets paid."

At that the guy halted. He revolved directly into the sunlight and had to shield his eyes with a hand. "Not a chance."

"Hey, Schoenberg," Finelli said.

"This man made a house call. He gave you his expert opinion." I looked hard at Finelli. "You planning to invoice him?"

"I'm not planning anything."

"Well, then, how about cash."

"Son of a bitch," the guy said.

"Cash always works. If you have it."

"You've got to be joking."

"Don't worry. It's not much. What is it, Finelli."

"I dunno."

"What would it be."

He pushed up and pulled down the brim of his cap. "Maybe twenty bucks."

"How about that," I told the guy. "Not a bad price. For consulting? You kidding me? You ever work with consultants? Unheard of. You might want to pay that before it goes up."

"Listen. You know what? Fine. That's fine with me." He dug into a pants pocket. He set down the rod, which tipped and fell to the soggy lawn. "If that's what it takes to get a couple of rednecks off my lawn, that's no problem." He strode back toward us, holding his wallet in both hands. The sun caught brightly in his metallic hair, white sparks off his beard. "You fucking people are something. Know that? This is some operation. You know where to come, don't you. Who to hit up."

"Actually," said Finelli, his lips twisting into the start of a smile, "you called me."

"You know what you're doing, all right. Guy like me can shell out a bundle. Plenty in the bank, you're thinking. Well, you're right I got plenty." He parted his wallet to reveal, indeed, a veritable salad of bills: a wad of thousands, I'd guess. "And you're not getting it. You're getting twenty bucks. You think I care about twenty bucks?" He held up a twenty in the breeze. "You think someone like me is going to miss twenty bucks? A guy like me—let's put it this way—could pay you twenty bucks an hour, twenty-four hours a day, for the rest of your sorry lives and not notice it. Not even *notice* it. How about that?"

"Sounds pretty good," I admitted.

"Dream on." He dropped the bill onto the wet lawn. "Guy like me could change your life. That's what you're thinking." He spoke to us earnestly, now, a sweatered psychiatrist, peering gently into our faces. "And you're right about that. But you know what? I'm not going to. What do think about that? What do you have to say about that?"

I shared a look with Finelli. "I'm impressed."

"I'd bet you are."

Behind the man, in the house, the caterer passed by a window, carrying a vase of tall flowers.

"Amazed, really," I said.

The guy stuck out his lower lip, apparently satisfied.

"Amazed that you can talk this shit while you're losing money hand over fist."

"Come again?"

"Well, let's see. Let's talk revenue streams for a second here. Since you brought up income. So. Television-station owner in upstate New York. You got a soft national ad market that's making you no money. Election-year ad spending is a long time away. You got the lower compensation payments from the big networks: there's a revenue stream that's getting choked off. Investors can't be too happy about that. Not to mention the flight to satellite TV. Makes for pretty grim earnings these days, I'd expect." I was strangely calm, pleasantly dizzy, back in the thick of it, clashing swords and measuring dicks once again. I tried to think what else I'd overheard in Mark's office. "That co-branded Web site making you any money? No? Really? That's a shame. Because local news is getting costly. Live traffic reports, price of helicopters. Those costs are going to start to show. And without decent quarterly cash flow, old buddy, your debt expense is going to go sky high." I looked off into the distance, as if watching the debt expense go sky high, there beyond the hills, past Finelli where he stood and stared at me. "And I don't have to tell you that the easiest thing to do in a downturn is lop off the head. Your head, I mean. Start your restructuring from the top down. That's about the clearest message your board can send to investors. Everyone knows that." I lifted my chin toward Finelli. "We know that, Finelli and I. So you must know that."

"Honey?" called the wife. The high voice surprised us all. The man fairly jumped. "It's almost time. You should really come—"

"All *right*," he said harshly without turning around.

She was leaning out the open door: combed hair, strapless shoulders. "I just think that the Michaelsons are going to pull in any minute. And I don't think—"

"Just a *minute*."

"I just don't *think*," she said firmly, not retreating from the doorway, "that the first thing the Michaelsons see when they get here should be the pest-control guys."

YOU CAN SMELL A BURNER

from clear across the county. There is a scraped sadness in the air, a charred sense of something wrong, a blackness you breathe without quite knowing you're breathing it until the pager goes off and confirms your very darkest fear. What you learn, sooner or later, is that a structure fire is more than the ignition of a house. It's the torching of expectations, the combustion of daily life. It's the fact that all our containers and property, our habits and marriage, every one of our constructions can suddenly go up in flames.

"Sixty control Harristown: firefighters needed at number thirty Apple Hill Road, three-oh Apple Hill, for a possible structure fire. Repeat: sixty control Harristown, manpower needed at three-oh Apple Hill Road, off Route eight, for a reported structure fire."

I was thrown hard enough by the announcement of an actual house fire that I had trouble starting the car. I jammed down the gas and twisted the key and finally heard the phlegmy catch of the motor as the starter turned the flywheel and the spark from the distributor hit the cylinders and pushed down the pistons and I was off. I remembered my new light and snatched it from the passenger seat, reached up and out the window to clap its magnetic bottom to the roof. As it whirled blue, my pager reminded me harshly of the coordinates. I sped out of Ridgepoint, seat belt on, and took the hard left down Apple Hill and slid— *Apple Hill Road, off Route eight*—to a stop.

I wasn't going to the station. I was on Apple Hill Road.

And there it was. Number 30 was one of the sad little houses I passed several times daily, a ramshackle combination of various limp types of wood with one front step broken, a rusty oil tank at the corner, lame little garage. The windows were black. And then, within one of those dark squares, the confirming lick of orange. The house was on fire.

I was out of the car and standing there on the thin grass and rocks of the driveway and wondering what the Christ I was supposed to do now. A whole side of the house was seeping smoke. I held my pager toward my mouth, but it wasn't a radio. I threw it furiously into the dirt road, turned back to the burning house. Ribbons of gray crept from the windows, seeping up the house and roof, dimming the sky. The whole place seethed with what it contained. Another flash of orange lit the black heart of the place. There was a snapping and popping sound. I didn't have my gear.

What you're supposed to do when you first get to the scene of a structure fire is circle the residence—a size-up, as outlined in the workbook's unit nine—which will give you a better sense of conditions and approaches to consider. Blown-out windows let you know where the flame's been. The heaviest smoke tells you where it's spreading. The butt end of air conditioners show the living areas to be searched. Consider the architecture and building materials, wind direction and water supply. Or else just walk to the front door, as I did, take the last breath of your goddamned life, and go in.

The door, to my surprise, was not particularly hot to the touch. Another surprise, then, when I gingerly opened it, was to be hit by the temperature inside. The heat was a plank in the face. I couldn't go in without gear. I wouldn't be able to breathe without a mask. But I was breathing, and when my knees hit and I began my belly crawl, I found that there was enough warm air by the floor to keep going. I was in a living room. The house felt empty apart from the chuckling of the fire and the haze that gathered in faint waves along the ceiling. I hurried toward what turned out to be the doorway to the dining room. You're supposed to search clockwise or counterclockwise, keeping it consistent throughout the house. I crawled a hard right against the wall, banged into a chair, saw nothing, noted the hotter air and the louder sounds of the fire. I checked inside a cabinet that held nothing but plastic place mats. Children can hide in cabinets. I moved into the next room.

I found myself at the bottom of a set of hideously carpeted stairs. I pulled myself up, step after step, by the elbows. Here it was excruciatingly hot. There were two bedrooms, it seemed, and the bathroom that I crawled into first. It was getting hotter by the second, and darker, the smoke dense now over my head. I smacked open the cupboard beside the bath to reveal a stack of towels. Back out in the smoky hall, I crawled as fast as I could.

"Hello?" it occurred to me to shout. I yelled louder as I crawled: "Hello! Hello! Anyone here?" It was my own improvised siren as I raced forward: "Anyone! Hello!" My voice caught and I coughed. The smoke had descended to head level. My scalp and face were burning. Two bedrooms to go.

The first was the small master bedroom. The closed door meant that I had to stretch upward into the wavering layers of fumes—more gagged smoke and coughing—but also that the fumes were not as bad once I was inside. I pulled open a couple dresser drawers, flailing for ideas. Checked under the bed. Pair of panties, magazine, comb.

"Anyone here!" The closet door flung open to reveal no hiding and frightened child but women's clothes everywhere: fishnet sweaters, wrinkled blouses, black pants, sharp-heeled boots. There was no man of the house, apparently. Only a single woman—whom I glimpsed, then, turning and spotting the photo on the bedside table. It was a shot of Paula and PJ (a bit blurry, but no doubt about it) mushing a kiss on the lips. This was their house.

The hallway was now fully toxic. The air was evil black from floor to ceiling. I couldn't see the hands and arms that I plonked down on the floor to move along. I was fairly certain my hair was on fire: the pain of it drilled me to the brain. Baring my teeth, I crawled into PJ's bedroom, identifiable through my tearing eyes by the overly stickered pink book bag left in the middle of the room.

"PJ! You in here!"

I checked her closet and under her miniature desk before making my way out. I was coughing unstoppably, unable to take in anything but more sour smoke, swallowing it whole, poisoned more thoroughly with each forward lunge. The smoke was rushing up the far stairwell when I got there. You could see it chugging upward, piling in, and by the time I slunk headfirst down the first couple steps I was too bleary to do anything but let myself go.

I landed, after an endless series of cracks on my miserable back and a head bang against a banister, on solid ground. I was conscious enough—the bang to my head seemed to revive me— to crawl. I wiped my face, felt the blood on my forehead. I could breathe as long as I kept my face to the hot wooden floor. And then the air was on fire. I screamed and crab-crawled backward. Ahead of me, fully alight, was what had to be the door to the cellar. The flames bellowed orange and streamed onto the walls, lashing out in all directions. The ceiling over my head was fully ablaze. Flames sprinted in even lines across the beams of the house, highlighting the bones of its construction. It was a heaving roof of death, flattening me, pinning and killing me right there, until I managed to get myself turned around and painfully away.

"PJ!" I gave out one last time as I made it into the living room, my face wet with tears and bleeding, my beard dripping with it now. I headed for the front door. My throat was hurting badly. I reached up for the handle, paused to wonder if the imitation brass knob would scorch me, decided that was the least of my problems and grabbed it. As I pulled open the door, still on my knees, I heard the scream of the siren of the truck coming up the hill. I could have wept with gratitude. But before I could pitch forward into the clean, cool air, I heard—or thought I heard—a different scream.

"PJ?" I called back into the house. "PJ!"

The cry came again. And another, I was pretty sure. I moved to my left, jammed a hand over one ear in a futile attempt to block out the ticks and cracks of the fire.

"PJ!"

Storming toward me from the open truck, then, was a fully suited and tanked-up firefighter. He was short and stocky enough to be Sully. There was no one with him. He had driven the truck alone.

"There you go," he said, struggling to lift me by the armpit.

"Where is everybody?" I croaked. My throat felt as if it was bleeding.

"Took too long," Sully shouted through his oxygen mask. He was grinning. "They can drive themselves in the other truck." Then he frowned at my weight. When he had successfully hauled me partly through the doorway, I looked up to see Paula, her face smeared with soot, hair wild, running like a madwoman back and forth in the drive. I planted my feet and tugged free and fell back into the house.

Sully crashed to the floor beside me. Looked me in the face. "She's still in here," I said. His expression was hard to see through his mask. It may have been raw fear, although that was the inevitable impression of the labored pops and sucks of breath. Something else, then, passed across his piggish eyes. Resolve, I would like to think now.

Two grown-ups crawling through a room is an elephantine

comedy. I felt safer for crawling behind his shifting bottom, as if that quilted ass could block and defend me from fire. I reached forward and grabbed him by the base of his tank as we neared the dining room. We had passed a door that I hadn't noticed during my first trip through the house. I pointed to it now. Flames were growling across the ceiling above us.

"Closet!" Sully shouted.

But no closet door had a lock. I reached up for the knob, grimacing in the heat. The door swung open. It led, as I thought it might, to the garage.

Sully wallowed down the two steps after me. It was cooler and quieter with the inferno a room behind us. Apart from the car, some kind of mid-'80s sedan, games and activities had been assembled out of junk far and wide. Milk crates were lined up with action figures trapped beneath them. A sidelong refrigerator box was painted on and knifed apart to make windows.

"PJ! Come out!"

"PJ!" called Sully. His voice was muffled by his mask. "PJ!"

To hell with clockwise or counterclockwise: we split up and crawled off in all directions. Sully, I saw, had forgotten to close the door behind us, and the fire leaped and surged at the appeal of the fresh air. In no time, the flames were on the ceiling, crawling overhead as we crawled around on the floor. It was, I saw then with terrible clarity, a race.

"Come on, PJ!"

"PJ!"

Sully had found an old dorm refrigerator. He looked back at me from his knees before he yanked it open. Nothing.

"PJ! Come out! Fucking—PJ!"

Their recycling, sloppy piles of newspapers and vodka bottles, filled a rusty metal shelf that I overturned to reveal nothing but the wall. A broken dollhouse leaned in the corner, too small to house her. There was a single window halfway up to the ceiling, too high for her to get through. Sully pulled over a plastic trash can and looked inside. He found a rolled-up carpet and spent way too long unrolling it. The fire engulfed the ceiling, finding the beams and thriving along them, surging and snapping, eating its way down the walls. A pair of sleds leaned against the wall by the door we'd entered. I crawled back and reached up to knock them over one by one. Down with a clash came the metal saucer. Behind the red plastic toboggan, when I bonked it away, there she was.

"PJ! What the fuck are you doing!" I was shouting at her small dirty face. "Come out when we tell you to!" She was almost smiling, eyes lit, as if amused by the game. Or else shocked by my bloody appearance. Terrorized—that's right— by the fire.

"Grab her! Let's go!" came the hushed yell of Sully.

I snatched her up, standing now, my whole body baking. The fire was seeping down the walls, tightening brightly around us.

"It's too hot," said PJ.

"Be quiet. I know. I'll get you out."

"But it's too hot."

"Be quiet."

Sully stood up as well and was the first to lumber to the big garage door. He tugged upward on the handle. He looked back, over his breathing tube, at me. He pulled again, shaking the door, not budging it. It occurred to me, then, that this was going to end here.

Sully headed back across the room. I fell to my knees with PJ. It was too hot; she was right. I watched Sully smack his gloved hand against the garage-door button on the wall. The boxed mechanics of the electric door opener blazed on the ceiling. Behind him, the wall fire had dropped to the level of his helmet. It roared in a full rectangle around the door frame leading back to the living room—which also appeared, from the ferocious glow of the room, fully involved. This was our last stand, our last sit, here in Paula Dickerson's garage. These were our last couple of minutes.

You're supposed to bring tools on your search-and-rescue operation in case of situations like this. I thought of that, then, saw clearly the relevant page of the workbook. I shuffled my body, carrying her body, over to the unraisable door to the outside. I banged on it with my bare fist. I pushed hard and felt the push back. I coughed and covered my hurting face and ears with my hands. The fire had climbed onto the top of the garage door, just above me, and was lapping downward. With my arms and elbows I hugged PJ, who was crying and coughing, reduced to the baby she was.

My head seemed to explode then. Did heads have boiling points, shattering like Paula's clay pots when they went above several hundred degrees? I creaked open my eyes—they seemed to have cooked closed—and felt another whack to the back of my head. I looked into PJ's face, tearless and openmouthed. Another wallop sent me forward; my head bounced back and hit the door. I slid us away, coughing hard, and turned to see an ax blade stick for a second in the chopped wooden door before it disappeared. It cracked back in a few inches to the left. Someone was trying to hack us out.

It was too late, of course. This was over. The fire was a few feet above us, all around us, the smoke too deep in our spasming lungs. Sully was hunched in the corner to the left of the door, his gloves braced against both walls, eyes wild behind the bright orange reflection on his mask. The ax had opened a jagged crack in the door through which I could see, for an instant, a narrow slice of turnout coat and working arms. In a whoosh the fire sucked down and out the thin hole, running for its life. Curses poured in. Finelli.

I dragged PJ with me toward the middle of the room. There was no room to stand. I was burned, or at least burning, grinning hard like a mummified corpse. I stretched to kick Sully's boot as I passed, a signal to come with me. In a minute we were side by side, perched on our hands and knees in the middle of the flaming room. PJ was back to wailing between coughs, sheltered by the size of my stomach, clinging upward like a baby chimp. I screamed at Sully to run for it. He had no idea what I meant.

"You and me!" I shouted. "Now!"

"There's nowhere to go!" came the softer shout behind his mask.

"Here we go! Right at him!" I lifted my hips like a sprinter, pulling up PJ with the rest of my strength. I was the Bull, I told myself. I was once the Bull. The ax appeared once more, splintering downward, extending the crack by another foot. When I took a hot breath to shout *Go,* Sully took off.

It was five long steps to the fiery door: just enough time, enough flung momentum for me to catch up to Sully and smash into the flames and wood a split second before him. I threw my shoulder into it, turning and pumping my legs, hand over PJ's face and flames all over me. And then, with the mighty sounds of breakage, we were clear, we were through, knocking Finelli backward and rolling, all three of us, all four of us, in the ashy mud on the ground.

I could open my eyes. Above me, thankfully receding, was the billowing black sky. There was me on my back. There was PJ on me. There was the white-helmeted chief, there was Henry gunning the hose at the house, and there was Gary in his fire suit, struggling and failing to hold back Paula, shouting after her as she ran, hair streaming, arms spread wide, to us.

WITH THE ONSET OF APRIL

came the overeager smells of the new season. Leaves sweetened the trees, fresh fat bushels of them for free, green hands extended like beggars, demanding more green. The rain came and went, leaving things beaded and clean. This was early spring, this cool jewelry, these wavering trees.

And so I took a drive. I had begun to take these aimless automotive tours with some regularity. I drove the way others walked: beard up, sharp breaths, cruising in the sun-shade-sun of an improvised route. I got to know the roads off Haymeadow that ran into dead ends by the quiet forest. I drove laps around the lakeside houses in Wheaton Valley, their front porches caked with goose shit. I toured the mud-colored entirety of Dovertown one day, inspected Grayville's ducks-in-a-row developments, like Lego houses, the next. I could give Pete Karl a run for his money on a quiz show on our residential geography. I settled for waving him to death, waggling full-palm salutes whenever our vehicles appeared in each other's windshields and slipped out of them to reappear in our rearview mirrors and shrink away.

That afternoon I headed for the river. I reached the glimmering water and turned south with the current, finding and losing and rejoining the roads that would keep me in sight of the ripples and shine. The air blew warm through my window, reeking of grass. At this rate the place would be changed within weeks: overrun once again by the lazy wealthy, by lawyers, by speed walkers with hand weights, by expensive dogs who for six months had lain like bear rugs in luxury apartments, by women who lofted operatic complaints about the lack of yellow peppers in stores. Astonishing to think, as I did while driving and gazing downriver, that I could simply wade in and grab a sizable piece of driftwood and be carried eventually back to the city, bobbing down through Columbia and Putnam counties, sliding past the Bronx, washing up on the coast of Manhattan by nightfall. Unthinkable that I could return.

A few of the guys had given me the cover of the *Gazette* as a keepsake, and these were the papers that startled and scattered like birds off the kitchen counter when I pulled open my front door. Unfunny jokes—"Got helmet?"—were scrawled on several of them. Others had PJ's badly reprinted school picture or the KILN FIRE headline circled for emphasis. There was an on-site photo of Paula, looking like a black-faced lioness, above the accompanying tale of her escape from the fiery basement. I jerked open a couple of windows for air. I brought in firewood and plonked it down in the den. A frayed edge of a log caught my Harristown Fire shirt and tore in it a second hole. I assembled and lit the fire, dirtying my hand bandage, before returning to the kitchen to start a pot of soup from a half onion, can of broth, a chopped carrot and a fistful of rice.

With Paula's help and sarcasm I had picked out a novel at Tommy's Antiques, a ragged old paperback of Jack London's *Call of the Wild*. I sank into an easy chair in the slowly warming den and was four pages in when the double beep of a car came from out front. I flipped the page. I ignored the hum of the engine in the drive. A visitor to the neighbors, once again, had gotten the wrong driveway. In a second I would have to unlock the door and tromp out onto the stoop to nod and smile and indicate the next house over. Then I heard the car engine shut off. I plowed forward through another paragraph until a knock sounded.

"Fuck me."

By the time I'd made it through the dining room and the smell of cooking soup the guy was actually pushing open my door, having somehow picked the lock. I crossed the kitchen with the urge to run full steam and smash the door closed, crushing the emerging arm and shoulder——but those, I saw now, belonged to a woman. The fingernails were French manicured. The jacket was green canvas and familiar.

"Hey," came her voice.

The door had swung all the way open.

"Pippa," I must have said, because the word hung loudly in the house.

Pippa was in my kitchen. Her kitchen, she would have said.

She fingered her house key, stuffed it into a jacket pocket. I was surprised—and this is strange—by how *small* she appeared. She seemed to have shrunk by an inch on all sides, her body thinned by her jacket, her face made daintier by makeup. A therapist would probably tell me she had previously loomed larger than life and had now simply withered to normal stature. Any other man would call her a knockout. To me she looked like a sophisticated kid, a slightly miniature look-alike of the woman I used to love.

Eventually I asked: "What are you doing here?"

"Aach, just in the neighborhood." It was an attempt at a joke. A clean flash of teeth. Then she looked at the floor. She was wearing rubber boots of a green that matched her jacket. Mud speckled the side of one of them: yard mud, my mud. I knew she was wondering what I'd done with the pineapple-shaped welcome mat that I had hated and crammed into the garbage my first day here. She pushed her hair back over her shoulder. "Whose car, hey?"

"Mine."

"*Reeee*-ly." She gave another bright smile. "And who drives it?"

"I drive it."

With an effort she took this in stride. "Bit beat up, hey."

"It's a used car."

Her eyes blazed the green of the jacket and boots. The gig was up. "You did *not* buy a used car."

I put my hands on my hips, considering my rebuttal. "*I* used it," I said. In the ensuing silence I looked past her and out the door for our old car, that garage-dwelling behemoth, the Lexus the size of a living room that I now wondered what it might have been like to drive. Instead there was a white moving truck, its edges sparking in the sun. The shadows played as if someone might be moving within it.

"Is there someone else here?"

Her face tightened almost imperceptibly, then relaxed. "It's just Julius."

"Oh." Julius was Pippa's assistant, fey and irritable, as brittle and efficient as his boss. "You figured you needed a bodyguard."

This got a tense laugh. "Aach, no," she said. "Just a helper."

"To help you with what."

"Just stuff, hey."

By stuff, it dawned on me, she meant her stuff. "You're here to take all the furniture."

She was staring at me intently. Then I remembered the Band-Aid on my forehead, the cut on my cheek. Not to mention the beard. I brushed off my ripped T-shirt with my book. I must have looked like some kind of vagabond version of my father; what she remembered of him from photos, anyway, if she remembered him at all. She, by contrast, was growing younger, defying logic: defying, I couldn't help but think, me. It was hard to picture this blond girlwoman ever angry, or yelling the way she had. Hard, even for me, to remember the venom with which she had spat: *You're no man.* She had cut a few inches off her hair, I noticed, honey colored after the long winter. She would have in her Palm Pilot an appointment for highlighting. In her purse would be eight to ten reference pages, ripped from magazines, that demonstrated the desired shade of blond. I knew her, I thought, like the back of my bandaged hand.

I was aware I ought to put up a fight about the furniture. I could hear the gaspy voice of Leonard—*any personal property you would like to protect and retain*—but I didn't have it in me. "You are not taking," came my firm pronouncement, "my bed."

She thought it over. Actually thought about it. "'Kay."

"*Any* of the beds. Or." I looked around. "The coffee machine. Those things are not moving."

"'Kay."

It felt ghostly to be speaking with her, to be having this conversation. In the past two minutes she had regained some of her size. I had, of course, imagined the previous shrinkage; or else she had inflated, as do certain furred and feathered animals when confronting an enemy in the wild. It was so familiar, this quiet battle, this mutual loathing in tender tones. To have her so close, and yet so far away that she thought nothing of throwing a cold, hard look at her watch.

"Listen, hey. I should *reeeely*—"

"Right. Sure. Hell."

"—just look around for a quick sec. Then I'll go get, ah." Her eyes wandered the kitchen, drifted into the dining room and back to the stove. Her face had tensed once again. "Who's making soup?"

So that's what was distracting her. She thought I had someone else. I could have laughed aloud. I liked the idea of being caught on this fresh Saturday morning with a woman in the house. She would be dozing facedown, tendrils of brown hair everywhere, wrapped in a twisted cord of bedsheets upstairs. She'd be gallivanting in one of my dress shirts, quarantined in the second-floor sitting room with rushed instructions to keep quiet. She was a hell of a cook, that's right, Pippa. A real do-it-yourselfer, equally at home under the hood of her '86 Chrysler LeBaron and at a woodsy picnic behind Reyfeldt Farm with her messy daughter. In fact, that right there is one of her handmade soup bowls. Have a look, Pippa. Right there on the counter. But Pippa wasn't looking. She was waiting for an answer, arms folded, from me.

"I made the soup," I told her.

"I don't think so, Bill."

My name, from her mouth, had always been *Bull*.

"Well, then, you can't have any."

"Aach, come on."

"What."

"Who's making your food?" She peered toward the den.

"Why don't you just take your things," I said. "If you need me I'll be reading my book upstairs."

I was on the third step when she called, "You don't read books." She said it almost warmly, like an old pal calling my bluff. I turned to see the gleam in her eye, the need for this to all be a joke: me surviving in the country, living without her; capable of driving a car on daily basis, of subsisting, of soup making, of reading a novel and—perhaps most impressively—of turning to bang up the rest of the stairs without another longing look back.

I sat on the end of my bed. She was right: I couldn't read. I stopped trying. I held the open book below my face as if positioning a satellite dish to more clearly receive her warbled comments.

"What happened to the Turkish rug?" she called when her inspection reached the den. "And the muslin drapes. Those were my muslin drapes, hey. Aaach, did someone repaint? What happened in here?"

Then nothing, for a while, but the fashionable squish of Wellingtons. It took another couple of minutes for her to find, with another shout, the ruined dining room table. "*Sjoe*—what the hell, Bill. What the—*shit*, Bill." Eventually she climbed all the way to the third floor, counting out loud in the closets, keeping an eye out for my mistress and finding only her own belongings. She even whisked open the bathroom door in a surprise attack, to no avail. Again I fought the urge to laugh. If she was hoping to catch Paula in the house, she was out of luck. A week early, to be precise. PJ and Paula would move in, as I had offered and Paula had brusquely accepted, until the reconstruction of their house was completed: a few months, by the estimate of the hoary work crew I'd vigilantly harangued and more quietly helped pay for. Mother and daughter would be across the hall from each other in the guest room and maid's room on the first floor, a safe distance from my personal space and yet probably there at breakfast time—which was fine, as I was fast perfecting my cinnamon oatmeal and was working hard on ham and eggs. There was plenty of room (once Pippa cleared out the furniture) for them and all their salvaged belongings, plenty of rooms in which to stash PJ's four thousand unmelted plastic toys, Paula's new kiln, and an unthinkable amount of girlish clutter. There was the sense, now, in this hollow house, of expectation, of wholehearted habitation at last. Certainly that's what Pippa's keen, narrow nose had picked up. That was the angry loudness of her boots on the stairs as she stomped back down.

The next sound I heard, far off on the lawn, was the rattling hand truck of delicate Julius as he embarked on the first of sixty-five laps for his boss.

"You want to tell me what you're taking?" I yelled. I wasn't moving. She could come talk to me. She could make the trip to my room. This, all of a sudden, seemed important. For twenty goddamned years I'd catered to her, approached her gingerly, supported her fiscally, catered to her dislikes and growing agitations and tolerated her leaving long before I left. I had killed myself (think of the *work* hours) for this woman, for the sake of the marriage that she swept aside as breezily as a muslin drape. She had cheated on me. Yes, true, I had wronged her in turn. I had allowed calamity. But she had gone out in search of it, embraced it, undressed and lain down with it, chosen it over me. She could come the fuck upstairs. I wasn't going downstairs. Until I heard the bang of the door.

I reached the kitchen a minute later and almost ran face-first into Julius.

"Hello, Mr. Schoenberg," he offered in his high reedy tone. He had a box open on the floor and was wrapping wineglasses in stiff manila paper that they must have brought.

"Where is she."

"Oh, she just—" He motioned limply outside. "She'll be right back."

I threw open the screen door.

"She'll be right *back*," he repeated shrilly, apparently trying to stop me from exiting my door.

My broken front stoop was piled with prefolded boxes and blankets. "Pippa?" I barged toward the moving truck. The hand truck, stacked high with small boxes, stood abandoned by the vehicle's open back. "Pippa, I think I have the right to"—but she wasn't in the truck. I stormed around the front of the cab, but she wasn't on the far side either. I looked down the driveway, and there she was, striding casually back.

"Were you looking for me?" Hands in the pockets of her coat, hair swaying, she was the picture of nonchalance. Out for a country stroll. "Hey?"

I had to crane my neck to see past her, such was her swingingly girlish approach. There, badly hidden, parked halfway behind the fat-trunked tree where my driveway met Ridgepoint Circle, was a gleaming sedan. Mercedes S-Class, if I wasn't mistaken. I had memorized the luxury cars of my neighbors. That was not one of them.

"Who's that?" I asked her.

"What? No one, hey. Asking directions."

I nodded vaguely. She gave a sunlit smile, beaming confidence. Which is when I decided to run for it. I bolted right past her, shrugging off what might have been an attempt to grab and stall me. It had been years since I'd felt the start of her hug. I sprinted the length of the driveway, bearing down on the car. I was close enough, now, to see that it was Leonard in the front seat, madly fussing with his keys between panicked glances up. "No, Bill," he called out his open window, a strange and fearful yelp. He had come to help Pippa: to protect her, if necessary, from me. It was him, I had time to realize. Leonard and Pippa. Leonard the whole time. He was hiding from me, there behind the tree. He had been hiding from me for months. I'd be damned if I'd let them take a stick of furniture. I'd smack him and send them back the way they came. Leonard dropped from view and found his keys on the seat. "No-no, Bill." He scrabbled to get the car going. His fingers couldn't work fast enough. Mine, as I charged the car, packed themselves into a fist.

There is a feeling, here in the country, at the brisk start of spring, that you can do anything you want if you can just catch up to it; that life is slipping along, just barely within your grasp. It's the sense, as solid and ecstatic as the trees, that chances abound as long as you hurry. And it's the knowledge that you're going to get there in time.

THERE ARE MORE PEOPLE

in this town than one might expect; and more types of people, and more startling clusters of them, arriving with their shaven-head boyfriends and uniformed softball teams, on souped-up motorcycles and rented mountain bikes and in more crowded family vans than I'd have thought the local economy could support. Most of them went for the wine first thing. I had foreseen this and had assembled my wares accordingly. My tabletop displays of rare and prizewinning vintages were along the edge of the lawn closest to the driveway. There were nearly a hundred bottles for sale, worth somewhere near $100,000. Thus far, three and a half hours into my firehouse fund-raiser, I'd banked $122. I had sold a 1961 Château Latour (originally purchased for $750) for eight dollars to a nearly toothless woman who looked like she could use it. My 1964 Haut-Brion had gone to Henry, along with a case of ancient Chateauneuf for around one thousandth of its auction value and for the sake of having a good red by the glass the next time I hunkered up to his bar.

From the wine tables people moseyed across the lawn and into a maze of luxury furniture. The chief, first one there, vowed to repair and resell the dining room table that he packed into his store truck along with two divans and a chaise longue. Sully's mother made off with an armoire that basically doubled the net worth of her home. Finelli, of all things, had a taste for ottomans, and he spent some time contrasting the suede with the leather before I ended his sneering debate with an offer of two for one. Sully helped out, somewhat, pestering me for prices and miscommunicating them to customers when he wasn't parked in the folding chair next to mine. Paula emerged from the house every so often. She served us cold beers in lop-sided ceramic mugs, checked on PJ where she romped from bed to bed in the bed section of the lawn and returned, with a sharp-eyed half smile in my direction, into my kitchen—our kitchen—to pour herself something stronger.

I had the sense that, if I sat here long enough, I'd see everyone I'd ever met north of New York City. Even Freddy from the frozen river slunk by, dutifully looking at rugs with his mom. The fat woman in the wheelchair would be here any minute: I knew it, I was counting on it, expecting it with every clomp of a closed car door. Then the idea that she was spending this bright Saturday home with her husband came to me, spilling over me with the cool-edged warmth of the sun. Wikowsky dawdled on my porch, scratching his neck at the artwork, and left with a farewell burp. Gary pushed apart the beds in PJ's bouncing game to make her screaming leaps a greater challenge: one to which Sully, with an odd giggle, soon rose. Several of my neighbors watched this circus with a predictable combination of panic and disdain. I caught sight of them in their windows, aghast, in the moments when they weren't placing calls to their realtors and relocking their front doors.

It was the beginning of the high season, after all, and other than the ugly jumble on my lawn the town appeared to be rising, as if slowly baked by the weather, to the occasion. From my hill at its very top I squinted over the blue-and-green glowing world. I sipped my beer. The air was pleasantly singed. Something somewhere was burning. Something always was. My concern was not that, at the moment, but rather my announced fund-raising target of ten thousand dollars. I would make up the difference, of course, when I wrote the check; but in the name of dignity, it'd be nice to net a clean thou. Even $800, I figured, and I could call it quits. I would give it till the end of the day. Or till $500, whichever came first. I could pull in $300 and be home free. I would give it till darkness and be home.

BOOKS BY NICHOLAS WEINSTOCK

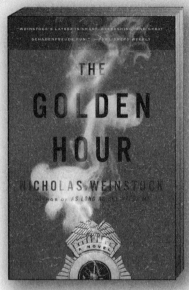

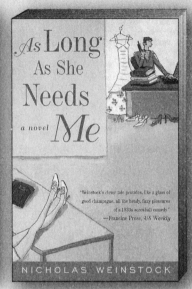

THE GOLDEN HOUR
A Novel
ISBN 978-0-06-076087-8 (paperback)

Thoughtful and suspenseful, hugely entertaining and beautifully constructed, *The Golden Hour* is the story of one man's power to ruin and regain his life.

"A novel of self-discovery that glides by with ease."   —*Kirkus Reviews*

"A charming, seductive fish-out-of-water tale . . . moving and funny."
                        —*Booklist*

"Mining a divorce story for laughs can be risky, but Nicholas Weinstock deftly does so in *The Golden Hour*."   —*Daily News*

AS LONG AS SHE NEEDS ME
A Novel
ISBN 978-0-06-095783-4 (paperback)

Juggling his duties as a publishing assistant with those of a pro bono wedding planner, Oscar labors to pull together his boss's wedding. Help arrives in the form of wedding columnist Lauren LaRose. As the two work together, they stumble into a romance of their own.

"The perfect marriage of not just smart, but brilliant and hilarious writing and a riveting plot. Weinstock's earnest protagonist is an irresistible combination of Dr. Jekyll and Mr. Right."
              —Jennifer Belle, author of
                        Going Down